MY SUMMER JOB IN HELL

GAIL KELLNER

DIVERTIR
PUBLISHING
Salem, NH

My Summer Job in Hell

Gail Kellner

Copyright © 2021 Gail Kellner

Cover image by
Megan Spaniol
http://meganspaniol.com

Published by
Divertir Publishing LLC
PO Box 232
North Salem, NH 03073
http://www.divertirpublishing.com/

ISBN-13: 978-1-938888-31-1
ISBN-10: 1-938888-31-6

Library of Congress Control Number: 2021946170

Printed in the United States of America

TABLE OF CONTENTS

CHAPTER ONE

I COULD HEAR the screaming all the way from my bedroom. High-pitched, shrill, and furious. The kinds of screams that make you think of werewolves and demons that steal your soul.

My feet were propped on my pillow as I lay in bed facing my Kate Upton swimsuit poster. I wished she were my girlfriend, but that didn't seem likely considering I was voted most likely to be overlooked by my high school class.

Okay, not really. For one thing, I'm a junior. I won't be voted most likely to be overlooked until next year.

Maybe I should introduce myself. My name is Fynn Hardin. I'm a sixteen-year-old guy with no girlfriend and no car. I have hair the color of dirt, a long face with a pointed chin, and a smattering of freckles. If this brings to mind an image of an adolescent giraffe, you're not far off.

I was throwing a ball against the wall and catching it with one hand. It's something I do to entertain myself. I've gotten pretty good at it. It helps block out the screaming.

"Noooooo! No! No! No!"

This ended in a screech so loud I thought my head was stuck inside a Boeing 747 engine. I sat up, grabbed my pillow from under my feet, and flopped back down, pressing it over my head. Which made me wonder—could I still catch the ball if I couldn't see, like, by using Spidey-sense or the Force or something?

Thwack.

Apparently not. I'd have to work on that.

"Fynn! Dinner!" I debated not going, but I was hungry, so I blew Kate a kiss and shuffled downstairs.

"Hi, Fynn." My mom was taking a chicken pot pie out of the oven, while my dad wrestled a screaming Madelaine, aka Maddie, into her highchair. *Sweet.* I love chicken pot pie, so I slid into a chair and helped myself to a large portion. The smell of hot, delicious, mouth-watering chicken met my nose. Ahhh…

"Fynn!" Dad barked.

I jerked my head up. "What?"

"Could you help me here, please!" Maddie had her feet on the edge of her high chair, her fists of fury flailing around my dad's head and her little body

1

bending in an arc. I made a face at her, stuck out my tongue, crossed my eyes, and poked her in the stomach. She laughed and relaxed enough for my dad to pop her into her highchair. When she realized what just happened, she got ready to scream again, but I shook some Cheerios onto her tray and she brightened.

"Thanks, Fynn," Dad said, wiping the sweat off his forehead. Dad was ten years older than mom, and he always said that he totally lucked out when she married him. I could kind of see it. Dad's balding and has a belly, plus he works long hours and has no sense of humor. He's a salesman for a printer business.

"You know, you're very good with Maddie," Mom said. I could tell by the way they exchanged glances that something was up. Should I just pretend not to notice? Probably. I shoveled another forkful of chicken into my mouth. My dad made a sort of "hmmf"ing noise.

"Okay, what?" I put my fork down.

Mom cleared her throat. "We were thinking that for the summer you could hang out and take care of Maddie. You know, while I go to work to earn money for your college education."

I stared at her, then at my father, searching for confirmation that this was a joke. My dad smiled at me like this was some fantastic opportunity that I would be a fool not to jump at. My twelve-year-old brother, Kevin, looked at me and laughed. His mouth was full.

"Are you kidding?" I managed.

"No, actually we are not," Mom said.

"I'm getting a job for the summer. You know, so I can save money and buy a car and…stuff."

Maddie was born fifteen months ago. Last summer, Mom was on maternity leave and could look after her own baby. Now that she was back at work she wanted me to do it?

"It won't be so bad looking after your sister. She's a pretty easy baby," my dad said, as if I had not just witnessed the war to get her into her highchair.

"Seriously? How am I supposed to save for a car if I'm running around after Maddie all day? Are you going to pay me for my services?"

"Because everyone…" They both started talking at the same time, so Dad stopped, nodded at Mom, and said, "You go."

"Because we're a family, and everyone has to do their part. We can save money by not sending Maddie to day care for the summer. Money which we can then use to send you to college." She brushed a lock of her cinnamon-colored hair out of her face. She works nights as an ICU nurse at a local hospital and was always tired. "You can borrow my car when I'm not using it. They'll be plenty of time for you to go out with your friends."

"It's not a bad deal," my dad said, as if he were trying to convince himself.

I sighed. My mom drove a ten-year-old minivan. I bet girls would be falling all over themselves to be seen with a guy who drove his mom's minivan.

There was another reason I really needed a job, but I didn't want to tell my parents. Three months ago, they had given me a line of credit on one of their cards for "emergencies"—gas and school expenses. Well, define "emergency." Is it an emergency if all of my friends are playing the same video game and I am in imminent danger of becoming more of a social misfit than I am already? I thought so. Anyway, somehow I managed to spend $400 on Steam. Yeah, I know. But it's not really my fault. Where did my parents get this misguided idea that I was responsible?

Obviously, the credit card people wanted their money. I had been yanking the bill out of the mailbox before my parents got to it so far, but obviously that wasn't going to work for much longer. I wanted to get rid of the debt before my parents noticed, or at least pay it down enough so that the total could be construed as gas and school expenses.

I have to admit, I also felt a twinge of resentment about this whole babysitting idea. Was it my fault they had a baby last year? No, it was not. So why was my summer going to be sacrificed? Because it was convenient for them?

"I didn't ask for you to have a baby," I said, almost instantly regretting it.

"Well, if that's how you feel, I'll just quit my job to take care of the three of you. Of course, next year when you want to go to college, I won't be able to help you." She gestured at me with her fork, and the expression on her face said she would have cheerfully stabbed me with it.

"You know, Fynn, sometimes you have to step up. You have to make sacrifices for your family," Dad said.

Peace and quiet, I thought. It seemed to me that's what I was sacrificing, not to mention steady income and self-esteem. Instead I grunted. Kevin looked at me, suppressing a giggle, which brought up an excellent point.

"What's Kevin sacrificing, exactly?" Kevin kicked me under the table.

"Don't you worry. Kevin will have responsibilities as well." Kevin stuck his tongue out at me. Maddie waved her spoon around and flicked chicken pot pie all over the table. My mom sighed and got up to get a cloth. Maddie smiled, pleased with herself, and banged her sippy cup on the tray of her highchair.

"There's a summer job fair this weekend at school. I was planning on going." I glanced at Mom and Dad. This was the delicate moment, where my summer and my self-respect hung in the balance. Were they going to let go of this idea that I would be Maddie's babysitter so I could go be a normal high school student with a summer job, meeting summer girls, and saving for summer cars?

"Fynn…" Mom appeared to be wrestling with saying what she really wanted to say, versus trying to be supportive. She sighed. "If you want to get a job so that you can contribute to your college fund, that would be…okay. I mean, we could work around it. You could get a job in the evenings or something."

Great. My parents were on board with my summer job search. The fact they thought I'd be sacking away money for college instead of a car was an issue I could deal with later. Right now, I looked forward to finding a summer job.

CHAPTER TWO

I KNEW THE job fair was at 8:00. I mean, seriously, who has a summer job fair at eight o'clock in the morning on a Saturday? Franklin Regional High School, that's who. My plan was to get there early, scope out all the jobs, and then pick two or three of the easiest ones and hope for the best.

I set my alarm. I know I did. I don't know why it didn't go off. When the first glimmer of consciousness pierced my sleeping brain at 10:30 a.m., my first thought was, *It's so light out.* Then I woke up and thought, *Shit!* I threw on the clothes I was wearing yesterday, conveniently lying crumpled up next to my bed, and ran out the door as fast as I could. The job fair only lasted until 11:00 a.m.

By the time I got there, the gym was nearly deserted. The only people left were the faculty monitors and the last of the job fair employers, who were throwing applications and poster board into folders and making a beeline for the exit. Mrs. Hinson and Mr. Clark were sucking on paper cups of cold coffee, waiting impatiently for the job fair to end so they could go about the rest of their weekend. They looked at me with derision. I know what they were thinking, that I was a screwup who couldn't even show up to a job fair on time. It was sort of true, but there was no reason to be so judgmental about it.

I glanced out the windows of the gym and saw my friend Josh outside, so I went to join him. It was a beautiful day in mid-May, one of the first nice days we had. It had been a rainy, cold, and depressing spring, but today was gorgeous. The sun was shining, bathing everyone in warmth and happiness. Birds were singing and flowers were cautiously poking their heads up through the sandy soil. A few clumps of students were standing around enjoying the weather, talking about whatever awesome opportunity had undoubtedly just unfolded before them.

"Hey," I said, without enthusiasm.

"Hey, where were you?" Josh said. "The job fair's mostly over."

"I know. I think I accidentally set my alarm for 7 p.m. instead of 7 a.m."

"Bummer. Don't despair. You can always go directly to the job sites."

"Yeah, I guess. How 'bout you? Did you get a job?"

"Yup. Computer Tech hired me on the spot." He flashed someone's business card and grinned.

"Of course you did," I said a bit sourly. Josh was brilliant. No matter what problem someone was having with a computer, he could always figure it out. Every time. It was simultaneously both really annoying and really convenient.

Just then, my cell phone pinged with a text message from my mom. *How was the job fair?* I winced. Should I just tell her I slept through it? For a second, I thought maybe it wouldn't be so bad hanging out with Maddie all summer. Then I remembered my $400 debt. I imagined the lecture I was in for when they found out I used their credit card for video games. Not to mention what a schmuck I was for missing the job fair in the first place.

My fingers hovered over my phone. *Great!* I texted. Hopefully, she wouldn't ask me too many follow-up questions. Thankfully, my phone remained silent.

I stood and wondered what to do with myself. I needed a job. I needed a job so I could pay my debt and get a car. I needed a car so I could get a hot girlfriend, because what hot girl dates a guy with no car?

Josh's mom pulled up, so Josh nodded at me and said, "Don't sweat it. You'll find something."

"Yeah. I know," I said, even though I was picturing myself spooning strained peas into Maddie's mouth and being single for the rest of my life. I waved half-heartedly and watched them drive away.

I wandered around aimlessly, not wanting to go home. Mom would frown, ask me if I had gotten a job, and give me a look of fatalistic disappointment. It occurred to me I had forgotten a book I needed for a paper that was due Monday, so I tried the front door. Locked. I tried the side door and the door to the cafeteria but found them locked as well. I walked around to the gym. Locked. However, the small gym, the one that's mostly used to store mats and deflated volleyballs, was unlocked. *Sweet.*

Walking down the hallways to my locker, I grabbed the book and shut the door as gently as possible. It made a crashing metal-on-metal sound anyone left in the building would've heard. I froze, expecting Principal Jones to come barreling around the corner, shaking his finger at me and yelling, "Hardin!" Not that I ever had that happen. But all was quiet.

I don't really know what I was thinking after that. It was weird being in my high school when it was empty. I peered into some of my classrooms, tried the door of the Main Office, found a few pencils, and basically wandered around. Lost in thought, I read posters I didn't usually have the time or inclination to read. The drama department was putting on a revival of *Into the Woods*. Baseball tryouts were next Wednesday, Thursday, and Saturday. The jazz band needed a guitarist. I wish I played guitar, but I had never quite gotten around to that.

I came to an elevator to the right of the main stairwell. It was usually locked, but for some reason it was standing open. *Weird*. So I got in it. Why not, right? I stabbed the button for the basement, thinking I'd find a bunch of cool old stuff stashed down there. The elevator dropped and started to descend. And descend. And descend. I swear I was in the elevator for ten minutes. My heart hammered in my chest and sweat ran down my neck as I stabbed the "stop" button, then all the other buttons, but nothing happened. I couldn't breathe and thought I might pass out when the elevator finally stopped. So happy to be out of my little metal prison, I damn near threw myself out of there.

Half a second later, I turned around to get back into the elevator. Sitting in front of me was the most bizarre secretary I'd ever seen—assuming that's what she was. She had blueish skin, like she hadn't seen the light of day in about a thousand years, and lime green hair, like her punk phase had lasted her entire life. She was wearing thick eyeglasses and large hoop earrings, and she was talking on the phone. She held up a finger to indicate she would be with me in a minute. I tried to shake my head as a way of saying, *I don't need anything, lady*, but too late. She hung up with whoever she was talking to and said, "Welcome to Hell. Can I help you?"

I stared at her, open-mouthed. "Uh…what?"

"I said, welcome to Hell. What can I help you with?"

Like most people, I had imagined what Hell would be like from time to time. I always thought it would be like a dungeon, with molten lava coursing through it in a river and the worst people humanity had to offer falling into it, screaming. I did not expect a receptionist.

"What…how did I get here?"

"I don't know, hon. You took the elevator, I expect." She looked me up and down, taking in my converse all-stars, my wrinkled t-shirt, and my cargo pants. I know, cargo pants went out of style a long time ago—I like the pockets, okay?

"More importantly, how do I get back out?" What if I was trapped in Hell? I couldn't breathe again and needed to sit down.

"The same way you got here—on the elevator." She said this as if explaining it to a kindergartner or to someone who had just recently come out of a coma. Feeling a smidge better, I glanced around, curious.

The receptionist was sitting at a normal-looking glass-topped desk with two chairs facing her. Behind her were bookshelves, and underneath everything was a tasteful-yet-bland beige carpet with a dotted pattern on it. It could have been any office in America. Further down the hall to the left there seemed to be a conference room, and to the right was a brick archway that led to a tunnel. Some kind of subway system?

"Did you need something?" The lady asked pointedly.

"I need a job," I blurted out without thinking.

She brightened. "Well, you've come to the right place. We need help."

"You do? Hell is hiring?"

She smiled, sort of a wicked smile, and said, "We sure are. Here." She rummaged around in her desk and put a piece of paper on a clipboard, stuck a pen to it, and handed it to me. "Just fill that out and give it back to me. I'll give it to my boss."

"You mean Satan, right?"

She smiled and shook her head. "No one calls him that. You can sit there," she said, pointing to one of the chairs.

"Uh, I don't...I won't be...you know..." I mimed using a pitchfork. "Torturing anyone, will I?"

"No. That's an upper-level position. You would be strictly entry-level."

"Oh. Great." I took the clipboard and sat down. It wouldn't hurt to look over the application, would it? I have to admit, I was curious. What sort of jobs were there in Hell? The first part was all the standard stuff—name, address, phone number, emergency contact.

I had a sudden thought. "Um, I was interested in summer employment. Are there summer jobs here?"

"Oh, yes. We usually hire several high school and college students to work for us during the busy season."

I wondered what made summer "the busy season," but I focused on the application.

What skills do you have? What skills *did* I have? Not many. I was pretty good at Minecraft. *Employment history?* None, I wrote. Already it was looking unlikely they would hire me anyway. *What special talents or abilities do you have that would benefit Hell?* Was this a trick question? I wrestled with that for a while, and finally I wrote, "I'm a people person."

I gave it back to the lime-haired lady. She glanced it over and said, "Okay, thank you...Fynn. How many hours a week are you looking for?"

"Well...thirty to forty a week, I guess. Just for the summer, though."

She nodded again. "Okay. My name is Dorothy. Is this a good number to call you at?" She indicated my cell phone number. I nodded. "We'll be in touch."

"So, I just hit the button to...you know. Get back to earth?"

"Yup, same way you came."

"O-kaaaay." I stepped back into the elevator, wondering if they would hire me and if I would want to work there if they did. But at least I had an application in somewhere.

CHAPTER THREE

MONDAY MORNING, I woke up at 7:03. School started at 7:19. Sixteen minutes. Totally doable. I grabbed my jeans—very neatly thrown over the top of the dresser—pulled on a clean*ish* shirt, stopped in the bathroom, and grabbed an apple on my way through the kitchen. Our cat, Shadow Chaser, came out from under the kitchen table and wrapped around my feet, so I nearly tripped.

My mom had just gotten home from work, and my dad was just leaving. He passed Maddie off to her, kissed her on the cheek, and drove off. Mom got started on feeding Maddie and then noticed me.

"Fynn, aren't you going to eat breakfast?" Mom asked as she tried to feed Maddie a spoonful of vanilla yogurt. Maddie tried to push her tray away from her chubby little body with both hands and said, "Out! Out!"

"No time, Mom. I gotta go."

I heard Maddie's telltale shriek as I jogged down Ellis Road. We only lived about a mile and a half away from Franklin Regional High School, thank goodness. If I could break a four-minute mile, I'd be right on time.

"Hey!" A black pickup truck pulled up next to me. I glanced over and discovered Josh grinning at me like he just won the lottery.

"Hey! Did you just get this?" I yanked open the passenger side door and climbed in.

"Yeah. My parents lent me the money, now that I'm working for a living." He smiled.

"Sweet!" It was, too. I was pretty sure my face turned all shades of green. Why couldn't my parents be cool like Josh's? There was no way my parents were going to buy me a car. Part of me knew Josh's parents didn't mind lending him the money because he would pay it back. But you'd think my parents could at least sympathize with my plight as a non-car-owning student in high school. If I had a car, I wouldn't be on the verge of being late every day, now would I?

We managed to walk in just as the bell was ringing. On my way in, I saw Amanda Kaneko, a totally hot Asian chick I sat behind in American History.

9

"Hi!" I said, too loudly. She glanced around until her gaze landed on me. She looked faintly puzzled.

"Do I know you?"

"Yeah. American History, second period?"

She hesitated, then nodded and smiled, but I could tell she still had no idea who I was. So I just nodded and said, "See ya."

High school sucks.

The rest of the day passed by uneventfully. After school, I learned Josh had to go straight to work and couldn't give me a ride home.

"But, I'll swing by your house tomorrow to pick you up. 7:05 a.m. sharp! Or I'm driving off without you!"

"Yeah, I'll be ready." I walked home, pushed my way in the front door, and discovered the house was unusually quiet. Where was everyone?

Kevin didn't get out of middle school until 2:32. He had to ride the bus, so he didn't get home until almost 3:00. I peeked in my parent's bedroom, wondering if Mom was taking a nap, but she wasn't there. She must have taken Maddie somewhere.

The landline rang. I walked over and saw "Free Rein Credit" on the caller ID, so I grabbed it.

"Hello?"

"May I speak to Mr. Hardin, please?"

"Yeah?" I lowered my voice an octave to sound more like Dad.

"Is this Mr. Hardin?"

"Yeah, this is Mr. Hardin." Well, I was *a* Mr. Hardin.

"Mr. Hardin, my name is Colton Reed with Free Rein Credit. I'm sure you know that your son," there was a pause here, as if he were frantically searching his paperwork to find out what my name might be, "Fynn, has rung up debt on his Student Freedom card. We were just calling to let you know, and to ask when we might expect payment."

Shit. "Oh, of course, we know. Ha ha, silly Fynn. Uh…how long do we have to pay it?"

"Mr. Hardin, the loan is already two months behind."

"Right. Well, I firmly believe Fynn should pay that himself. I will not bail him out. Look, I…I mean he should have a job in a few weeks."

A sigh on the other end. "Mr. Hardin, I would hate to have to report this to credit agencies. I am only giving you as much leeway as I am because of your prior credit history with us. But I can only delay so long."

I calculated quickly. I had a few dollars left over from my birthday. "I can pay thirty dollars now, and then I…I mean Fynn…can make payments starting

June 15th." This was wildly optimistic, considering I had so far only applied to one place, but whatever. I didn't even want to think about what would happen when my parents found out what I had spent $400 on. They would look at each other, then at me, and instead of disappointment or shock, they would have a look of resignation on their faces, as if they always knew I would be a screwup and I was just living up to their expectations.

A sigh on the other end. "Thirty dollars now?"

"Well, I have cash. Do you take cash?" I knew they didn't take cash over the phone, but I thought they had a branch office downtown. "I can make a payment tomorrow in the Franklin branch on West Street."

"I'm making a note of this in the computer."

"Great!" I said.

"Okay. Thirty dollars now and then payments starting June fifteenth. Thank you, Mr. Hardin."

"Yes, sounds good. Have a great day!"

I disconnected.

I seriously needed to find a job.

CHAPTER FOUR

OKAY, I'M NOT an idiot. Usually, anyway.

I knew Hell would be a terrible place to work. I knew that. Everyone knows that. So, in the weeks that followed, I applied for every single summer job I could think of. I applied for retail jobs, restaurant jobs, janitorial jobs, stock boy jobs, but I heard the same thing, over and over.

"Sorry, but we've already hired our summer crew."

I did find a few places that took my application and said, "We'll be in touch." One was a Chinese restaurant run by immigrants with a sketchy reputation as far as what went into the Pork Fried Rice. The owner smiled at me in such a nice way, and I think she said, "We call you."

Another was a retail store, Big Bargains. The manager looked at me skeptically but promised he'd look over my application and call if anything came up.

I was batting a thousand.

I applied as a summer camp counselor, too. It wasn't what I was hoping for, but weren't girls often employed as summer camp counselors? Cute girls? Girls in bikinis? It was worth a shot.

As May dragged into June, my mom started talking like it was all settled. I would be Maddie's full-time de-facto babysitter. "Fynn, I want you to go over this stacking game with Maddie—it's good for her fine motor skills." "I just got a cool new app that teaches language skills. Come look at this." "Fynn, you know Maddie likes strained sweet potatoes for lunch." And on and on.

I hadn't heard from anyone—not one place I applied had called me back. It was starting to mess with my self-esteem. I know I had no job experience, but how much know-how did it take to stock shelves? Why didn't anyone want me?

I paid my thirty dollars to the woman sitting behind the counter at Free Rein. She looked at me like she had just found me under her refrigerator, rotted and shriveled. "First payment, June 15th."

"Great. Uh, is there a grace period?"

She glared at me. "Five days."

"Thank you."

The first Friday in June was one of those perfect near-summer days that people write poems about. The sun dappled the earth with puddles of light and warmth. There was an optimism in the air, a promise of better weather and carefree afternoons spent napping in the sun. I finished school and went home—I wanted to hang out with Josh, but he was already working his summer job at Computer Tech. I threw my backpack on the kitchen table and started poking around in the cabinets for something to eat.

"Fynn? Is that you?"

"Yeah, hi Mom." Why couldn't we have decent chips for once? Why did we always have to buy store-brand chips? Oh, well. I ripped open the package and wandered into the living room.

Mom was in her pajamas, and Maddie was concentrating on a puzzle. She had one piece gripped in her chubby fist and was studying the puzzle board. Carefully, she placed the piece near the border, almost perfectly. She looked up at me and grinned. I had to hand it to her—she was a smart little kid. I knelt on the rug next to her and handed her another piece.

Just then my cell rang, so I dug it out of my pocket. It said "Dorothy" and a number I didn't recognize. I tried to think who I knew named Dorothy when it occurred to me—Hell's receptionist. With a bit of trepidation, I answered.

"Hello?"

"Fynn Hardin?"

"Yeah?" Oops. I cleared my throat. "Yes, this is he." I could see Mom watching me so I went up the stairs to my room.

"This is Dorothy Leningrad, the Office Manager from Hell. How are you today, Mr. Hardin?"

"I'm go…well. I'm well. How are you?"

"I'm doing fine. Thank you for asking. I believe I have good news for you, Mr. Hardin. We'd like to offer you a job."

"Oh? I mean, great! That's great. Uh…so, what sort of job?"

"We'd like you to come to Orientation, which is a week from tomorrow, and we'll assign jobs and set your hours then. Sound good?"

"Sounds great! Thank you! Thank you very much." I clicked off.

I ran downstairs into the living room, where Mom was looking at me expectantly. "Who was that?" she asked.

"I just got a summer job!" I crowed.

"Oh." She glanced at Maddie. "That's great. I'm happy for you."

I felt a pang of guilt. "Uh…we'll be okay, right?"

She smiled and said, "Of course we will. We'll figure it out. Kevin can keep an eye on Maddie a little if I'm right upstairs sleeping, you can do it occasionally, I'll take vacation time—we'll work it out. I'm happy for you. Congratulations."

So, that's how I got my summer job in Hell. Next up: Orientation.

CHAPTER FIVE

I SPENT THE next week filled with a combination of excitement and dread. I was going to work in Hell! Oh, crap—I was going to work in Hell. Well, maybe it wouldn't be so bad. Wait, what am I, nuts? Well, it couldn't hurt to show up on Saturday and find out what it's all about.

Saturday arrived. I slammed my hand down on my alarm clock and sat up, knowing I couldn't be late. Dorothy said to arrive at 9 a.m. sharp, and I was determined not to be a screwup. I put on my nicest chinos and a button-down shirt, and I made my way back to Franklin Regional High School. Naturally, every door was locked. It was Saturday morning, and nothing was going on at the school that would've led to a stray door being open. I tried the front doors, the side doors, the door hidden under the stairwell to the cafeteria—all locked. And before you ask the obvious, yes, of course I tried the door to the small gym. It was locked too.

I was on the edge of panic. I couldn't be late on my first day, and it was almost 9:00. Trying every door, I was literally tearing around like a madman—anything to find a way in. I was just about to give up and resign myself to a summer of loneliness and diapers when I saw a window on the first floor just slightly ajar. Now how to get in? I searched for something to stand on, saw a trash can tucked under an overhang, and pushed it under the window. It would be just my luck to get stuck. Then someone would call the police about some kid with his butt hanging out of a window at the high school, and by Monday I would have to move to avoid the ridicule. Luckily, I'm pretty skinny and slid through.

I ran to the elevator near the stairwell, and thank goodness it was standing open, waiting, like an invitation. As soon as I got in it started to descend.

"Hello, Fynn. Nice to see you again." Dorothy smiled at me. Today her hair was blue, probably to match her skin.

"Hi, Dorothy." I tried to surreptitiously sniff under my armpit to make sure I didn't smell, and I followed her down a dark hallway to a large auditorium. To my surprise, I was not the only one here for Orientation. There were about fifty kids seated in the blue velvet seats, looking around, talking to each other in that way that people who have just met do—anxiously and eager to be liked.

I took a seat next to a tall redheaded girl and said, "So, you come here often?" She rolled her eyes and immediately started talking to the person on her other side. *Nice going, Fynn*, I thought. I really had to brush up on pick-up lines. As I was mulling over what I should've said, an overweight, balding man appeared on the stage in front of us.

"Your attention, please." He grabbed the microphone, which screeched in protest. People started nudging each other and quieted down.

"Good morning, and welcome to Hell! This is going to be a very exciting summer. My name is Marshall Dodd, and I run the Soul Destination Department here in Hell. Now, I'm sure you're all wondering what you're going to be doing. We've sorted you as best we can into departments where we feel your skills and abilities will be put to the best use. We have openings in the kitchen, transportation, sorting, packing, and admissions. At the end of this brief introduction, I'll identify what departments you'll be working in, and you'll finish your orientation there. But first, I'd like to introduce you to a very important being here in Hell—indeed, probably *the* most important being. Would you please give a warm welcome to The Prince of Darkness himself, Lucifer!"

We all leaned forward, curious, as the first few notes of "Sympathy for the Devil" played over the loudspeaker. I must admit, I expected to see a horned giant blowing smoke out of his nose, twirling a pitchfork, kind of like a mutant minotaur. Instead, the most handsome man I had ever seen in my life appeared and walked confidently to the podium. Lucifer wore a black suit, and his hair was neatly trimmed. He was tall and moved with an easy grace. He shook hands with Mr. Dodd and then held his arms out as if extending an embrace to us all.

"I would like to personally welcome you to Hell. Call me Luke. I hope you'll find Hell is a great place to work. If you have any difficulties, I hope you'll feel like you can come to me. We want you to be happy, efficient workers. Hell is a busy place. We process over half a million souls a year, and you'll be an integral part of that."

As he went on, there was something absolutely mesmerizing about him. I looked around and saw that we were all enthralled, both males and females leaning forward in their seats, slack-jawed, elbows on their knees and staring in some kind of hypnotic trance. He was pleasant, and the words were welcoming, but at the same time there was a faint malevolence, a coldness behind his friendly eyes.

He didn't talk very long—I got the sense he had better things to do than welcome new employees to Hell. He hurried off, and as soon as he did the spell was broken. People relaxed back in their seats and again looked faintly disinterested. Mr. Dodd took the stage again.

"I would like to introduce you to the department managers. These are the people you will report to directly. Our culinary director, Ms. Analisa Santiago." In all my fantasy novels, women are always oversexed, half-dressed creatures nearly bursting at the seams of their suggestive clothing. But this was a stout, middle-aged witch wearing a heavy hooded caftan. Her eyebrows almost met in the middle of her face, right above her hooked nose.

"Transportation manager, Mr. Roger Abbet." He had white hair, smoothly tied into a ponytail, and a stubble of white on his chin. His lined face was high-lighted by his ice-blue eyes. "Soul sorting, Mr. Billy Pae." A slim man with no mouth stood up and waved. I didn't know what happened to his mouth at the time—I learned later he lost it in a bet with the next guy to stand up.

"Security, Mr. Andre Markov." A gigantic man, probably seven feet tall and as wide as your average subcompact car, grunted at us. He was carrying an ax that was the size of a bus. I was hoping I wasn't in security. "Finally, Soul Destination, that's me, and we've already met." He smiled at us like this was really funny.

They sorted us into our departments, so we could get oriented to whatever job we were going to do. I wound up in Soul Destination. There were three of us—me, an overweight kid named Tom, and a girl with dyed black hair, a nose ring, and a tattoo on her neck. I wondered if she was single.

Dutifully, we followed Mr. Dodd along on the tour. The auditorium and the cafeteria made up two halves of a circular whole. They formed a central hub, with corporate offices and reception around the outer circle. They were clean, modern, and sterile—about what you'd find in any office in America. A small bay just outside of the cafeteria was where transportation was housed.

Dodd punched a passcode and a small, driverless taxi appeared before us. It was just big enough for the four of us to squish into, with me and Tom facing Dodd and the girl, who I learned was named Jenna. It was so small our knees were almost touching, which was about as awkward as it sounds. Dodd punched some numbers in the keypad by the door, and immediately a thrust sent us off.

"These hovercrafts are so efficient. Before we had these, we had an ancient railway system, and it took almost a whole day to get from one side of Hell to the other. Now, we can do it in about an hour. And the railway was always breaking down. I had one orientee who got stuck on the train in a really remote area, and a week went by before anyone noticed she was gone." He saw our faces and said, "Oh, but don't worry, that doesn't happen anymore."

We zipped along so fast I couldn't see anything—just a blur of dirt brown. Finally, we stopped at central Soul Destination.

I'm sure you're wondering, as I did, that if Hell has been around since the beginning of time and a certain percentage of people go there after they die, then Hell must be really crowded. Where do they put all these people? Hell is really big, but even so—if it's been in operation for thousands of years, there must be millions of people down there.

The answer is no there isn't. Hell has six levels, according to how dreadful people were on earth—the farther down you go, the worse humanity is. The outermost level has your internet trolls, tax evaders, the chronically late, and people who leave their Christmas lights up until April. The next level has adulterers, drug addicts, and the like. The third level houses thieves, armed robbers, and narcissists. On the fourth level, you start to get really unpleasant people— people who were cruel to animals, stalkers, and people who committed manslaughter. The fifth level is where murderers, pedophiles, and rapists go, and the final level is where they put the absolute worst of the worst—serial killers, mass murderers, and tyrannical dictators like Hitler and Mao Zedong.

So, everyone gets a sentence in Hell depending on their level of offense. The level one people get a year, or a few years, where they suffer depending on their crime. It varies, but having people being bitten by mosquitoes and flies constantly, keeping them cold, and keeping them hungry are some favorites. The lower the level, the worse the torture. The sixth level is probably closest to what you think of as Hell—people are burned in hellfire, drowned in lava, etcetera. Lucifer himself takes care of the sixth level.

Obviously, for torture to work effectively, you need a body. Otherwise, there is no pain or suffering. So everyone brings their corporeal body with them to Hell to be subjected to whatever stress has been deemed appropriate. When they have served out their sentence, the bodies are burned, and the ashes are part of the dirt that coats the floors. The souls are packaged up neatly, put in boxes, and shipped off to their final destination. Some of them eventually go to Heaven, some to Purgatory, and some return to earth. A few are dissolved and their energy returns to the universe.

My job would be to package up the souls, put them in boxes, and label them according to destination. Mr. Dodd gave us our schedules. I would be working Monday, Tuesday, Thursday, and Saturday from 8:00 a.m. to 6:00 p.m. My first day would be the Monday following the end of the school year, and I could quit August 27th—two days before school started. I looked forward to my first day at work.

CHAPTER SIX

SCHOOL ROCKETED TO its usual end-of-the-year conclusion. I spent my time catching up on all the work I never got around to before final grades were due. Most teachers were pretty accepting of my lame excuses, but one, Mr. Ericson, peered out at me over the rims of his glasses and grunted.

"Is there a reason you were not able to complete your project on time, Mr. Hardin?"

"Uh, well, you know my mom works nights and she had a baby last year, and sometimes I have to take care of my sister." I smiled in what I hoped was a winning fashion. It worked for every other teacher. I had no reason to doubt it would work now.

"Really?" He gestured with his pen at a desk that was usually occupied by Michaela Cleary. I looked at her desk and looked back at Mr. Ericson. I had no idea what he was getting at.

"Did you know Ms. Cleary had a baby last July and still managed to turn in her project on time? Furthermore, she got one of the top grades in all my classes. What was your excuse again, Mr. Hardin?" His eyes bored into me, daring me to make up some bullshit excuse. Damn Michaela Cleary and her over-achievement.

"My excuse is…uh, lack of character?"

At this, Mr. Ericson laughed. His eyes crinkled at the corners, and for a second he looked like a nice guy instead of the history taskmaster that he actually was. He took off his glasses, pinched his nose, and then put his glasses back on and looked at me.

"You do have some charm, I'll give you that. If you turn in your project by Monday, you can earn half credit. By Monday! No more excuses."

"Yes, sir, by Monday. Thank you." Great, now I had four days to throw together a project that I should've spent weeks working on and for only half credit.

I spent that weekend feverishly working on my history project. Originally I was going to do an Allied Forces vs. Nazi Chess set, but then I realized that would take way too long forming all the little model chessmen. So instead, I wrote a journal from the perspective of a soldier in the trenches during WWII, loosely based on the movie, *All Quiet on the Western Front*. I was in a hurry. It wasn't great, but I got it done, although Mr. Ericson rolled his eyes at me when I turned it in.

Free Rein credit called, and I answered it before my parents could. I assured them I—Fynn—had a job, although I didn't mention where it was, and said his first payment would be forthcoming after his first paycheck. This would make it only slightly late.

"We will report this to the credit agencies if we don't get the payment by June 15th." The disembodied voice hissed into the phone. Okay, so with the grace period I had until June twentieth. I could totally do that.

Before I knew it, it was the last day of school, and people were hugging while girls were carrying on about staying in touch. C'mon, we all have cell phones. You're gonna be texting these people forty times a day. Making my way past the parking lot, I started my walk home. I could've taken the bus, but I would be surrounded by freshmen and other nerds with no cars. So I walked instead. I wasn't even a quarter of a mile away when Josh pulled up in his pickup truck.

"Need a ride?" He grinned and leaned out his window.

Josh got all the breaks.

A small part of me knew Josh actually worked hard for what he got, but the rest of me shoved that thought out of my head and wondered why Josh was so freakin' lucky. Why couldn't I be lucky?

Josh dropped me off, and I went up the steps and into the kitchen. There was an end-of-the-year party later, and I was thinking of a nap. I grabbed a bag of chips—naps require a full stomach—and threw myself onto the sofa. I was just about to crash when Kevin came home. He threw his backpack down and started to head up to his room.

"What's the matter? You're looking a little down for someone with the whole summer ahead of him." He looked down at his feet and shrugged.

"It's nothing. I'm fine, just tired. I had a final today."

"Jesus, they have those in middle school now?"

Kevin nodded and yawned. "Yeah. I'm gonna lie down for a bit."

I watched him as he mounted the stairs and disappeared into his room. I thought he looked down, but I chalked it up to him thinking he didn't do well on the final.

That night I went to a party at the home of a girl Josh knew peripherally from Calculus. It was a good party, although I stayed out too late, and when I woke up in the morning my head was pounding. I spent the day recovering, mostly lying on the couch and eating cheese snaps until my mother yelled at me to find something productive to do. I said I would clean my room, and I did, for a few minutes. Then I stretched out on my bed and played video games.

Sunday passed by in a blur—it was a graduation party for my cousin Tim. His mom was my dad's sister, and we were pretty close. He was going to go to college out of state. Tim had red cheeks and red hair and freckles. He was wearing a baseball cap because he tended to burn in the sun.

"Did you find a job yet?" he asked.

"Yup." I felt no further elaboration was necessary. Weren't all summer jobs pretty much the same?

"Okay. Where?"

"Hell."

He laughed. "No, really. Where are you working?"

"Hell."

"All right, fine, don't tell me."

"Seriously. Somehow I got a job in Hell."

He looked at me like I was nuts. "Yeah, I'm going to college in Hell."

I gave up and shrugged. "Just kidding. I'm working at McDonald's."

"Oh, so you are working in Hell." He laughed, I laughed, and that was the end of that.

Before I knew it, it was Monday morning. I got up on time and got dressed in my cargo pants, a long sleeve shirt, and work boots. Only the boots were really required—just in case of sparks.

I went to the high school. Once again, I had trouble finding a way in. Finally, I found a window cracked open. I thrust it open as far as I dared, and then I propped it opened with a pencil. I would need to go back later and try to disguise it so that it looked closed, but since I was going to need some way to get in four days a week, I might as well try to set something up for myself. Anyway, I shimmied in and then took the elevator to Hell.

"Fynn! Nice to see you," Dorothy said as the elevator doors slid open. Today she had striped hair—wide Rainbow Brite stripes of pink, purple, and orange. Her lipstick was red and her skin was lavender.

"Hi, Dorothy."

"Is this your first day?" she asked.

"Yeah. I'm a little nervous."

"You're going to do fine. You'll need to take a hovercraft…" She pointed somewhere behind me with a pencil, "and enter 9A on the keypad. Soul Destination is department nine, A level. Got it?"

"9A. Yeah, I got it. Thank you."

There were a few other people waiting in line for a hovercraft. I stood behind a tall woman with dark brown hair. She glanced at me, gave a lukewarm smile, and then turned back around.

Hmmf. Nice to meet you, too.

I took a seat in the hovercraft. It was metal and shaped like a bullet. My fingers fumbled for the keypad and I entered 9A. Almost immediately the hovercraft took off. I gripped the edge of the seat cushion to keep from falling over.

Hell is dark and made up of hundreds of subterranean tunnels going every which way. There are lanterns to light the way, and it is someone's job to just go around making sure every lantern is lit. I was riding in my hovercraft with June Samuels, a gray-haired woman with glasses that hung from her neck on a chain, and Grover Thoreau, a man who looked to be 160 if he was a day. He had crepey, wrinkled skin that hung off his frame. He was wearing an old black suit and a fedora. He reminded me of a crow, sitting there in the hovercraft and staring at me as if I were lunch. Was I going to be surrounded by senior citizens all the time? Were there no girls my age in hell?

I got off the hovercraft at Soul Destination, and Mr. Dodd greeted me and led me over to a table. On the table, there was packing tape and a magic marker. In front of the table were a stack of empty boxes and a series of bins. Each bin was marked 'green,' 'yellow,' or 'blue.'

"Okay, here's what you do," Mr. Dodd said. "You take a soul and put it in a box. Green is for Heaven, Yellow is for Purgatory, Blue is for Universal Return. You pick up a soul, put it in a compartment, and grab another soul of the same color until you fill a box. Eight souls to a box. Then you tape it up, write on the tape where it's heading to, and then stack them up, here." He showed me a storage room off to the left. "Delivery picks them up at the end of the day. Any questions?"

"Do you know when we get our first paychecks?"

He frowned and put his hands on his hips. "It usually takes a week." He gave me a long look and pursed his hips. "Any other questions?"

"No, I don't think so. It seems pretty straightforward," I said.

"Great. There are three of you working down here right now. This is Adrian." He nodded at a tall black man with a beard. "And this is Sierra," he said, pointing at a middle-aged woman with mousy brown wash-and-wear hair and a hint of a mustache. "This is Fynn's first day, so answer his questions and try to help him out, okay?" They both nodded, went over to their tables, and started working.

I peered into the bin. I don't know what I was expecting to see. It was basically a box of nothing. Cautiously, I stuck my hand in and scooped. A white, smoky thing came out of the box.

What does a soul look like? Sort of like a shadow, or a ghost, gray and gauzy. It feels kind of slippery, but it's as light as air. This soul was marked 'blue' so a blue light was pinned to it. If you didn't know better, you would think there was a blue light hovering in space. I thrust it into the box marked 'blue.' Each soul gets its own compartment, kind of like an egg carton. I got another soul and continued working.

By lunch, I felt I had gotten the hang of Soul Destination. For lunch, we could go to the cafeteria, which required hopping on a hovercraft, or we could go to the employee break room, where there were vending machines and a microwave. I elected to go to the break room.

CHAPTER SEVEN

I WALKED DOWN one of the tunnels and found the break room, the second room on the right. There were vending machines on one wall and a few metal tables and chairs in the center. A vague smell of chicken filled the air. But I barely noticed any of these things, because at one of the tables was a girl so pretty my heart immediately jumped and my muscles froze. My mouth dropped open and I stared, transfixed.

She had glossy, light-brown hair that hung halfway down her back in waves. Her eyes were the color of the turquoise blue right in the center of a peacock feather. Her lips were the most luscious color pink. She looked up at me, a chip halfway to her mouth, and raised her eyebrows.

"Hello?" she said. "Dude, what's the matter with you?"

I finally found the power to speak. "N-Nothing. Sorry." I gestured at the chair across from her. "Okay if I sit here?"

She shrugged. "Do you see anyone else here?"

I sat down in the hard plastic chair and busied myself opening the bag of corn chips I had just gotten from the machine. "So. You work around here somewhere?" *Clever, Fynn*, I thought. *Why don't you ask her what her sign is?*

"Yeah. Admissions. You?"

"Soul Destination."

She wrinkled up her adorable little nose. "Is that boring?"

"Well, not so far. It's my first day."

I thought her eyes widened just a fraction, but I may have imagined it. Suddenly she leaned forward. "Really? What brings you to Hell?"

"Summer job. I've gotta save for…" I almost said a car, but then I changed it to 'college' because I thought it sounded smarter. "How about you? What brings you to Hell?"

She paused for a second, took a sip of her soda, and said, "Same as you, mostly. I needed a job."

"So, Admissions. What do you do there?"

"We evaluate the people who come in, and then we figure out what level of Hell they go to. Every sin has a score, according to severity, so we count up their sins and tally up their scores. Then off they go—we never see them again."

"I just sort the souls according to color," I said, although she hadn't asked. She smiled and got up, gathering her wrappers and water bottle.

"Wait! What's your name?" I said as she started walking to the door.

"Lily." She paused. "What's yours?"

"Fynn. Fynn Hardin."

She smiled and nodded. "Okay, Fynn Hardin. See you around."

I watched her walk away, fascinated by the motion of her hips swaying side to side. When I couldn't see her anymore, I said, "See you, Lily."

I gathered all my trash and sped back to Soul Destination. We only got nine minutes for lunch, and I didn't want to be late.

"Hey," I said to Sierra and Adrian. "Wow, only nine minutes. That really flies by. Hey, either of you know a girl named Lily? She works in Admissions?" I was talking too fast, I could hear myself, but the words just kept flying out of my mouth as fast as they bubbled to the surface. They both looked at me and shook their heads.

Bummer.

I worked as quickly as I could for the rest of the day, thinking about Lily and wondering when I would see her again.

CHAPTER EIGHT

ONCE I GOT the hang of it, Hell wasn't really that bad—at least, not at first. It was probably like any other summer job—yeah, it sort of sucked, but it was kind of fun, too. As soon as I got my first check, I ran to Free Rein and paid them a hundred dollars.

The woman behind the desk entered my payment into the computer and then looked at me over the tops of her glasses. "Don't run it up again," she said sternly. Oh, really? Darn, I hadn't thought of that. Why do adults always think they have great advice to give to teenagers like we've never heard it before? We have the Internet, you know.

I got the hang of sorting souls, which wasn't really that difficult unless the indicator light had gone out. On a good day, I could package up to three hundred souls. In addition to Adrian and Sierra, depending on what day it was, I also worked with Tom and Audrey. Tom had a big nose, and his hair looked exactly like someone stood behind him with a blow dryer every morning and blew all his hair forward. Audrey was kind of a stickler for rules, which was annoying unless we—meaning me and whoever else I was working with—were making fun of her. Then it was a riot.

"You're supposed to fold the soul into thirds," she said, crinkling her nose like she just smelled moldy cheese.

"Oh, I am so sorry. I didn't fold the soul into thirds! Whatever shall we do?" I said to Adrian.

"We will need to reassess our lives," Adrian said gravely. We cracked up, and Audrey didn't speak to us for the rest of the day, which was fine with us.

Adrian was a pretty cool guy. This was his third summer working in Hell. "You don't want to work somewhere, I don't know, normal?" I asked him.

"Nah—Hell pays marginally better and besides, I have the hang of it now. It's kind of like a break from reality."

Apparently, when he wasn't sorting souls in Hell he was an Accounting major at the University of Illinois. He already had a girlfriend—which was good, because there was no way I wanted to compete with some college dude for Lily—and a car, although he tried to make me feel better by telling me it was a piece of shit.

Sierra was fine, mostly quiet, and kept to herself. I guess maybe because she was older she felt she didn't have anything in common with us. She just kept her head down and sorted, although sometimes I swear I saw her trying to hide a smile.

This was Tom's first summer in Hell, and what he really, really wanted for next summer was to work somewhere else. As you might guess, it's freaking hot in Hell. They have fans and such, but it's still stiflingly hot all the time. It smells like ammonia and ash. They have a claustrophobic subterranean tunnel system that feels hot and closed and makes a lot of people freak out if they don't like tight spaces. And it's dark. There are lanterns every couple of feet, but it's kind of like working in a closet. There wasn't any cell phone reception—we were too deep underneath the earth. So, you couldn't text or call anyone your whole shift. I guess Tom was concerned because he had just started dating some girl—who he said was gorgeous—and he couldn't talk to her when he was at work.

"Just tell her your boss is really strict." Frankly, I was only mildly sympathetic. At least he *had* a girlfriend.

"Yeah, I guess." He still wasn't happy. I will say he tore out of there the second his shift was over, like a bat out of Hell.

Although I went to the break room instead of the cafeteria every day I worked, I didn't see Lily again. Not for weeks. I had almost given up when suddenly there she was, her lips wrapped around a straw in a soda, giving her a pout that made my head spin. It was a good thing there was a chair right next to her because my knees were like peanut butter.

"Hi!" I said, too loudly.

She looked at me appraisingly and said, "Hi, yourself."

"How's it going?" My words were coming out too fast. Crap, slow down. I sounded like Minnie Mouse.

"Going well. You?" Her eyelashes were stunning.

"Good. Things are fine in SD. How's Admissions?"

"Good."

What was with these one or two-word answers? Did she not like me? Why didn't she like me? Maybe it was my breath? I tried to breathe into my elbow to see if my breath was offensive but I didn't smell anything.

I cast about for something to say. "Do you go to school somewhere?"

She hesitated for a second and then said, "Yeah, I do. I go to high school... uh... in Springfield."

I could hardly dare to hope she meant Springfield, MA, but since Hell is big, she could be going to school anywhere on earth. "Where's that?"

"Nebraska."

Major bummer. "Oh, right. Nebraska. I don't know anyone who lives in Nebraska. Is it nice there?"

"Sure."

I was totally striking out. I don't really know what made me keep talking. "What do you like to do when you're not in Hell?"

Again, a hesitation. "I like to…you know. Normal stuff. Shopping, hanging out. What do you like to do?"

"Mostly the same. Well, I'm not so much into shopping. I like video games. You like Halo 6?"

She shook her head and asked, "I've never played it. Is it fun?"

"Oh, yeah!" I enthusiastically described my exploits as Locke and my missions for the next fifteen minutes. Eventually, it occurred to me that I was droning on and on—maybe she wasn't that interested. "So, anyway, do you play any video games?"

"I play—what's that new one? The one with the weapons?"

"They all have weapons. What platform?"

"Xbox?" she said.

"Are there Aliens involved?"

She nodded.

"Maybe Prey?"

She nodded again.

"Wow." Oh, my God. The woman of my dreams—she played video games!

Abruptly, she got up from the table. "I have to go back to work. See ya, Fynn." She gave me a wave and—I could've sworn—a flirtatious look over her shoulder. I pondered that for a while, and then realized I was late getting back to SD.

"You're late," Audrey said.

"No shit," I responded.

She made her prune face again, and then said, "The rule is people returning from break late will be forced to stay an extra thirty minutes."

"What? I was only like, five minutes late."

"It's the rule," she said stubbornly and started feverishly throwing souls into boxes.

"What the—never mind. Whatever." Honestly, I didn't much care. I was filled with a light, ballooning optimism about this girl I met. Maybe things were finally going my way.

CHAPTER NINE

U P UNTIL NOW, I had been getting to work, reporting directly to Soul Destination—SD for those of us in the biz—working my hours, and then getting the hell out of there, pardon the pun. Today was pretty slow, and curiosity got the better of me, so I decided to explore a little. After all, Hell was a big, bustling place. There could be dateless girls all over Hell who needed me to come and rescue them from a life of loneliness and desperation.

Or maybe I was just bored.

I wandered out of SD and took a left down the hallway. Hell's subterranean tunnels were claustrophobic. They were dark, like medieval-castle dark, and lit by the same sort of lanterns glowing every so often. They smelled like copper and smoke. They were supported by carved-out stone, so I supposed they couldn't collapse. I could picture myself buried under a pile of rubble and stuck in Hell somewhere for the rest of my life.

I wandered down the dimly lit tunnels, which seemed to wind around and around. This meant you couldn't see very far ahead of you. I was almost knocked over by a couple of afreets. These demons are responsible for delivering all the supplies to and from everywhere in Hell. They are short—very short, only reaching up to my kneecaps. They have potbellies and usually have beards, even the lady afreets. They have solid, thick feet. This combined with their short stature makes them very hard to knock over, but as effective as bowling balls at whacking people out of their way. Two of them came barreling past me, pushing a cart loaded with supplies. I leapt out of the way just in time.

"Watch it!" One snapped, and before I could reply they were gone.

Bastards. I continued on and came to a fork where the tunnel split in two. For no reason, I chose left. Eventually, I came to a door marked Level One. I peered in the window and almost immediately wished I hadn't.

I saw sad, soulless people staring at me with hollow eyes. The room—about the size of a football field—was filled with snow and ice. The wind was blowing snow around them, into their faces, into their hair, and onto their skin. Their skin was exposed—they had thin rags to cover themselves, but they were shivering so violently that if they weren't already dead I was sure they would've frozen to death. Fingers and ears and bare feet were black and blistered. They stumbled around, mumbling to themselves, bumping into each other. If any one of them tried to sit down, a goblin was there to poke them with a stick and make them continue their exhausted wandering.

"Jesus," I whispered to myself.

"We don't use that name here."

I spun around and found myself looking at a slim man of middle-eastern descent. He was taller than I am—5'10" in case you were wondering—and was wearing a simple sort of toga. He would've looked completely normal except for his long twisted fingernails and the two small horns sprouting from the middle of his forehead.

"Whoops, sorry." I jerked my head at the collection of miserable souls in the room. "What did they do?"

"Various things. Some were unrepentant liars and philanderers. Some of them were constant complainers. So, we give them something to complain about. Who might you be?"

"Fynn. Fynn Hardin, Soul Destination."

"Ah. Nice to meet you. I am Belphegor. I oversee levels one and two, or the junior achievers, as we like to call them." He smiled a little, pleased with his little joke. He waited a second, expecting a laugh, and when no laugh was forthcoming, he said, "I have a pick-up for you. Shall I give it to you now, or send it via afreet?"

"Uhm…send it via afreet, I guess. I have a few stops to make."

Belphegor bowed and said, "Excellent." Then he pushed the door open and disappeared into the snow-filled room. I heard more intense moaning when he entered, but I didn't want to know so I hurried on.

I could've sworn I was going in circles. Losing my bearings, I couldn't have made it back to SD if I tried. Maybe my own personal Hell would be getting lost in Hell for the rest of my life. I also worried about getting in trouble at SD, although if I remained lost, surely someone up there would wonder where I went. And send out a search party. Maybe.

I got the sense I was descending. The hallways seemed gloomier, closer. The ceiling was lower, and the dirt that made up the floors was damp. And what was that utterly nauseating smell? It was the kind of smell that crawled down your throat and stuck there like a blade.

Eventually, it occurred to me that if I was going down, what I wanted to do was reverse direction and try to go up. So, I turned around and went the way I had come, but after only a minute or two I came to another fork. Which way did I come from? I couldn't remember. The right-hand fork seemed to be headed in an upward direction, so I took it. I walked on, slowing down, trying to make heads or tails of Hell's intricate hallways.

Eventually I came to another door. I peered in. It was a large, empty white space. I looked closer. Nothing. It was a room filled with nothing. Pondering this, I wondered where all the bodies had gone. I thought about going in to look, but I was afraid I might never get out. Later I learned this was where the narcissists went. No one can see them, hear them, or smell them. When I heard that I made a mental note to volunteer to feed the homeless or work with underprivileged kids or something. You know, just in case.

I pressed on, trying to head upwards, but I felt almost as if I was upside down. Was I going up or down? I couldn't tell. The walls closed in. I felt dizzy and a little nauseous. Where was I? I walked on and on. I came to another door. This one had just a hole in the door—the glass would've melted.

It was a deep cavern. I couldn't see the bottom, but hot lava flowed by the floor. There were rock formations. I couldn't see anyone here either.

Suddenly a face appeared in the hole, so close to mine that I gasped. I was nose-to-nose with a face contorted in agonizing pain. The mouth was open wide, and the lips were pulled back in a rictus scream exposing rotting teeth and oozing gums. The stench of fetid breath hit me and I gagged. A hand reached out and clawed at the hole, scratching desperately at the wood.

Just as suddenly as it appeared, it was gone. I stood shaking, the screams echoing, and I shook my head, trying to rid myself of the image of pure torture. My skin was clammy and my legs suddenly felt like Jell-O. I had to get out of here. This wasn't a fun little field trip anymore. It was seriously creeping me out. I mean, I know I *worked* in Hell, but I had never given all that much thought to what might be going on down in those lower levels. If you buy a T-shirt for five bucks, do you seriously think about all the children in third world countries who worked for a dollar an hour to make it? No, you think, *T-shirt*! *Five bucks*! *Score*!

I wound around and around, seriously lost. Why wasn't there an elevator or something? Where were the hover crafts? Didn't they run everywhere in Hell? This must be how people felt about taxis in New York—why were they never around when you needed one? My head hurt. I needed to sit down.

I came to a door. Carved deeply into the charred wood was the name "Governor Gaap." I was thinking over whether I should or shouldn't knock when the door swung open, and before me stood a man who resembled a boulder with giant bat wings growing out of his shoulders. They flapped once and then were still.

"Can I help you?" he said.

"I...I'm lost. I can't find my way back to Soul Destination." I managed.

"Soul Destination. That's on Level One. You're on sub-level Five, a long way from there. Let me summon you a hovercraft." He clapped his hairy, clawed hands, and immediately a hovercraft appeared, humming and ready to go.

"Wow, thanks Mister, uh..."

"I am Governor Gaap. I'm in charge of southern Hell."

"Southern Hell...so, there's a Northern Hell?"

"There's an upstairs." He smiled. His lips were black. "That's where you work. I suggest you get back there as soon as possible. Nice meeting you, young man." He turned and walked into his office.

I was going to tell him my name, but then it occurred to me that maybe I really didn't want him to know. I sat in the hovercraft, and right away it took off like it was on a mission. It whipped along the hallways of Hell, which, did I mention had a vast multitude of turns? Before I knew it I was extremely motion sick and hanging onto the roll bar for dear life. My stomach lurched wildly. I squeezed my eyes shut and prayed for the ride to be over.

Finally, I was dropped off, miraculously right outside SD. I lurched out of the hovercraft, which immediately took off. Adrian and Sierra both stopped sorting and looked up as I pushed open the door.

"Where have you been?" Adrian said.

"I was just wandering around and got lost." I wiped the sweat off my forehead. I had never been so happy to see SD. Furthermore, today was Audrey's day off, so no one was around to harass me for falling behind on my quota.

"Word of advice: Don't go poking around Hell," Adrian said.

"Good advice," I said.

CHAPTER TEN

WORKING EVERY MONDAY, Tuesday, Thursday, and Saturday was okay, but I never really got a weekend, or even more than one day off in a row. I thought about complaining, but I was worried about what happened to people who complained about the working conditions. There was no precedent. Furthermore, since I didn't have a girlfriend, I didn't have anything to do anyway.

Tuesday started like any other day in Hell. I was working with Tom and Sierra, so it was nice and quiet. Around mid-morning, Dodd came down from his office and stood in the middle of the room until we all stopped working and stared at him expectantly.

"I need someone to run this over to Marketing, ASAP." He was holding an envelope in one hand and hitting the corner of it into his palm.

Marketing? Hell had a marketing department? What would that entail? All I could picture was a TV commercial and some disembodied voice saying, "Are you tired of making good choices in your life? Had it with noble intentions? Determined to be miserable? Come to sunny Hell! You'll enjoy our warm and flaming atmosphere, our friendly non-human staff, and the total conviction that nothing will ever be good again!"

Tom, Sierra, and I all looked at each other. After the last disaster of getting lost in Hell, I was reluctant to venture past SD. I don't know what was up with Tom and Sierra, but they didn't look excited either.

Exasperated, Dodd said, "You just have to cross the central hub, and Marketing is on your right, next to Admissions. It's not far. It'll take you ten minutes."

Admissions? Did he say Admissions? "I'll do it!" I said.

"Thank you, Fynn," Dodd said as he handed me the envelope. I nodded and tried not to seem too eager. Taking a left out of SD, I followed the hallway down into the central hub. Dorothy smiled and waved.

"Hi, Dorothy!" She had pink hair and orange skin today. She kind of reminded me of Dunkin' Donuts. I liked Dorothy, but I didn't want to stop to chat—I was on a mission, so I waved but didn't break stride.

I went down the west hallway where most of the corporate offices were. There were signs on the doors, and I finally found the marketing department.

It looked like a more or less normal office. I walked in, and the office manager turned to me and blinked slowly. A frill covered the top of his dry green head. He didn't say anything, but I was pretty sure his forked tongue flickered. Cautiously, I handed him the envelope. He hissed and nodded at me. I turned around quickly and left.

Now to say hello to Lily. I found Admissions just fine, but before I got to the door I was stopped cold. A fearsome-looking chimera with the head of a lion, a goat's head on its back, and a snake for a tail was strutting down the hallway. His snake tail was nipping at the backs of a few forlorn-looking people. They had their heads down as they studied the floor. I stared. One of them looked kind of familiar.

"Uncle Seymour?" I said.

The man in the middle jerked his head up and stared at me. He resembled a praying mantis. He had a broad forehead that tapered down to a pointed chin and large eyes that asked, "What's in it for me?"

"Fynn?" He asked in amazement.

Uncle Seymour was the kind of relative you only saw at weddings and funerals and hardly at any other time. He wasn't even my uncle; he was my mother's uncle, so my great uncle. Still, I thought he was a great guy. Unlike a lot of relatives, he would take time to talk to me, squatting down so we were at eye level and really listening when I told him about my fascination with insects. Okay, I was a dorky kid. But Uncle Seymour made me feel like it was perfectly normal to be obsessed with the mating rituals of a male water strider. I went to his funeral a few months ago.

"What are you doing here?" I asked.

He glanced at the chimera. "What are *you* doing here?"

"I work here. What…are you…" I said awkwardly. Obviously, Hell didn't get many visitors. Uncle Seymour had gone to Hell! I wondered what he did to get him here.

"Oh, Fynn. I'm so sorry." He shook his head with a knowing smile. His rheumy eyes bore into me, and he grabbed my wrist and leaned closer. "What are you in for?"

I shook his hand off and jumped. "I *work* here, Uncle Seymour."

"Sure you do, son."

"I do!" I snapped. I felt my stomach muscles clench and my face grow hot, although that may have been because I was standing too close to a lantern.

At this point, the snake-head tail of the chimera bit Uncle Seymour, and he yelped and started walking. He turned around and stared at me until he and the group of inductees disappeared around the corner.

Damn, talking to Uncle Seymour had chewed up all ten minutes Dodd thought it should take someone to drop something off in marketing. Much to my chagrin, I would have to find Lily later, although I did try to see into the office as I passed it but didn't see her.

I pondered what unfortunate life choices Uncle Seymour must have made that landed him in Hell. I don't know why, but I never thought I would run into anyone I knew in Hell. It was unsettling, to say the least. For the rest of the day, I kept my head down and just concentrated on hitting my quota.

§ § §

Wednesday afternoon, I was sprawled out on the living room couch, eating nachos and watching a reality show called *Celebrity Truck Drivers*. It wasn't very good, and I was just about to doze off when I heard the door slam. I opened my eyes to find Kevin standing in the living room, clenching and unclenching his fists. His bottom lip stuck out a little and he was breathing hard.

"Hey, Kevin, what's up?" I sat up.

"Nothing!" he snapped.

I studied him as he stomped up to his room. Was I this moody when I was twelve? In my head, I was a ray of sunshine and light, but I supposed it was possible that I was moody. I would have to ask Mom.

I dozed back off on the couch until I heard the front door and the telltale pitter-patter of toddler's feet gamboling down the hallway.

"Inn! Inn!" Maddie shrieked. She climbed up on the couch to say hi, patting my face with her chubby hands. Mom walked in after a minute. She smiled at me and sat down in the recliner.

"How was work?" Mom asked.

"Fine." Maddie climbed off of me and went to explore her toy bin. I pulled myself up into a sitting position. "Hey, I was wondering about Uncle Seymour."

Mom leaned forward, propping her chin in her hand. "What about him?"

"Well, what sort of a person was he?"

Mom looked at me in the exact same way you might look at someone if they just told you they were contagious. "Why do you ask?"

I shrugged and tried to appear nonchalant. "Just wondering. He was in a dream I had."

"Well, he was smart. He was funny and sarcastic. Actually, he kind of reminded me of you."

That's what I was afraid of. Was I destined to go to Hell after I died? Because I really didn't want to. Not only would I know everyone on the staff—*Hey, Frank.*

37

How's the torture going—which would be awkward, but Hell was no fun to spend any part of your afterlife.

"Good old Uncle Seymour," she said. Then she frowned as if she just remembered something.

"What?"

She glanced at me and shrugged. "Oh, nothing. It was a long time ago. Anyway, can you keep an eye on your sister while I throw together something for dinner?"

"Yeah, sure. C'mon, Maddie. Let's play with something noisy."

CHAPTER ELEVEN

"IT'S SO HOT." I moaned and rolled over onto my back, thus almost flipping off the chaise lounge. I was at Josh's house, hanging out with him and his girlfriend, Courtney. Courtney had long, tanned legs that extended out from her cut-off jean shorts and ended in pretty feet, painted with hot pink nail polish. A plaid bikini top gracefully curved around her breasts, not that I was looking or anything.

"Is it hotter than Hell?" Josh asked. Out of all the people I told, Josh and Court were the only people who really believed I had a job in Hell. It was only June, and it was so hot outside even the mosquitoes seemed lazy and unmotivated.

"Hell is hot, but it's a dry heat."

"Right. It's not the heat, it's the humidity," Josh said. I threw my empty water bottle at him. Court laughed.

"You must be used to it by now," Court said.

"Not really." I sat up and wiped my face, which had sweat running down it in little rivulets. We were out by his pool—technically, his parents' pool. The sun shimmered off the water and reflected onto the concrete. It was ninety-two degrees out. Josh's parents' house had a typical suburban backyard. The pool was plopped in the sunny part, meaning on hot days it was twice as hot. I jumped in the deep end, making a huge splash. Courtney squealed. Josh then jumped in, and Court followed, still wearing her shorts. It was so cool, wet, and refreshing. New life surged through us as we splashed and goofed around, enjoying the respite from the suffocating heat.

When we finally dragged ourselves out of the pool we dried only our faces with our towels. I flipped my towel on the chaise lounge and stretched out, feeling much better. The heat was tolerable, almost friendly now.

"So, Fynn. Have you met anyone, down in Hell?" Courtney giggled as if this was absurd.

"Well, maybe."

"Really?" She sat up, interested, lowered her sunglasses a smidgen, and peered over the top of them. "Who is she?"

"She's not a demon, is she?" Josh asked.

"No! She's nice. I mean, I…I like her but…I don't know much about her. We just met." I didn't mention dreaming of her at night, Lily's long hair wrapped around my hands, feeling her body pressed against me, her mouth hungrily tasting mine.

"Where is she from?" Maddie asked.

"Nebraska."

"Nebraska? I didn't think anyone lived in Nebraska," Josh said.

"That's what I said!"

"Nebraska. So it would be a long-distance relationship I guess, then, huh? That's rough," Courtney said. I hadn't really thought about it.

"Well, we're not at the dating stage yet. But…I don't know. She could just get off the elevator at my stop, if she came to visit, couldn't she?"

"I guess. Or you could go to Nebraska. Hang out in cornfields and shit," Josh said.

"Yeah. Nebraska." I paused. "Is there anything in Nebraska?"

"They have Omaha. They probably have, like, McDonald's and stuff. Other than that, no. There's nothing there," Josh said. I knew Josh had never been to Nebraska, but he was smart so I figured maybe he looked it up once, or something. "Why don't you ask her? That would be an interesting topic of conversation. 'Hey'—what's her name?"

"Lily."

"Hey, Lily, what on earth do you do all day?"

"I assume she goes to school. Or, wait—how old is she?" Court asked.

"I don't know. Around our age, I think. She plays video games."

"Oooo—a shared interest!" Josh said.

"Yeah. I mean, if anything ever comes of it."

"Don't worry Fynn. You'll find a girlfriend one of these days." Josh smirked.

"Not without a car," I said glumly.

"Well, you're working on that. How much money have you saved?"

"Not enough."

"Well, keep working. Do they have overtime?" Josh asked.

"I don't think so." Actually, I hadn't looked into it. Maybe they did. I'd have to ask Dodd about it. I could use more money to put away. While I had paid off my debt to Free Rein, so far I had only saved $1000, which is obviously not enough for a car.

Courtney smiled at me sympathetically. She had really white teeth. "Hang in there, Fynn. Things will get better. You'll see."

I didn't know it at the time, but things were about to get worse. Much worse.

CHAPTER TWELVE

JUNE CREPT INTO July, and I still wasn't making any progress with Lily. So, when Josh said he was having a Fourth of July party and that I should come, I said sure. Why not?

Josh's parents were on vacation in Mexico—Cancun, Josh said. It didn't matter; the point was they weren't home, which meant a fun night of debauchery and mayhem. At least in theory.

Josh lives in a nicer neighborhood than mine. In my neighborhood, all the houses have fences that surround the small-ish yards, and there are at least two cars in every driveway. All the neighbors wave as they pass you going down the street. In Josh's neighborhood, the cars are tucked away in the garages, and the yards are huge and only fenced in if there's a dog. No one waves.

I didn't have a car, but I knew a kid near me who did. His name was Liam. He agreed to give me a lift if I walked over to his house. He had red hair and freckles and the annoying habit of saying, "Am I right?" after almost everything he said. But he had a car, so I went. After a thankfully short ride—"Nice house, am I right?"—we parked on the street a few houses down from Josh's.

I heard music in Josh's backyard, so I went around back towards the pool. There were about thirty to forty kids, some I knew from high school and some I didn't. I looked around for Josh. He was over by the gas grill, flipping burgers with one hand and drinking a beer with the other. "Hey, Fynn!" He called out. "C'mon over! What can I get ya? Beer, burger, hot dog?"

"I'll have a beer." I didn't really like the taste of beer all that much, but it was alcohol, and damned if I was going to look like a lame duck. Josh opened a bottle and handed it to me. He looked busy so I wandered around, saying hi to some kids from school.

"Hey, Fynn. How's it going?" my friend Tony asked.

"Good. You?"

"Can't complain," he said as he threw his arm around a very pretty brunette. I think her name might've been Julie, but then again it could've been Robin. He nuzzled her behind the ear and she laughed. "Haven't seen you around much."

"I've been working a lot." I took a huge chug of beer.

"Where ya working?"

41

"Hell."

He laughed. "That bad, huh? Well, cheer up. It's already July."

I nodded but walked away, not terribly interested in watching Tony and Julie/Robin/whatever-her-name-was slobber all over each other.

A couple of kids were playing chicken in the pool. It looked fun, but then I'd be stuck sitting around in wet clothes for the rest of the party. I wandered over to one of the snack tables and helped myself to a handful of chips and some cocktail wieners, wondering what to do with myself. I always felt awkward at parties. Do you just go up to people and start talking? Stand around looking like a wallflower, hoping to God someone starts talking to you? I promised myself that if I wasn't having fun in, like, 45 minutes, I was leaving. I'd be having a lot more fun playing Mall Zombie by myself at this point.

Just when I was about to throw in the towel, find Josh, and tell him I was going, a cute girl I had never seen before approached the snack table. She had wide brown eyes, blonde hair, and dark eyebrows. I love that look.

"Hi," she said shyly as she stuck her hand in the chip bowl.

"Hi." I wondered where she was from. I searched for something clever to say and went with, "So, how do you know Josh?"

She shrugged and smiled. "I don't, really. My cousin goes to school with him, but I'm from Canton." Canton was a town over. Good sign.

"Oh. Who's your cousin?"

"Hailey Lyons?"

"Oh, right, Hailey. I think she was in my Algebra class." Maybe.

"So, what's your name?" she asked me.

I told her my name was Fynn and she said her name was Cassidy. Cassidy Evans. We talked for a bit as we ate snacks. Then, in a fit of social competence, I said, "Why don't we sit and I'll get us some beers?" Two chairs next to each other had just been vacated. She nodded, and I went to go fetch the beer. I was relieved when she was still waiting right where I left her.

We talked. Her parents were divorced, and she lived with her mom and two sisters. Her mom was a doctor, and she thought maybe that's part of the reason her parents divorced—not only was her mom more accomplished than her dad, she was also working all time. Her dad was a high school teacher a few towns away.

"So, you live with your mom but you never see her?" I asked.

"Not much. She's an ER doctor. She works a lot."

I filled her in on my family, my mom being a nurse working nights, so I sort of knew where she was coming from, and my dad being in business. I told her about Kevin and that Maddie was a surprise baby.

"How old is Maddie?" she asked.

"Uh…a little over a year. Fifteen months?" I guessed.

"My son Blake is eighteen months," she said, looking at her shorts.

I wasn't sure I heard her correctly. Did she just say she had a son? I stared while I waited for inspiration to hit me.

Cassidy looked up and said, "It's okay. It's just something I like to get out of the way."

"Oh. No, it's fine. Wow. A son, huh? That must be hard. How do you, like, go to high school?"

"My high school actually has a day care program, which is great."

"Yeah. So…" Now what? Do I ask her if she's single? Because in light of her having a son, I wasn't sure what the protocol was. Was I supposed to assume Blake's father was involved and that she was just out for a pleasant evening to make new friends? For that matter, what was *my* intention? I mean, just taking care of Maddie was difficult, and she wasn't even my kid. I couldn't imagine trying to date someone with a son. Did that make me a future step-dad? I didn't think I could handle it.

Lucky for me, Cassidy seemed to read my mind and said, "I haven't talked to Blake's dad since Blake was a month old." She took a long sip of her beer.

Well, I guess she was single. The rest of my questions just tumbled around in my buzzed brain, the words rearranging themselves in different ways. I think Cassidy noticed my mental wrestling match because she said, "I know—it's a lot to digest."

I nodded and decided to keep talking to her for a while. We talked a lot, actually. I liked her, but I couldn't help but compare her to Lily. Lily was more beautiful, but then again, I wasn't really getting anywhere with Lily. I hadn't even seen her in a few weeks. Plus she lived in Nebraska, whereas Cassidy lived about ten minutes away. Cassidy was easy to talk to as well—easy for me, who stumbled and stuttered and looked like an idiot in front of girls most of the time. But she had a kid. I couldn't imagine I was mature enough to date someone with a kid. Half of the time *I* needed supervision.

The party flew by. When it got dark Cassidy and I watched the fireworks that you could just barely see over the trees. Some kids lit illegal fireworks in the backyard until one of them lit the grass on fire and Josh got pissed.

"Well, I gotta go. See ya, Fynn." She started to walk away.

Should I call her? Should I ask for her number? Shit, what do I do?

Really, I was still infatuated with Lily. But what if it didn't work out? How could it even work out? But…I was still pondering Cassidy being a mom. That seemed like an awful lot to take on.

I stood there and, while I was still thinking about it, Cassidy disappeared around a corner.

CHAPTER THIRTEEN

I WOKE UP the next morning, hot and sweaty and tangled in my sheets. My mouth felt like I had been eating cotton balls, and there was a repetitive throbbing going on in my head. I rolled over and stared at my Kate Upton poster. Somehow the banging in my head grew louder. I covered my traitorous head with a pillow and told it to shut up.

"Fynn!"

Oh, God.

"Fynn!"

"What?"

"Will you watch Maddie for about an hour? I have to run some errands, and I don't want to take her."

I slowly dragged myself into a sitting position and blinked. It felt like someone had poured sand into my eyes while I was asleep. "Yeah, give me a minute."

What day was this? Where was my phone? I grabbed it off my side table and saw it was nine o'clock on Sunday, July 5th. Rubbing the back of my sweaty neck, I pulled on some shorts and went downstairs.

Maddie was staggering around, weaving between her toys and other obstacles like a sailor with an inner ear infection. Mom was stuffing her cell phone into her purse. She looked irritable.

"I don't know where Kevin went, and your father had to work. I need to go to the grocery store and…some other places. I'll be back." She nodded at me and closed the door firmly. I suspected what she really wanted was to get away from Maddie. Making my way into the kitchen, I hit the button on the coffee maker. Before I could even sit down Maddie was grinning and making a beeline for the door to the cellar.

"Hey, no!" I said, steering her away from the door. All I needed was for Maddie to plummet down the basement steps. She wasn't that good at stairs yet, and it's dark down there. I explained this to her, but she insisted on running for the door about seventeen more times, shrieking with laughter every time I caught her and swept her back into the living room. I was already sweating.

"All right, that's enough." I herded her into the living room and put the baby gates on both sides so she couldn't get out. She howled.

45

"Hey, look. Look, Maddie! Isn't this great?" I held up one of her loud flashing light toys. She looked mildly interested. I sighed, finished my cold coffee, and pondered what life must be like for Cassidy. I hoped she had someone to help her when Blake engaged in toddler terrorist behavior.

The front door slammed and Kevin walked in. He had a face on him like he just lost his dog.

"Hey, what's up?"

"Nothing."

"Kevin, what's the matter?"

"Nothing."

He sure was acting strange. I watched as he went up to his room, and I made a mental note to ask Mom about him later.

After a few hours, Mom was back. I think her hair was different. Maddie squealed, ran over to her, and Mom picked her up. I'm pretty sure Maddie's babbling was her telling Mom about being kept captive in the living room.

"Hey, Mom—do you know what's up with Kevin?" I asked.

Mom put Maddie back down. "Why?"

"I don't know. He seems off. Like, depressed or something."

Mom looked puzzled. "I haven't noticed, but I'll ask him about it."

"Good." Leaving my worries about Kevin in Mom's capable hands, I went upstairs and shut the door to my room. Peace and quiet, at least for now.

CHAPTER FOURTEEN

YOU MAY HAVE noticed, as certainly Josh pointed out about three hundred times, that even though I had been crushing hard on Lily for weeks, I had not actually asked her out. I was working my way up to it, I swear. But every time I went to say, "So, do you want to maybe catch a movie or something?" I stared into her gorgeous blue eyes, my mouth went dry, and instead I said something completely inane, such as, "Want a Cheetos?"

I really had to up my game.

"Just ask her out already," Josh said. "What, does she have a boyfriend?"

Actually, she didn't. This I knew, but only because we were talking about stuff we liked to do when we weren't working, and she said she liked to shop and play the video game *Zombie Death Mall* online. I managed to say, "Oh, does your boyfriend play that, too?" She said she didn't have one. This was weeks ago. I knew she was probably at least somewhat aware that I liked her, so I don't know why I couldn't close the deal. Because I'm a chicken shit, that's why.

"Cassidy really liked you," Josh said.

I sort of knew that, I guess.

"I gave her your number."

"Wait, what?" I said.

Josh sighed. "Look, you're not getting anywhere with this Lily chick, and you and Cassidy seemed to like each other, so when she asked me for it, I gave it to her. Sorry if I shouldn't have."

"It's okay." I *did* like Cassidy. But I still felt I should give me and Lily another shot. Or a shot, at least.

As July hammered on, I knew I had to do something. After all, soon it would be August. I would quit working in Hell and go back to school, and she probably would, too. So I had to act fast. Pretty fast, anyway.

I spent the morning in Soul Destination, working with Audrey and Tom. Tom worked quickly, almost carelessly, and he didn't make many mistakes; the reason I knew this is because at the end of every shift they reported our accuracy rate on an electronic board. Tom was always above ninety-four percent. Apparently if you slid below eighty-five percent they fired you. So far I had managed to hover above ninety-two percent, which wasn't surprising because separating souls was pretty straightforward. I was happy with ninety-two percent. Audrey, on the other hand, had a fit if she scored anything below a hundred percent. Naturally, we were very mature and supportive about this and harassed her mercilessly.

"Oh, my God! You should just quit, now. You're a failure. How do you live with yourself?"

"I don't know if I can continue on, in the face of such incompetence."

Then her nostrils would flare, her ears would get all red, and she'd say something like, "I am doing my best! I really don't understand why I didn't get a hundred percent." Then she would mumble to herself while we giggled and sometimes just outright laughed. Okay, we were jerks, but she really had to lighten up.

Lunch rolled around. I had the best luck finding Lily in the break room, so that's where I headed. Tom went to the cafeteria and Audrey—I really don't know where Audrey spent her lunch breaks, but anywhere not near me was fine. I walked into the break room and there she was. Lily. My heart jumped like it had paddles on it and my breath seized. God, she was luscious.

"Hi," I said as I made my way to the vending machines.

"Hi," she said.

I grabbed a ham and cheese sandwich and Coke and sat down next to her, focusing on unwrapping my sandwich. I couldn't very well start with, *Hey, you want to hang out sometime,* so I went to the standard lunchtime conversation starter. "What did you get?"

"Tuna."

"From the machine? It's not like, poison or something?"

She lifted the edge of the bread and sniffed delicately. "Doesn't seem to be."

"Oh, well, that's good." I took a bite of my sandwich. "Aren't there any condiments around here?"

She lifted her chin towards a table next to the vending machine. "I think so."

"Oh." I felt mildly stupid, but at least now I had mayonnaise. "So. How have you been?" I ventured.

She finished chewing and swallowed. "Good. And you?"

"Oh, I've been fine. Uhh…play any good games lately?"

She smiled, and I swear I heard angels. "Actually, I just found a new one I love! It's called Destruction."

"Ooo—that sounds fun."

She described the game to me, her face animated and lively, and I have no idea what she said. I was entranced by her mouth, her nose, and her face. I was in deep. Break time flew by as we laughed and discussed great video games of our time, and I guess I made appropriate responses. I glanced at the clock. My break was up in three minutes. I took a deep breath. "We should hang out sometime."

There was a pause. She stared at me for a second, and I thought, *that's it. It's over. I've blown it.* But to my surprise, she smiled shyly and said, "Yeah, okay. I can come to Massachusetts."

I laughed, but then I thought, *this is a challenge, her living in Nebraska and me in Massachusetts.* "Sure! You could come to my house and hang out for a while, and then I could bring you back to the elevator. You could take it to Hell and then to your home." That didn't really explain what would happen when school started and I quit Hell, but we could get to that later.

She gave me a long, appraising look. "Okay. When?"

"How about today?" No time like the present.

"Sure. Where shall I meet you?"

"How about…how about right here? At 6:00 p.m.? What time do you have to be home?"

"My curfew is 10:00 p.m."

Four hours with Lily! I had died and gone to heaven.

CHAPTER FIFTEEN

I SPENT THE rest of the day counting down the hours and fantasizing about my date with Lily. Obviously, this made me incredibly distracted, and my accuracy rate slid to eighty-seven percent.

"You really need to focus," Audrey said, pursing her lips and looking judgmental.

"Yup, you're right," I said cheerfully. Even Miss Judgmental Supreme herself couldn't spoil my fantastic mood. I was going to hang out with Lily! I was going to hang out with Lily! This sing-songed through my head, and I would smile to myself, which I think made my coworkers think I had some kind of mental disorder. But I didn't really care. The culmination of all my summer fantasies was coming to fruition! Lily. Lily. Lily.

Finally, 6:00 p.m. arrived. I bolted to the time clock, punched out, and then hightailed it to the break room.

Empty.

I looked up and down the hallway. Waiting a minute or two, I looked up and down the hallway again. I sat at a table, taking out my cell phone before I remembered Hell didn't get any cell phone reception. Still, I could play Candy Crush. I played for about 45 seconds, and I got up to check the hallway again.

I knew it was too good to be true. She stood me up. I didn't know where I had gone wrong, but obviously somewhere. Maybe it was too soon? Maybe too late? Maybe she was put off by the thought of having a relationship with someone seven states away from hers—I had Googled it. Or maybe it was my approach. I tried to remember how much I had talked about myself. Did I let her talk enough? Did...

"Hello."

I jerked my head up and there she was. Lily.

I jumped out of my seat. "Hi!"

She laughed. "Afraid I was going to blow you off?"

"No, no, of course not. Are you ready to go?"

"Sure."

We walked out of the break room and caught a hovercraft to central corporate. Waving at Dorothy, I noticed she was sporting purple hair and green skin today.

"You look nice," I said as I boarded the elevator. I couldn't help but notice that Lily's hand was firmly gripping my elbow, and I liked it. It made me feel like I was hers.

Dorothy smiled and said, "Thanks, Fynn. Have a nice evening."

"I will!" I said as the doors closed. I glanced at Lily and a thought occurred to me. "Hey Lily, what's your last name?"

She hesitated, just a fraction of a second. She glanced over my shoulder and said, "Case."

I always got motion sick on the elevator, so I was momentarily quiet while I focused on not throwing up on her shoes, because I was pretty sure that would ruin the whole date. Luckily, I held it together, and finally the elevator stopped.

"Okay, Lily Case, welcome to Massachusetts!" We got off the elevator in the basement of Franklin Regional High School. She looked around, taking it in. Since it was a little after 6:20 p.m. in July, it wasn't dark yet, but obviously there weren't any lights on. It gave the whole place a deserted feel, like somewhere you'd film "My High School Horror Story" or something like that. But she seemed interested, asking questions like what subjects I had taken and what I would be taking in the fall. I brushed over my lackadaisical grades and mentioned that I enjoyed study hall. But she didn't laugh.

"Are you hungry?" I asked her.

"Uhm, sure."

"Great! I have just the place in mind."

As I might have mentioned, I have no car. There isn't a lot of public transportation in Franklin, so I called an Uber and we went to my favorite pizza place, "Al's Pizza." It was small and cozy and smelled delicious. We grabbed a table, and I ordered us a medium pizza and two cokes.

I sat across from her and stared at her beautiful blue eyes and button nose and said, "Okay, Lily Case. Tell me everything."

She laughed.

"No, seriously, I want to know everything about you. What do you do every day? What's it like in Nebraska?"

She started to talk, hesitating a little at first and then gathering some steam. She said she was a pretty good student, about a B average, but if she wanted to go to college she felt she would have to leave Nebraska. However, her Dad had a heart condition, and she wasn't sure she wanted to go far from home. I almost said, "There's a ton of great colleges in Massachusetts," but I managed not to. It might be a little over the top for the first date. Maybe I would save it for the next one. She said she had a little sister named Kathy who was grade-A annoying. She lived in a small town about an hour away from Omaha.

The pizza arrived—her favorite toppings were pineapple and bacon, so that's what I ordered—and we talked on and on. I drank three cokes, and between us we finished the whole pizza. Before I knew it, it was 9:30 p.m. and time to take her back to the high school so she could go to Hell.

"I guess it's time to go." I couldn't stop myself from smiling at her. I was having so much fun.

She stretched her arms over her head. Wow, she had long arms. They kind of bent towards her head, like they were put on backwards. They looked like antlers. "Okay."

We got back to FRHS and I tipped the driver, who grunted at me as he drove away. I walked her back to the elevator, trying to walk slowly. For one thing, I was trying to stretch out the time as long as it could go. And, hanging over my head was the age-old question, do I kiss her or not?

I really, really wanted to. But other than hanging onto my elbow as we boarded the elevator to get here in the first place, she hadn't touched me or made any affectionate overtures. Maybe she wasn't really into me?

I felt the warmth from her body as she walked next to me. I looked at her from the side. She smelled delicious, like flowers in the spring. She had a beautiful profile. Her nose was a perfect little ski slope, and her cheekbones were so sharp you could ski off them. Her lips were a great shade of pink, soft and full, and so kissable it hurt.

"I had a good time," she said.

Good? She had a good time? Not a great time? "So did I," I said. If she was going to play it casual so was I.

She stood in front of the open elevator doors, about to step into them and head back to Hell and then to her home. It was now or never.

I took a step towards her. She didn't step back, so that was good. I leaned in and closed my eyes. Go, go, go—touch down. I felt my lips press onto hers. They were soft and warm. No slobber. Great kisser.

She put her hands on my shoulders and said sweetly, "I have to get back. I'll see you tomorrow?"

"Yeah. Tomorrow," I breathed. I trotted away, and my feet never touched the ground. Never had I so looked forward to going to Hell.

CHAPTER SIXTEEN

I HAD TROUBLE sleeping that night, partly because I was so excited I felt like I had wings. I'm sure the fact that I had three cokes had something to do with it, too, but really it was because of Lily. I went over every part of the date in my mind, over and over again. Especially the kiss. It was wonderful. My lips met hers, and my nerves sang out in a joyous emotional chorus. I saw the faces of angels smiling down at me, gracing me with their warmth. My heart swelled with love.

I almost skipped off to work the next morning. I came off the elevator into Hell and saw Dorothy. She looked...well, terrible. Whereas usually her hair was done in an elaborate style and in a color dyed to contrast with her skin color of the day, today her skin was a mottled blue and her hair was gray. She looked like a giant bruise.

"Dorothy, is everything all right?" I asked. Maybe she was sick.

"Fynn. Oh, my, it's just been crazy around here." She leaned forward conspiratorially and whispered, "A demon escaped last night."

I stared at her for a second. I didn't think demons could escape Hell. Isn't it where they belong or something? "How...how does a demon escape?"

She looked puzzled. "I'm not sure, but it has sure thrown management into a tizzy, I can tell you. Demons can cause all sorts of problems. If a demon escapes and gets to earth, it has some plan, and not a good one."

I mulled that over. Wouldn't a demon be noticeable if it escaped? I thought of the afreets, and then of all the demons I had met. I couldn't imagine any of them blending into polite society, or impolite society.

Distracted, I waved to Dorothy and went to SD. I saw Tom and Sierra were working with me today. Thank goodness, no Audrey. I opened my first box of souls and started sorting them, all the while pretty much just counting down the minutes until lunch. It took forever and was like time had stopped. I had always sorted souls; I would always be sorting souls. It would go on forever.

Naturally, it didn't, and eventually lunchtime arrived. I went to the break room. No Lily. Figuring she was late or something, I got myself a protein bar and soda, sat down, and starting munching. A few minutes went by, and still no Lily. I knew sometimes Admissions fell behind if there were a lot of people that entered Hell at once. So I waited. And waited. We only got nine minutes for lunch, so when eight minutes had gone by I decided to check to see if Lily had gone to the cafeteria instead.

Hell's cafeteria is a large oval room with different serving stations. There was one for salads, one for sandwiches, and one for the hot meal of the day. Today was Tuesday, so that meant meatloaf. I glanced around the seating area, but I didn't see Lily.

Of course, it wasn't that unusual that I didn't see her at work. She had explained to me once that Admissions had a rotating lunch schedule, so sometimes she went early and sometimes she went later. We didn't always have the same break period. Still, we'd just had a date last night, and you'd think she'd try to talk to me or something. Maybe dating was different in Nebraska.

From time to time, the Hornissens poked their heads in, looking for the escaped demon. I guess they were thinking it didn't really escape but was hiding somewhere. Hell's security task force, the Hornissens, was the biggest, scariest bunch of prison guards ever. They were each over seven feet tall, with long faces that ended in pincer jaws. They would use these to rip apart any demon or dead person foolish enough to try to escape. They had hulking shoulders, massive chests, and they carried bandoleers strapped across their torsos. They traveled in groups of three and marched with military precision. You could hear them coming by the "click, click, click" of their jaws beating a rhythm in the hallways. They were terrifying.

Honestly, though, I didn't give them much thought. They marched by a few times, and I just kept my head down and continued working. After all, I personally was not an escaped demon, and I didn't know of any escaped demons. I was mostly wondering where Lily went and when I would see her again. The inner workings of Hell were above my station.

Finally, 6:00 p.m. rolled around. My shoulders were stiff from bending over the packing table all day. I rolled them out a little, but they were like boulders. Walking to the elevator, I looked over my shoulder now and then to see if Lily was around. When I got to the elevator, three Hornissens were stationed there. I moved to get by them, and one of them stopped me with an insect-like claw on my shoulder. Then they frisked me, which made no sense to me. Did they think I stuck a demon in my pocket?

Once that was over I went home, a little dejected. I thought Lily and I had a really good time yesterday, but maybe she didn't think so? She said she would see me today, didn't she? But then where was she?

I trudged out of the high school and started my walk home. So far this summer I had put most of my money away, only spending a little bit here and there on fast food and a few random things. I had been thinking of all the places I could show Lily if I had a car. We could go down to the beach I always went to when I was a kid. There were acres and acres of smooth, grassy fields where we used to picnic, and then there was the beach and the salty waves and the marshland. I used to try to catch crabs in the shallow waters, putting them into my yellow plastic pail and keeping them until it was time to go home. Then I would gently let them go. They seemed happy, waving their claws around, probably waving to their families and friends, "Here I am! I'm back!"

I could show her the summer carnival they had every year in Bradford. The smell of fried dough and cotton candy coming down the midway. Dozens of kids, small ones walking around with their parents, wide-eyed with wonder. Teenagers laughing with their friends, holding giant plushes they won at ring toss and the water gun races.

I walked the rest of the way home, feeling a little sorry for myself. I turned over every aspect of our date. Had I said something wrong? I looked for clues in her behavior, but I came up with nothing. She seemed to have fun. Maybe not as much fun as I did, but fun.

I pushed through the front door. Mom was sitting on the couch in the living room, watching Maddie play with her xylophone. Someone who clearly doesn't like us gave it to her for her birthday.

"Hi, Sweetie. There's chicken and stuffing in the crock pot if you're hungry," mom said.

"Thanks." I was starving. As I was heaping a large portion of chicken onto my plate, my phone pinged. I finished scooping, took my phone out, and looked at it. It was a text—from Lily. She hadn't forgotten me!

Hey, sorry I didn't see you at work. I had to call in sick. See you soon?

My heart soared. I couldn't type fast enough.

"For sure! Feel better."

I was so relieved that I celebrated by eating two helpings of dinner and then finishing up with ice cream.

CHAPTER SEVENTEEN

I WAS HAPPY I was dating Lily—if that's what we were doing. Never had a girl pulled me in so completely. It was like I was under a magic spell cast by a particularly cute witch.

Of course, Cassidy was a problem. She was a nice girl. I didn't want to hurt her feelings. But then, we weren't like, a thing, were we? We just texted back and forth while my erstwhile girlfriend was on sabbatical. Did that mean I had to text her and say, oh, by the way, I can't talk to you anymore? Was that necessary?

I wrestled with this question quite a bit during the next few days. At some point, Cassidy texted me. "How's it going?" So, I did what I usually do when faced with uncomfortable choices. I was very mature, so I ignored her completely. For once I was happy that Hell didn't get any reception as I went to work. I was also beyond thrilled that Lily said she could come over after I got off work. As far as Cassidy went, I knew I had mentioned not being able to text while at work. She just thought it was because my boss was really strict.

You have no idea.

Hell gave me a respite from the guilt I felt. After all, I couldn't do anything about Cassidy if I couldn't talk to her, could I? I focused on my work, sorting soul after soul. I packed them neatly in their little compartments and sent them on their way. Sometimes I wondered about the souls—who they were and what sort of a person they had been to be sent to Hell. The ones I especially wondered about were the ones marked for Universal Return. These were people who, after serving a sentence in Hell, had still not made up for the pain they had caused in life, so they were returned to be absorbed into the universe. I heard some of them went on to become another life form and some just kind of vanished. Their souls went into the ether to create some form of life, but not necessarily conscious life.

Sometimes I thought of these things. Other times I just packed the souls into the cartons and stacked the cartons for pick up. After I finished up work and came home, Lily appeared at the front door.

"Hi."

"Hi."

"You look delicious," I said. She smiled. I wondered if I should kiss her.

59

Just do it, Fynn. Just take her by the arms and pull her in for a kiss. While I was wondering how to go about that, she turned so that I couldn't reach both of her arms. *Okay, maybe later.*

She was wearing cut-off jean shorts and a tank top that tied in the back. Her legs were long and tan, and the cut-off shorts perfectly showed them off. And did I mention how amazing her butt was?

"What do you want to do?" I asked her.

"Hmmm...I don't know. What do you want to do?"

"You want to meet some friends of mine? My friend Josh has a pool. We could go swimming." *You could wear a bikini.*

"That girl isn't going to be there?" she asked.

Had I mentioned Cassidy? I didn't think I had, but I might have. Half the time I didn't really listen to myself when I talked—I just stared into Lily's eyes and my mouth went on autopilot.

"No, just my friend Josh and his girlfriend Courtney. It'll be fun."

She made a face. "I don't have a bathing suit."

I allowed myself to entertain all sorts of fun possibilities before saying, "We could stop by a store and buy one."

"Okay, sounds good."

We took Mom's minivan, and I apologized as Lily got in. She laughed good-naturedly and said it was no big deal. I explained I was saving up to buy a car of my own, not wanting her to think I was driving a minivan by choice. We pulled into the local version of a department store. It was called Abbotts and had seen better days. Nowadays, mostly semi-retired office workers and housewives prowled through it, looking for easy wash and wear clothing that they could get on sale. Even the clothing seemed to sense their heyday had passed. They huddled together on the racks, looking nervous and forlorn. But it was close by so here we were.

She pulled a few bathing suits off one of the racks in the Juniors department and headed to a dressing room. I sat on a chair that seemed to be put there for the boyfriends and husbands of women trying on clothes.

I took out my cell phone and saw that I had a text. From Cassidy, naturally. "What's up with you? You wanna hang out?"

My insides clenched. *Crap.* I should tell her something. I should definitely tell her something. What, though?

Sorry, I have to work. Work was a pretty good excuse for being unavailable. I hit send.

"Oh, bummer." I breathed a sigh of relief. Then, "What about tomorrow?" *Crap, crap, double crap.* What to do now?

No, I have… What did I have? Band practice? Medieval jousting? Driveway re-graveling? *To watch Maddie tomorrow. Sorry.* I hit send and waited anxiously for a reply.

"What do you think?"

I jerked my head up from my phone and stared. Lily was standing in front of me in a hot pink bikini. Her stomach was as flat as Florida, and her skin was smooth and tan.

She was a vision.

"You look gorgeous," I said, barely trusting myself to speak. She seemed pleased until she saw my phone clutched in my hand.

"Who were you talking to?"

"No one!" I cleared my throat. "No one, just Mom told me to put gas in the car."

Her eyes narrowed. "Really?"

"Of course, really. Wow, you look great," I said, anxious to change the subject. She walked to the three-way mirror and inspected herself from all angles while I admired her from all angles. I surreptitiously tucked my phone in my back pocket and forgot all about Cassidy.

We paid for the bikini and went to Josh's house. His mom greeted us at the door.

"Fynn! So nice to see you. Did you have dinner? I have some leftover pasta salad if you're hungry. And who's this?" she asked, gesturing to Lily.

"This is my…" I hesitated for just a fraction of a second, but I got the sense that Lily noticed it. "Friend Lily. Lily, this is Mrs. Hayes."

Lily smiled and shook her hand. Mrs. Hayes said, "Are you hungry, dear?" Lily shook her head.

"Josh is out back, by the pool."

We headed out to the pool. Josh was sprawled on a lawn chair, trying to toss a ring onto a floating pole thing in the pool. Courtney was in the pool, throwing the ring back every time he missed.

"Hi," I said, keeping my voice casual, although what I wanted to do was shout, "This is Lily! Look, it's LILY! Isn't she awesome?"

"Oh, wow," Josh said and scrambled off his chair. "You must be Lily, who I've heard so much about."

Courtney came over to the edge of the pool. "Oh, hi."

Lily smiled shyly and said, "Hi."

"Lily, this is Josh and Courtney."

Josh immediately said, "Yup, I'm Courtney." And Courtney chimed in and said, "And I'm Josh." They clearly thought they were hilarious. I will say one thing I admire about Josh and Court's relationship is that they both have the same stupid sense of humor.

"Nice to meet you, Josh," she said, nodding at Courtney. "And Courtney." She nodded at Josh. I was relieved she was cool. They laughed, pleased with their own joke.

"So, you guys want to swim or something?" Josh asked, "Or you want something to drink? I got Cokes, Sprite, Iced Tea, Uh...water...?"

"I'll have a water," Lily said.

"Me, too," I said immediately. See, I was nothing if not supportive of her drink choices. I sat on one of the striped lounge chairs and gestured that Lily should sit in the one next to me. She sat carefully, unscrewed the cap, and took a delicate sip from the water bottle.

"So, Lily." Josh sprawled out in the lounge chair on Lily's other side. "You seem normal enough. What on earth do you see in Fynn?"

She looked a little uncertain, but she smiled and said, "Well, sometimes he shares his chips."

"Ah, the old chip-sharing-seduction bit. Classy. So, what do you do in Hell?" Josh asked. I looked down at the concrete pool deck and studied an ant carrying off a tortilla chip crumb.

"I work in Admissions," she said.

"Oh, cool. So, do you actually decide where people go in Hell?"

"No, no—there's a set protocol. We just take their information and pass them along to the next stage, which is sorting them by level, and then someone else takes them to whatever level of Hell they deserve."

"Huh. Interesting. Like a point system?"

"Sort of. Like, anyone who killed someone gets ten points, right off the bat. Meanness, spite, anger, bitterness, laziness—they all get assigned points. If there are special circumstances—like, you accidentally killed someone or you were a soldier or something, then they get evaluated by hand. I don't do that—I don't really have any input."

They chatted back and forth for a while, and then we decided to go get something to eat. There was the dilemma of whose car to take. We could all fit comfortably in the minivan, but then we'd be driving around in a minivan. Or we could squash into Josh's pick-up truck, which would be tight since he didn't really have a back seat, just an extra storage area with seats that flipped down. Naturally, we squashed into the truck.

Josh and Courtney got in front, while me and Lily sat facing each other. It was so close back there that our knees touched. We sat, both of us pretty much squished by the seat in front of us. Luckily it wasn't far to Nonnie's, which was a diner in town. Its claim to fame was that it was open until 3:00 a.m. every day and didn't mind serving drunk people, as long as they didn't get too obnoxious. And the food was pretty good.

We sat and drank milkshakes and ate burgers dripping with ketchup. Lily was charming, funny, and sweet, and I could tell Josh and Courtney liked her. As we drove back to Josh's house and pried ourselves out of the truck, Courtney said, "That was really fun! We need to do this again."

"Yeah, we do," I said. I glanced at Lily.

"For sure."

"You guys want to hang out, or you have to get back?" Josh asked.

"No, I really have to be getting home," Lily said.

"Well, another time," Josh said.

We all agreed that we should definitely do it again, and then Lily and I hopped in the minivan.

"So, how long have you known Josh?"

"Uhm…since third grade, I think? We met in Miss Reynolds' math class. I was terrible at math and Josh is brilliant, so he helped me out. He's a good guy."

"Yeah, I can tell. And Courtney?"

"Josh has been dating her for, oh, let's see…almost a year now. She's great. They make each other laugh. And she's really cool, too."

"Clearly." Was there an edge to her voice?

"What? Courtney is great. Why? You don't think so?"

"She's lovely. I said she was lovely." She picked at the threads of her cutoffs. Sometimes this girl made me nervous. I shrugged it off, though. Maybe she was just nervous, being introduced to people I had been friends with forever. Which made me think of something.

"So, when do I get to go to Nebraska with you?"

She laughed. "You want to go to Nebraska?"

"Yeah, I do."

She rolled her eyes. "There's not a lot to do in Nebraska."

"Well, I want to see where you live, where you go to school, meet your friends…all that."

She sighed. "Well, Dad's still not well, so why don't we give it a week or so, okay?"

I forgot her Dad was sick. I'm an idiot. "Oh, right. Yeah, whenever he's better. Until then, you can hang out here."

She smiled. "I'd like that."

We pulled up to the school parking lot. I got out and ran around to the passenger side, but she had gotten out already. She smiled at me as I reached for her hand, and we walked to the school. Now that I was coming and going into a locked school pretty frequently, I had jammed a lock by the gym so I could always get in and out. I took her there and we walked towards the elevator.

She turned to me. "Well, thanks. That was fun."

"Yeah." I was fascinated by the bluish-turquoise of her eyes. And her eyelashes. God, she was beautiful. I grabbed her other hand and pulled her closer. She giggled. "You are so beautiful," I said.

"Thanks. So are you," she said.

I was thinking, *How far could I reasonably go on the second date?* She turned abruptly and said, "I have to go."

"I know," I said. No kiss? None at all?

"I'll see you tomorrow?" she asked.

"Yup. Tomorrow." I was disappointed. I mean, this was our second date. We had kissed, a little, on the first date, so there should be more, right? Lily waved as she stepped into the elevator. As the doors closed I called out, "See you in Hell!"

It never got old.

CHAPTER EIGHTEEN

SINCE THE NEXT day was Wednesday, I didn't have to work. I slept late, the bed covers over my head, blocking out the driving July sun. Mom knocked gently on my door to wake me. "Fynn?"

I sat up groggily. What time was it? 9:32 a.m. I groaned. Was I not a member of the workforce, and as such, was I not entitled to sleeping late on my day off? I rubbed the crusts off my eyes and wondered if I could pretend I wasn't home.

More knocking, louder this time. "Fynn?"

"What?"

"I need you to watch Maddie for a while, okay? I have an appointment, and Kevin went out."

"Fine, whatever." I slid my feet to the floor and sat up. Damn. It felt early, probably because I had been up late the night before. I kept thinking about Lily.

"Can you make her something to eat?"

"Yeah." I wondered how Maddie felt about leftover pizza. I yawned, stretched, pulled on sweatpants, and went downstairs. Maddie was looking indignant and trying to push herself out of her high chair. Her little fingers curled around the lip of the tray, and she screamed in frustration as she discovered she couldn't make it move.

"She has been a bear this morning," Mom said as she dove into the refrigerator and threw a yogurt in her tote bag. "I don't know why—she slept well."

Great. That meant she probably wouldn't nap.

"Thanks, hon. I'll be home around two o'clock. You gonna be okay?"

"Yeah, we'll be fine." I scooped Maddie out of her highchair, and she showed how grateful she was by grabbing a fist full of my hair. Carefully, I pried her fingers open and set her down on the floor. She followed me as I looked in the cabinets for some kind of baby food to give her that wouldn't require a highchair. I grabbed myself a slice of pizza. Maddie gurgled and pointed.

"Pizza? You want pizza?" She stretched out her hands towards the pizza. Was pizza bad for a baby? I couldn't think of any reason why, so I picked off the pepperoni and gave her a small slice of pizza. She gnawed happily while I made myself coffee and set up my laptop at the kitchen table. I checked my phone for texts from Lily, but there were none.

I opened Facebook, Instagram, and every other social media outlet I could think of. I entered "Lily Case" into every social media search engine. There were lots of Lily Cases, but none of them were *my* Lily Case. How could someone not have any social media accounts? She didn't seem to be anywhere. I Googled her—nothing. I tried to remember what town she told me she lived in—Springfield, Nebraska. So I looked up the high school and searched the yearbooks for the past four years. Nothing. No candids, no mention of her being in any clubs, no sports, nothing.

It was like she didn't exist.

I was so wrapped up in my virtual pursuit of Lily that I forgot about Maddie until I heard a thump and a small groan. I jumped up from the table and ran into the living room. She had fallen over while trying to climb up on the sofa. She didn't seem any worse for wear. Thank God.

"Okay, look. Let's watch TV." I sat down on the couch and pulled her up on my lap. She grinned at me as I put on *The Wonder Pets*. She clapped her hands and tried to sing along. I made her dance by holding her hands and having her balance her feet on my thighs. She wiggled and laughed, delighted with herself.

I spent the day looking after Maddie and obsessing about Lily. She didn't answer one of my texts. I didn't want to seem needy, but she seemed a little distant at the end of our last date. Or maybe her Dad was sick? She mentioned him having a heart condition. But she could at least answer a text, couldn't she?

Eventually, I dozed off on the couch with Maddie curled up next to me. This is how I remember it, anyway. The next thing I knew, I heard someone come in. While I was still in my half-sleep haze, I heard Kevin say, "Oh, Maddie, no!" I sat up and looked around. No Maddie. I ran into the kitchen to find Kevin trying to stop Maddie from shoving a cat toy into her mouth.

"Maddie!"

She screamed, frustrated her new toy was being taken away. After all, there's not a lot of difference between a cat toy mouse and a baby toy. They both had bells, and the cat toy even smelled better. But, cat saliva. I found her a baby toy—some stuffed animal of indeterminate species with a rattle in it—and gave it to her instead.

After a few minutes, Kevin came into the living room, looking dejected.

"Hey, what's up?" I asked.

"Nothing," he mumbled, starting to head up the stairs to his room.

"Take my advice—upstairs sucks. What you want to do is stay here and let me beat you in a game of *Zombie Action 5*."

Kevin smiled at that and said, "Like that would ever happen. I can beat you with my eyes closed."

"Oh, really? Care to make a wager on that? Loser has to do the winner's chores for a day?"

"You're on." He plopped on the sofa next to me, and we got down to destroying each other with undead zombies. It was glorious. I didn't get a chance to play as many video games as I would've liked, and I almost never got a chance to play with Kevin anymore. I was usually working, or hanging out with Josh or something, and Kevin was hanging out with… come to think of it, I hadn't seen Kevin hanging out with anyone lately.

"So, how's your summer going?" I asked while I drove a screwdriver through one of his zombie's heads.

"It's going okay, I guess." His character wielded a machete at my character's head, but I jumped out of the way.

"You watching Maddie a lot?" I knew when Mom was upstairs sleeping Kevin was in charge of Maddie. I felt a little guilty about it.

"Mornings, mostly." He stared at the screen and chopped my arm off.

"Oooo! Well, that doesn't sound so bad. How are Paul and Jimmy?" I counter-attacked and lunged at him but missed. I think he had been friends with Paul and Jimmy since, like, birth. Usually, they spent every summer together, riding bikes, swimming, and playing complicated tournaments of video game baseball.

"Okay, I guess."

I swung a machete at him. "You're not hanging around with them anymore?" I got distracted and he lopped my head off. Whoops. It was just as well, because I turned towards him a little and said, "What, do they have girlfriends or something?"

"No. Hey, I won. Sucker." He wiggled a little bit on the couch—his version of dancing.

"Yeah, okay. Where are Paul and Jimmy? They can't have jobs."

He sighed. "No, they do not have jobs."

"Well, then what?"

He stared at the carpet. "I don't know." He looked up. "Did you ever, like, have friends, and all of a sudden they get to be friends with someone else, and then they don't want to hang out with you anymore?"

I tried to think back to when I was twelve, but all I remembered was riding my bike around in circles with Nathan and a girl named Nicki. We were best friends that summer. We rode our bikes through the woods, to the town pool, and to the store. We hung out at each other's houses, too, watching YouTube and drinking lemonade out of tall, sweaty glasses. We were just three dudes, even though one of us was a girl.

Until one day, when suddenly she wasn't a dude anymore. Her formerly flat chest now had curves in the middle. She blushed and looked at the ground when she caught one of us staring at her newly forming breasts. Then we wouldn't know where to look. Eventually school started, and Nicki was swept away by a group of girls with long hair and coltish legs. Their heads bobbed up and down in the school hallways, and they giggled when I walked by and made my face get hot. Nathan moved away that year, and the next summer I started hanging out with Josh and a of couple other guys. Twelve was an awkward age.

"Sort of. Paul and Jimmy are hanging out with some other kid?"

"Yup."

"Well, just because they have a new friend doesn't mean they don't still want to be your friend, does it?" I couldn't help but think I sounded like Mom.

"Thanks, Mom."

"Well, maybe this new kid is…you know. A novelty. Did he just move here or something?"

"Yeah. Minnesota, I think."

"I bet by the time school starts they'll be tired of him already."

"Yeah, maybe. I'm taking a nap," Kevin said. He hauled himself off the couch and mounted the stairs.

"Upstairs sucks. It's hot."

"I'll point a fan at my head."

Well, at least I knew what was going on with Kevin, but that didn't explain why I couldn't find Lily anywhere. I opened my laptop up again and started to search. Was it possible to find a directory of Hell's employees on the internet? I Googled "Working in Hell," "Employees of Hell," and "Admissions in Hell." I didn't find anything, not that I was really expecting to. She said Admissions, right? Where the Hell was she?

CHAPTER NINETEEN

I WENT TO sleep thinking of Lily, although a gnawing anxiety was chewing away at my stomach. It did seem weird she had no social media accounts at all. Still, I wasn't that worried. There must be an explanation. I didn't think it bothered me, but I had nightmares almost all night long. Weird things were after me, trying to kill me. Some black, formless being was trying to suck me into a mouth filled with thousands of rotten teeth. I tried to scream, but no sound came out. It surrounded me as I tried to run, a black cloud of doom. I couldn't breathe, my chest hurt, and my lungs screamed.

I woke up sweating and grabbed my phone. 3:30 a.m. I flopped back on my pillow. Three hours until I had to get up for work. Thank goodness.

I fell asleep again. Almost immediately I was tormented by more nightmares. There was a tornado, and it was whipping around our house. All the stuff in our backyard kept flying around and around. Then I saw Mom and Dad fly by, looking confused and terrified. I kept saying, "I'm sorry, I'm sorry," and tears were running down my face. Then Dad was next to me saying, "You must have known. You must have known."

I woke up again at 4:45 a.m., so I lay back down and stared at the ceiling. There were still glow-in-the-dark stars stuck to it from when I was little. Should I bother trying to go back to sleep? There was about an hour and a half before I had to get up. I turned over and put a pillow over my head, but that made me feel like I was suffocating, so I threw it off and pulled my sheet over my head. I tried to go back to sleep—I was still exhausted—but I couldn't get comfortable. It was too hot. Then I couldn't decide where my arms should go. Eventually I just got up.

I wandered into the kitchen and made myself a cup of coffee, watching as the hot liquid filled my cup. The smell jolted my senses, and I started to shake off the fog. I tossed in a teaspoon of sugar and a splash of milk and then went out onto the porch.

I settled myself into a lounge chair and studied the backyard. The sun had been up for a little while, spreading light across the suburban landscape. I watched the neighbor's cat hunt something in the grass. He focused with the intensity of a lovelorn high school stalker, slowly setting one paw down and then the other. Closer, a step closer. Then he sprang forward, rushed at the chipmunk, and snatched it up in his mouth. He strutted down the driveway, pleased with himself.

I sighed. Circle of life, I suppose, but all of a sudden I wanted to go back inside. I took my coffee cup, went back into the kitchen, and rifled through the cabinets, looking for something to eat. There was a bagel in the freezer, so I nuked it for a few seconds and popped it into the toaster oven. I slathered it with a ridiculous amount of cream cheese and took it into the living room. Digging the remote out between the sofa cushions, I flipped around while I ate my breakfast.

By this time, it was almost 7:00 a.m., and I heard my dad getting up. He shuffled past me in his bathrobe and looked at me like he had never seen me before. "What are you doing up?"

"Couldn't sleep."

He grunted something in reply and continued to the kitchen. If Dad was awake, I knew I should hop in the shower before he did. I shook off my terrible night's sleep and got ready to go to work.

I washed up quickly, trying not to use all of the hot water. Dad was reading the news when I walked back into the kitchen.

"Did you know there were six accidents yesterday, just in Franklin?"

"Uh, no."

"Huh." He stared at his laptop. "Doesn't that seem like a lot?"

I hadn't given it much thought. Then again, I just found out about it twenty seconds ago. "Yeah, I guess so."

He shook his head and mumbled something. "Well, drive carefully."

"Dad…" I started to say I walk to work, and I don't have a car, but I gave up and just said, "I will."

Counting the days until I could go buy a car, I walked into the high school. I spent a lot of time looking up different models, reading the classifieds, and studying sales. I imagined myself cruising along in whatever car I was considering, driving up to the first day of school in my new wheels. "Fynn got a new car! He is suddenly overwhelmingly attractive. Let me at him!" At least, this is how I was hoping it would go.

I opened the back door of the cafeteria, went to the elevator, and went to work. When I first started, I figured working in Hell would be some non-stop adventure, but after a month it was pretty much a job like any other job. I went to Soul Destination, nodded at Audrey and Tom, and went to my work table. Naturally, Audrey had something to say as soon as I started.

"Oh, yeah—there's a new way to label the boxes. We're not using markers anymore; now there are stickers to put on. It's better this way—sometimes there was confusion before, you know, if someone didn't have good handwriting. And it's faster, too—just slap on a sticker. You get them over there." She gestured at a new box, which was in the corner.

"Yeah, okay, whatever."

She got that annoyed look she always did. "It makes a difference."

"Of course it does," I said.

She pursed her lips and frowned but didn't say anything. I grabbed a supply of stickers and brought them over to my station.

She looked annoyed again. "You're not supposed to get them before you pack the boxes. You're supposed to get a sticker after the box is already packed."

I sighed. Everyone probably works with an Audrey, but I didn't have to like it. "What difference does it make?"

This threw her a little. "Well, it…if you get the stickers first, you…" She spluttered. "You might not put them on the right boxes."

"I could just as easily put them on the wrong box your way, too."

I watched as she tried to process the utter incomprehensibility of doing something in a different way than she did it. It was kind of funny, like she was wrestling with a tricky math problem. I went back to sorting my own souls.

Lunch rolled around. Lily wasn't in the break room. She wasn't in the cafeteria, either. I sat at a table and ate my soggy, pathetic turkey sandwich from the vending machine and wondered why she wasn't here. Didn't she say, "See you in Hell?" Or maybe I said that. I couldn't remember.

After my lunch, I went back to work. Audrey was waiting for me with a triumphant look on her face.

"I checked with Dodd, and he said my way is better—you should pack the box and then bring it to the table and get a sticker."

"You must be very proud," I said as I continued to do things my way.

She glared. "If you're not going to take your job seriously…"

"Audrey, you're not my supervisor. We are equals here. In other words, I'm gonna do things my way, and you can do things whatever way you want. Got it?"

She got that indignant look. "Tom?" she said, appealing to him.

"Hey, I just work here. We sort souls. It's not rocket science. Mind your own business." He continued to sort his souls.

Audrey pouted for the rest of the day, which was actually great because she was quiet. Tom and I sorted out souls and stickered our boxes just as competently as she did, which I'm sure made her furious.

Finally, it was time to punch out. I passed Dorothy on my way out. Blue hair, orange skin, pink fingernails. "You look lovely."

"Thank you, Fynn." She beamed and patted her hair.

"Any luck finding the escaped demon?"

"Not yet, but don't worry. We'll get her."

My blood turned to ice water. "Her?"

Dorothy laughed. "Well, of course, silly. Demons come in both sexes. Didn't you know that?"

I guess I did but didn't really give it any thought before. "I just didn't know the escaped one was female."

Dorothy shrugged. "We'll get her. Hopefully not before too much longer. Demons tend to wreak havoc."

"I bet," I said as I got in the elevator. I waved and, as soon as the doors closed, I sighed.

A female demon. What a nightmare that would be.

CHAPTER TWENTY

I CHECKED MY phone about a thousand times the next day. Then I sent several texts to Lily: *Hey. What's up? Where are you? Are you working tomorrow?* I didn't get one response. Not one. I couldn't help but feel rejected and confused. She seemed to like me. This just brought up all my raging insecurities that no girl would ever like me and I had nothing to offer. But I tried not to panic. Finally, just before I went to bed, it occurred to me that I should just go to Admissions and look for her there. Simple, right? Great idea, Fynn. I fell into a fitful sleep.

I got to Hell early the next morning. As usual, Dorothy greeted me when I got off the elevator.

"Morning, Fynn!" She called out cheerfully.

"Morning, Dorothy. You look nice." She had her hair down around her shoulders. It was red and blue plaid, and her skin was a neutral beige tone.

She patted her hair. "Do you like it? I wasn't sure about the plaid."

"No, I like it. Have they had any luck finding the escaped demon yet?"

"No, but they'll find her. They always do."

"Always...this has happened before?"

"Well, not very often, but occasionally. I remember one time, oh, probably a hundred and fifty years ago or so when a devil sprite escaped with the trash. It took weeks to find him, but they finally did. He was holed up in San Francisco, trying to steal the patent for blue jeans from Levi Strauss. Of course, then they were called overalls. But I remember what a to-do it was until one of the Hornissens found him and brought him back."

A hundred and fifty years? "Dorothy, how long have you worked here?"

She blushed—at least, I think she did—and said, "It's impolite to ask a lady her age."

"Oh, right. Sorry. See ya, Dorothy." I had to get to work so I could go on break so I could go check Admissions.

"Bye, Fynn."

I know it doesn't make any sense, but I worked quickly all morning, somehow thinking the faster I worked the faster time would go by. Even Audrey noticed.

"What has gotten into you?" She seemed mildly affronted, as if I were

73

doing this on purpose just to annoy her. Although, to be fair, if I had known it would annoy her I would've worked this quickly all summer.

Finally, lunch arrived. I practically sprinted down the tunnel, darting around lanterns and jumping out of the way of other people passing by. I burst into the break room. No Lily. I went up to the cafeteria. No Lily.

This was my chance to ask about her in Admissions. I hopped on a hovercraft and sped off. My hovercraft stopped in front of what looked like the mouth of a cave. Above the door was a sign "Admissions." I went into the room and found a short, bald man sitting at a desk. He had a hat pulled down low over one eye. It may have been his only eye.

"Can I help you?" He looked me up and down and scowled. I guess being cordial wasn't a requirement of working in Admissions.

I cleared my throat. "I'm looking for someone who works here. Her name is Lily Case." The desk was so high that I was almost at eye level with him, even though I was standing up and he was sitting down. He must have been on a platform.

He looked at me and said, "Well, let's see." He opened up a ledger and ran his finger down the pages. It seemed to be taking a long time.

"How many people work here?" I asked, trying to be friendly.

He glared at me. "Now I have to start over." Again, he ran his thick finger down the pages. After a while, he slammed the book shut. "No one by that name works here."

I stared at him. "No, I know she does. She told me." I said stubbornly. "Look again. Maybe you missed her?"

He growled at me. "Kid, I've worked here a long time. There's no one here by that name."

"But..." My mind spun. She had to work here. She told me she worked here. I saw her in the break room. Why would she pretend to work in Admissions if she worked somewhere else?

"Are there interns or something?"

He chortled. "No. Most people won't entertain the idea of working in Hell for no money."

"Please, can you just...just check one more time? Please?" I must've looked desperate, because he sighed and opened up the ledger again. There seemed to be four pages of names.

"Nope, still nothing. Here, you can look yourself if you want." He pushed the ledger at me. It was an awkward angle, the desk being the same level as my head, but I could read just fine. I skimmed through every page once, then again more slowly. He was right. No one named Lily Case worked there.

CHAPTER TWENTY-ONE

I COULDN'T BELIEVE it. There had to be some rational explanation. Maybe she didn't work in Admissions; she worked in some other part of Hell? I wasn't sure why she would lie and tell me she worked in Admissions if she worked somewhere else, but maybe? Maybe she worked on one of the floors, hands on? That's what we called the employees who actually tortured people. Hands on. Maybe she thought I'd think less of her?

Or maybe she had a stalker and was just being cautious? I knew girls could be really sensitive about those things. Or maybe I was suffering from some giant, Hell-induced psychosis and hallucinated an entire girl. After all, the fact that I worked in Hell wasn't entirely normal either. It wasn't that much of a leap to think I conjured up an entire girl out of desperation.

Except I knew I didn't. I was positive I talked to her and had fallen, if not in love, then at least in a pretty large amount of lust. I remembered the way tendrils of her hair curled delicately around her sweet face. I remember the way her shoulder blades carved boomerangs across her back. The way she laughed, throwing back her head, her whole body shaking with delight. I remembered the way she moved, graceful yet methodical, with purpose, like a cat.

I knew I hadn't just imagined her. For one thing, my imagination didn't stretch that far. I had trouble thinking up stories in English class, and I usually just hijacked episodes of sitcoms and changed a few details. There was no way I could've imagined an entire relationship.

I was just baffled. Did she not like me? She seemed to like me. What was wrong with me? I was at least passable looking. I had a sense of humor and a pretty good personality, if I did say so myself. Part of me was thinking there was just some miscommunication, and when I saw her there would be a rational explanation. "Admissions? No, I said Munitions!" And then I could go back to my regularly scheduled summer, with my completely normal-but-hot girlfriend.

A few days passed. Every day I went to the break room and had lunch. I thought if I sat there long enough, Lily would turn up and say "Hi" super casually, and I would say hi, and everything would be great again. Naturally, this didn't happen. I remained hopeful, though. Call me an optimist. Or delusional. Whatever.

The next day was Sunday, so I slept late, waking up around 11:00 a.m. I love sleeping, but I also felt like I had nothing fun to do and nowhere interesting to go. Josh was working and Courtney was somewhere, but it would be weird if we started hanging out together when Josh wasn't around. At least I thought so.

I went downstairs. It looked like someone had made some bacon and eggs not too long ago. Pouring myself a coffee, I studied the counter for a few minutes, waiting for either the motivation to make my own breakfast or for someone to come in, take pity on me, and make me something. After a minute or two of this, I gave up and got myself a bowl of cereal.

I was eating and reading Reddit when Dad came in.

"Hey, Fynn."

"Hi, Dad." He started putting away the dishes in the dishwasher. I went back to my reading.

"Hey, do you have any plans for today?" he asked, as if struck by a sudden thought, which I knew was bullshit because he had been after me to help weed the gardens for a few days.

"I was uh…" I tried to think as fast as I could. I did not want to spend my day off weeding the garden in the July heat. "I was going to…meet a friend."

"Oh. Oh, well, then." He sounded disappointed. "What friend?"

It came to me, a stroke of inspiration. "Cassidy. I met her at Josh's Fourth of July party."

"Oh, well, that's good." He sighed. "I can do the weeding myself." He hated it as much as I did. I felt bad, but I really didn't want to weed. I felt I did enough for this family, keeping track of Maddie and…whatever else I did. Sometimes I mowed the lawn.

Dad puttered around the kitchen for a while, probably trying to put off the weeding, and I went up to my room. I sat on my bed and stared at the rug. What to do? Then I thought, *What if I actually did call Cassidy?* I had said it as an excuse not to work in the yard, but it wasn't a bad idea. I mean, if Lily was going to just go on not really existing, there was no reason why I couldn't see other women.

I had deleted her number. Would Josh have it? I texted him, and a few minutes later he texted back with her number and a row of pink hearts. *Asshole.*

I texted Cassidy. *Hey. This is Fynn. Wondered if you want to hang out?*

A minute went by. Two minutes. Shit. She was trying to think of a reason not to hang out. Then she texted, "When?"

Anytime. Today if you're not busy?

Another pause. "I can get my mom to watch Blake for a while. You want to meet somewhere?"

Where should we meet? I racked my brains. There was a pond I knew by the overpass. It was pretty clean, in case we wanted to jump in and cool off because it was already 87 degrees. I could pick up some picnic fare, sandwiches or something. I texted her the address and waited.

"Great. In about an hour?"

I couldn't believe it. Just like that I had something fun to do today. And Cassidy was cute. She was no Lily, but at this point I was so confused by Lily's disappearance that I figured maybe she didn't like me anyway.

We had a lot of fun. At least I did, and I think Cassidy did, too. If I was troubled by occasional thoughts of Lily, well, I just did what anyone would do in my situation—stuffed them way down deep and pretended they didn't exist. Besides, Cassidy was a great girl. She was smart, she was funny, and she was at least somewhat interested in me. I mean, I still was baffled by what was going on with Lily, but Cassidy was a balm to my bruised ego and hurt feelings. I thought I'd never see Lily again.

How wrong I was.

CHAPTER TWENTY-TWO

I HAD TAKEN my Dad's car to meet Cassidy—a completely generic sedan, about as uncool a car as could be found, unless it was Mom's mini-van—and he said I had to be home by 6:00 p.m. because he had some errands to run. So I got the car back to him with minutes to spare, and then I flopped on the couch in the living room, pondering my date.

I thought it went well. Still, I couldn't help but compare Cassidy to Lily. Lily was taller, and her voice was huskier. Her earlobes were smaller, and her collarbones stood out more. Her eyelashes were longer. Of course, on the negative side, I had no idea where Lily went, and she lied about where she worked. So, there was that. At least Cassidy had a working phone number.

I flipped on the TV, looking for some kind of mindless entertainment. Outside, dark clouds were gathering together in a pre-thunderstorm conspiracy meeting. It was humid, and the air was so thick you would swear it was a reality show contestant. Speaking of reality shows, there must be a re-run of one that I could watch. I finally found one that I could just watch without having to think about anything at all.

After a while, Kevin joined me. A few years ago, a summer thunderstorm whipped itself into a tornado. Kevin was at fifth-grade band practice at the time, and they wouldn't let anyone leave. He was locked in the band room with seventy-five other fifth graders for about an hour and a half. Our house didn't sustain any damage, but a lot of neighborhoods in Franklin had trees ripped up, and the roof of the high school was torn off. Ever since, Kevin has been anxious about thunderstorms. We sat on the couch and made fun of the contestants on the dating show we were watching. I wish I could get on a dating show. All the women were hot.

Dad got home after a while, dripping wet. He went upstairs to change and then joined us. He's normally too busy or too uptight for those kinds of shows, so it was fun to hang out with him, just three dudes watching a dumb show. Then Dad broke the whole just-three-dudes thing by saying, "Kevin, bring down your laundry, and Fynn, can you start the grill so we can do burgers?"

"Dad, there's a thunderstorm."

"Fynn, it's been over for about twenty minutes already. Look." He gestured to the window. Sure enough, the sun was now shining in full force, burning off the rain.

"Fine." I made my way outside. The earth had that refreshed feeling it does after a thunderstorm—softer, cooler, and less oppressive. I busied myself igniting the grill and chopping some burger toppings—red onion, tomatoes, and a few mushrooms. When the grill was hot, I slid the burgers onto it. After a few minutes, I flipped them over. They were sizzling, bubbling, and smelled so good. Nothing smells as good as a burger grilled outside. I added the cheese—cheddar, never American, American is nasty—and voila! Fynn's Fantastic Burgers.

Kevin, Dad, and I ate our burgers along with the potato salad Mom had left us before she went to work. It was a pleasant evening. Nothing remarkable about it, just me and my brother hanging out with our Dad, eating dinner together. I guess I remember it so clearly because it was the beginning of the worst month of my entire life.

After dinner, I wandered outside. Should I text Cassidy? Too soon? I was studying the screen, reviewing the texts, trying to gauge her level of interest. The dark clouds were rolling away, and the earth smelled clean and refreshed. I felt optimistic—I was interested in Cassidy and willing to forget Lily. Almost everything I made was being saved for a car, and I figured by the end of the summer I would have almost $4,000 saved up altogether. I just might be able to get a car with that amount of money. Not the car of my dreams, but a decent, non-dorky car. And I might even have a real, honest-to-goodness girlfriend by then, too.

I was walking down my quiet suburban street for no particular reason, enjoying the sun after the storm. The air was soft, and the humidity had dissipated. A shape flew out of nowhere—I felt a cold draft blow by my head. A brunette person with murder in her eyes appeared by my side.

"Lily?" I couldn't even comprehend it. I stood staring at her, amazed she actually existed and that she was right in front of me. "Where did you come from?"

She glared at me. I swear her eyes held a red glow, although I couldn't help but notice they were still like magnets and I couldn't tear my eyes away from them. She was hot. Even furious, she was hot.

"Who. Was. That. Girl!" Her eyes narrowed and smoke came out of her ears. Okay, not really. It took me a minute to figure out what she was talking about, because I had just been hanging out with my Dad and my brother.

"Huh? What girl?"

"The one you were just with," she hissed.

"Oh, you mean Cassidy? We were…wait a minute, why do I have to explain myself to you? I asked at Admissions if there was a Lily Case working there and they had never heard of you. What's up with that?" My feelings were shifting from one to another so fast I had no idea what I felt. On the one hand, I was glad to see her. On the other, she was acting psycho. I felt guilty for having a date with someone else, and then angry that I should feel guilty in the first place.

"I'm on sabbatical," she said, tossing her ponytail with a shake of her head.

"They have no record of you being there, *ever*. So either you work there under an alias, or you never worked there at all—in which case, why were you hanging out in the break room?" Yeah, good questions, Fynn. Let her try to explain that!

"You know Hell has terrible record keeping sometimes. Probably they just lost my name. It's not that big a deal."

You know when someone you really like tells you something, and you're pretty sure it's bullshit but you really like them so you want to give them the benefit of the doubt? I had never heard of Hell losing someone's name entirely, but I hadn't worked there that long, and it was a really big and bustling place bogged down in bureaucracy. I suppose it could happen. Which brought us to the next issue.

"I had a date. I haven't seen you in days, and I was beginning to doubt that you actually existed. Where the hell were you?" I was trying to keep that accusatory note out of my voice, but even I could hear it.

"I was attending to my father. He had a heart attack. I'm sorry I didn't have time to let you know."

I instantly felt terrible. Poor Lily. "Oh, my God. Is he in the hospital? Is he okay? What happened?" The questions shot out of my mouth as fast as I thought them up.

"He's okay. They released him this morning. He's going to have to take it easy for a while, but he'll be okay. I got here as soon as I could."

Great, here she was taking care of her ailing father, and then she seizes the first opportunity to come here to explain and finds I'm already dating some-one else. Boy, Fynn, you really are a world-class asshole.

"I'm sorry," I said. "Really, I had no idea. But you could've told me."

Her eyes narrowed a bit. "Okay, next time I have a life-threatening family emergency I'll be sure and call you first," she said.

"That's not how I meant that."

"Of course it's not," she said.

"Okay, look. You're obviously upset. You've been under some stress. Why don't we just go get something to eat or something and you can tell me about your dad?"

She sighed. She looked so cute when she sighed. Part of me was hoping she would say, "You know what? I'm done. Good riddance." Because while she was certainly adorable, I was starting to get the sense that she was super high maintenance. The other part of me noticed her cherry red lips, so soft and inviting, her long eyelashes, and her blue eyes, and I would have followed her anywhere.

After some apparent consideration, she said, "Okay. I'm hungry."

In spite of myself, I smiled and felt my mood soar. "Great!"

Chapter Twenty-Three

FYNN, HAVE YOU seen my car keys?"

I opened one eye and squinted at my alarm clock. Dad was yelling from downstairs about his keys. Why would I know where his keys were at seven o'clock on a morning I didn't have to work?

"No," I said into my pillow. About seven seconds later my Dad opened the door to my bedroom. "Fynn, have you seen my keys?"

"No." I was still hoping this was a dream.

"Are you sure? I left them where I always leave them, and now they're not there."

"I have no idea where your keys are."

"You didn't take them?"

I was feeling a bit defensive as I sat up. "No, I didn't. Did they fall, or maybe Mom took them?"

Dad ran a hand over his head. "Mom says she didn't."

"Well, I didn't either." He grunted and went back downstairs.

I tried to go back to sleep, but I kept hearing Dad's frantic slamming of drawers. Apparently the spare key was missing, too. Which was weird, I'll admit, but I didn't think it was impossible. Sometimes Dad was absentminded. Eventually, I think Mom gave him a ride to work. When I thought the coast was clear, I went downstairs.

I punched the button on the coffee maker and stared at my phone. I wondered if Lily was awake. Should I text her? While I was pondering this, I was surprised to see the neighbor's dog running around by himself. He's a malamute, and when he gets out he's gone for a long while. Last year they installed a six-foot fence to prevent him from ever getting out again. I wondered what happened.

I opened my laptop, scrolling through Instagram and the local news. A lot of weird stuff was going on in Franklin. For one thing, somehow all of the locks disengaged on the nursing home doors, and all of the patients who could walk were wandering around downtown. The ones in wheelchairs just rolled away. It took the staff and the police three hours to round them all up. The director was quoted as saying, "Thank God none of them wandered into traffic."

Another weird thing was that the local summer camp had two kids go missing. They were camping. When they all gathered for the evening dinner and sing-a-long, they realized that two of the campers weren't there. Anyone who could volunteer to look for them was told to report to the police station for instructions. I wondered if I should go. It's got to suck having your kid missing from summer camp. The kids—Jasmine and Cooper—were only about eight years old.

While I was thinking about that—do I have attention deficit disorder, I wondered—my phone pinged. It was Mom. The hospital called and wanted to know if she could work, and since she knew it was my day off she figured I could watch Maddie. I sighed, then texted back, *Fine.* I mean, I could call Lily, but then again she might be dealing with her Dad. Or something.

And how did she know I had a date with Cassidy? This occurred to me a few days after I saw Lily in the street. I certainly hadn't told her. Was she stalking me or something? That seemed ridiculous, but it bothered me. I couldn't come up with any rational explanation, so I shoved it right out of my head for the time being. And I was leery to even text or call Lily, for fear she would go back to not answering. So I didn't mind, too much, spending the day looking after Maddie. I managed to keep her entertained by playing the same movie over and over.

CHAPTER TWENTY-FOUR

I SAW LILY again the next day. Not at work, of course. I had pretty much given up on ever seeing her in the break room. But as soon as I got off the elevator, she was there, waiting for me. She smiled and immediately kissed me with her soft, cherry-sweet lips. Now this was more like it. She hasn't kissed me since our first date.

"Whoa. I missed you," I said, and kissed her again.

"Hmm. I missed you, too."

I think I felt fine at first. We decided to grab something to eat, so I took Lily to a fast-food chain. It was sometime around dinner that I started to feel like my head had vise grips around my temples, squeezing until I was certain my head would explode. I closed my eyes and lifted a hand to my head.

"What's wrong?" Lily asked.

"Ah, I just…I just have a headache. Like a migraine or something." It was difficult to talk. I'd never had a migraine before, but this must be what they feel like. The lights were boring holes into my head, and my stomach lurched, threatening to reintroduce the pizza I had just eaten to the world.

"Oh, I'm sorry. Maybe you should go home." When I was able to squint at her, she seemed sympathetic.

"Yeah…yeah, maybe I should. Sorry, Lily." I pushed away from the table and stumbled toward the minivan. As soon as I got into the hammering July sun, I threw up. My head felt unwieldy, as if it might fall off at any moment. I spit and then wiped my mouth.

You know how sometimes, when you throw up, you instantly feel a lot better? Yeah, no. I still felt like crap. I felt a tap on my shoulder and I flinched involuntarily.

"Fynn?"

"Yeah?"

"You want me to drive you home?" She sounded uncertain, and I wondered if I had offended her. I groaned. Mom would kill me if I let someone else drive the van—what if she got into an accident—but what choice did I have? I could barely hold my head up. I nodded and crawled into the passenger seat.

It felt like the drive took about an hour and a half, although in reality it was about fifteen minutes. I slouched in my seat, torn between holding my head or my stomach. Every time we turned a corner, I felt as if my whole body had turned gelatinous and was going to slide under the seat. Eventually we came to a stop. I looked up and saw my house.

"Thanks, Lily. I don't know what's wrong with me. Must be a virus."

"You look terrible." She put a cool hand on my hot head and nodded sympathetically.

"You'll be able to get back? You want my Dad to drive you?" I asked.

"No, no. Don't put him to any trouble. I'll be fine." I nodded gratefully and ran into the house.

I threw myself on my bed and closed my eyes. I felt better, and I chalked it up to being in bed in a room with the shades drawn. My headache had lessened and my stomach had stopped doing jumping jacks.

I think I fell asleep, because when I woke up it was almost 10:00 p.m. *What an awkward time for a nap*, I thought. Now I was going to be awake until two or three in the morning. Oh, well. I went downstairs, found my phone, and texted Lily.

Get back okay? She sent a thumbs-up emoji.

Great. Sorry about tonight.

"It's okay. People get sick. See ya tomorrow?"

For sure! Can't wait. I hesitated. Should I send a heart emoji, or was that a girl thing? Or should I tell her in person? By this time, I knew I loved her. I just hadn't told her yet. My fingers hovered over the keyboard. Nah, better to tell her in person.

Chapter Twenty-Five

THOUGHTS OF LILY paraded through my head, and I had a hard time falling asleep. I stared at the ceiling for a while and then turned over and stared at the wall for a change of scenery. Eventually I did fall asleep, although I don't know when. The last time I looked at the clock it was 2:44 a.m. Then the next thing I knew I was having a dream—something about waiting in line for turnips—and there was a loud noise, like an alarm. I turned to the dream person next to me and said, "What was that," and then I realized it was my alarm clock and it was time to go to Hell.

I yawned and stretched, trying to get the kink out of my back. I went downstairs to find Mom sitting at the kitchen table, drinking coffee and staring vacantly out the window. Sometimes her sleep schedule was all messed up.

"Morning," I said as I made a beeline for the coffee maker.

"Hi, honey. How are you? How's Big Box?"

It took me a minute to realize that was where I was supposed to be working. "It's fine. How's the hospital?"

"They're still trying to make us work short all the time." The nurses at her hospital had been fighting with the administration ever since they were bought out by a major corporate hospital. They did things like insisting nurses work until 7:30 a.m. instead of 7:15 a.m. Half the time, when there was supposed to be one nurse for every four patients, they had six or seven patients. Mom said it was compromising patient care, but the administration didn't care about things like that.

I sympathized. The administration sucked. "Sorry."

She opened her computer. "They found those kids. The ones missing from the camp," she added when she saw my blank expression.

"Oh, right. That's good."

"You're up early." She gazed at me appraisingly.

"Yeah. I had some kind of stomach thing last night, and I fell asleep early so I couldn't sleep last night."

"Bummer. How do feel now?" She tilted her head. I always thought my mom was beautiful. She had a wide smile, pretty cinnamon-colored hair, and blue eyes. I've seen pictures—she was a total knockout before she had kids. Really, she still is. But she looked tired.

"Better. Actually, much better." It was true, too. My headache was gone and I was starving. I rummaged around in the freezer for a bagel. I found a poppy seed, defrosted it, and toasted it. Then I slathered it liberally with cream cheese and sat across the table from Mom.

She watched me eat. "I wish I could eat like that."

"You can, like this, see," I said with my mouth full of bagel.

She laughed. "I could, but I would gain lots of weight. Then my knees would give out, I'd have to quit my job, and then we'd all go on welfare."

"Yeah, right."

We talked a little as I ate. I told her a little about Lily. Her only question was, "Does she treat you well?" I just love that about her. She could care less what she looked like, how much money she had—which was good because I really had no idea—where she lived, or anything. She just wanted to make sure Lily was good to me. As I got up from the table, I thought about how lucky I was to have a nice, normal family that loved each other. I know not everyone does and that sucks.

I went to work. Work was pretty boring—even Hell gets repetitive—and I watched the clock. I swear it was moving slowly just to spite me. I looked up and it was 1:17. Then about an hour and a half later I looked up again and it was 1:25. The whole day went by like a flock of octogenarians mall walking. I thought of quitting early, but no one ever quit early. I wasn't sure if people who quit early were fired, roasted alive, or what, but I decided not to chance it.

Finally, the day was over. Since my illness had ruined last night's date, I was very excited to see Lily. I eagerly jumped off the elevator and looked around the cafeteria. No Lily. I glanced at my cell phone to see if I was early or something, but I wasn't. It was just 6:07 p.m. I looked down the hallway. No Lily. I peered into the storage pantries and freezers. No Lily, although I did find a bag of leftover chips. So I ate those while I looked around. I even looked in the girls' bathroom. No Lily. I was just about to give up and start my long, hot, lonely walk home when someone came up behind me and covered my eyes.

"Guess who?" A sweet voice whispered in my ear.

"Miranda?" I said.

"What?" She let go and whipped me around to face her.

"Calm down, I'm kidding."

"Who's Miranda?" She wasn't quite mad, but there was a severity to her level of interest I didn't much like.

"A name I made up. Relax." I pulled her close to me and kissed her. She melted underneath me, and when we let go, she was smiling.

"Hmm…I don't know if I believe you," she said.

"Now, why would I go out with some imaginary girl named Miranda when I'm going out with the hottest…" Kiss. "Most beautiful…" Kiss. "Girl in the entire world?" Kiss.

This seemed to placate her. "Yeah, you're right. What do you want to do?" she asked.

It was really hot, so I suggested we go up to the lake and chill. She pouted. "I didn't bring a swimsuit."

I smiled. "So?" She hit me on the shoulder. I laughed.

"Well, if you're worried about attracting a crowd, I think your bathing suit we bought when we went to Josh's is still in the van."

She brightened and, after a brief stop at my house for bathing suits, towels, and sandwiches, we were on our way.

I was exaggerating when I called our destination a lake. Small Cove Pond is…a pond. The bottom is covered with rocks and creepy sea life that resembled snakes no matter if it's an actual snake or not. But a lot of people hang out on the strip of sand right by the water.

Tonight, though, there were just a few kids and their mom, and they looked like they were packing up. I spread out a towel, grabbed a sandwich from the gym bag I had thrown it in, and offered Lily the other sandwich.

After about ten minutes, I started to feel nauseous. The sun was beating down on my head so hard it felt like it was going to crack.

"Maybe we should move to the shade," I managed.

"Oh, okay." Her eyes narrowed. "Are you feeling alright?"

"No—I think it's the sun." We dragged the towels underneath a tree.

"Better?" Lily asked.

"Not really. But it's helping. Give me a minute." I sprawled out on the towel and closed my eyes. *Please feel better,* I told myself. How was I ever going to get past first base with Lily if I was constantly ill? And it couldn't be much fun for her, always hanging out with some guy who was sick all the time. I so wanted to feel okay. I willed my stomach to settle. I had to feel better.

It didn't work. My guts threatened to expose my partially digested sandwich and spew everywhere. Also, I was so weak I could barely sit up.

Lily sighed. "Fynn, I think you should just go home."

"No, I'm fine." I concentrated very hard on not looking pale and deathlike.

She put a hand on my head again. Her hand was so cool, so delicious I wanted to lick it. She shook her head. "You're really hot."

"Thank you."

She smiled. "At least you still have a sense of humor. But seriously, you must still be sick. Maybe it's some kind of recurring bug."

"Like a cockroach."

"No, cockroaches just never die. This dies and then comes back."

"Okay, so it's a zombie illness."

"Whatever. Why don't we go back? It's not going to be fun if you're asleep on the beach. Text me when you feel better."

I groaned. I really, really wanted to stay and hang out with Lily, but I really felt like I had just been run over by a train. Reluctantly, I nodded. She started gathering up our things and stuffing them into my gym bag.

"Maybe it was the mayonnaise." I almost couldn't stand up straight. I was so tired I just wanted to sleep.

"Maybe."

I felt like a puppy who'd been caught peeing on the floor. In addition to my weird illness, I had let Lily down. Some boyfriend I was.

She sighed when we got to the van. "You want me to drive?"

"Yeah." What Mom didn't know wouldn't hurt her. Probably. With a mighty effort, I got myself into the passenger seat and I closed my eyes and tried not to throw up on the way home. I didn't actually puke, so I guess there's that.

"Thanks. You want my Mom to drive you to the school?" I asked.

"Nah, I'm fine. Feel better, Fynn." She would've kissed me—I think—but I was already running to the bathroom.

"I'll text you!"

CHAPTER TWENTY-SIX

I STARTED TO notice a pattern.

I was lying on a deck chair in Josh's backyard. While I felt exhausted, I didn't feel nauseous or sick or anything. Since the date at the pond with Lily, there had been two more dates with Lily. Oh, did I say dates? I should've said attempted dates. It was the strangest thing. I would meet Lily, I would be thrilled to see her and excited to hang out with her, and then within thirty minutes I would feel like I was about to die.

"Maybe you're allergic to her," Josh said. He was also on a deck chair, wearing oversized shades and sipping a Coke.

"Thanks," I said.

"Maybe you're motion sick. Do you spin around when you see her?"

"Ha ha."

He shrugged. "I don't know what to tell you. It's weird, I guess. Maybe you should go to a doctor. Maybe you have Lyme disease. Or mono."

I wasn't sure what the symptoms were for Lyme disease—flu-like, I seem to remember—but I was definitely exhausted enough for it to be mono. "Yeah, maybe. But how come I always feel worse around her?"

"You have issues?" Josh hazarded.

"Probably. But that doesn't explain why I feel like crap every time we have a date."

Courtney, who I thought was napping, lifted her head up off the lounge chair. "When you brought her here, you felt okay, right?"

I tried to think. It seemed like a long time ago, although in reality it was about two weeks ago. "I think so, yeah."

"Well, what's different?"

Again, my mental wheels churned slowly into action. I remembered Lily being ticked off about Court. I remember kissing her at the end. No, wait—she didn't kiss me, she went into the elevator and waved. I remember being really bummed out by that. "Well, she didn't kiss me after. But before our first date she did kiss me. A little. No tongue or anything."

Courtney made a face. "Probably TMI, but maybe that's it. Maybe she has some weird virus that you have no immunity for."

I thought about it. Was it the kissing? I tried to think back. I never kissed her in Hell, and I never felt bad after seeing her. Our first date kiss was just a smooch, a quick peck on the lips. After that, we got more into it. Did I feel sick every time I kissed her? Was there some way I could like, take antibiotics or something? Or maybe Claritin?

"That would be a major bummer if kissing made you sick," Josh said.

"It's not kissing, it's kissing *Lily*." I didn't have tons of kissing experience, but I had kissed a few girls before, and I had never come down with anything. I thought about it for a minute. No, never.

"Still a major bummer," Josh said.

"Yeah." Yeah, it was.

CHAPTER TWENTY-SEVEN

I GOT HOME from Josh's to find Dad sitting at his computer, looking irritable. I thought about asking him what was wrong, but before I could, he barked, "Fynn!"

My shoulders hunched up around my ears. "What?"

"Have you been…doing something to my computer?"

"No, Dad. I haven't touched your computer. I have my own computer. Why would I use yours?"

He was staring at the screen mumbling to himself. "Must be a virus."

Well, at least Dad's computer and I had something in common, although if I stayed away from Lily I seemed to feel okay. I didn't think this boded well for our relationship, so I made an appointment with the doctor. If it was just an illness, then I could get some meds and enjoy Lily for the rest of the summer. Off I went.

§§§

"Breathe in."

I was wearing a johnny and sitting on the examination table. My bare feet swung underneath me—why do they make you take off your shoes? My feet are fine. Dr. Michaels, my doctor since I was born, clamped an icy cold stethoscope on my chest.

"Ah! Do you keep those things in the refrigerator?" I said as I jumped.

"Always the comedian. No, just for you I kept this one in the freezer." Dr. Michaels was probably in his sixties. He had gray hair that was growing closer to white every year, an easy smile, and an earring, a nod to his hippy past.

He took my pulse, my blood pressure, looked in my throat, all the standard stuff. "I can't find a thing wrong with you," he said.

"Really? What about a virus?"

"Hmm, no. You'd have a fever. You don't have a fever."

"What if I have the world's first fever-less virus?"

Dr. Michaels put his stethoscope back in a drawer. "Then I'll write it up in a medical journal and become famous. But there's no evidence you have anything of the sort."

"Oh."

He tilted his head. "Shouldn't you be relieved?"

"Yeah. I guess. But then why do I keep having these reactions?"

Dr. Michaels sat down. He flipped through my chart. "Maybe it's adrenal fatigue. I guess it could be bacterial—we should draw some blood. I don't think it is bacterial, but it wouldn't do any harm to rule that out. Or it could be something in the environment that you're allergic to. Or stress? Are you getting enough rest?"

"I think so."

He consulted the chart. "It says you've lost seven pounds since April."

"Yeah. I've been sick. Have you not been paying attention?"

Dr. Michaels sighed. "Well, let's get the blood work done. In the meantime, take it easy. Don't work too hard. Where do you work, again?"

I almost said, "Hell" without thinking about it and then caught myself. "Big Boxes."

"Well, they can work you pretty hard if you're not careful. Keep an eye on your hours."

"Yeah, okay."

He nodded and shook my hand. "Always good seeing you. You can get dressed."

I put my shorts and shirt back on. It was kind of weird to be hoping I had a bacterial infection, but the alternative was that Lily was somehow making me ill. Of the two, I'd rather have the bacterial infection.

I drove myself home. I was depressed. I finally get a hot girlfriend, and I have some gut-wrenching reaction to her. Sucks to be me.

CHAPTER TWENTY-EIGHT

THE NEXT DAY was Thursday, which meant work. I overslept, and when I did wake up I felt like a zombie. A shower, meant to wake me up, just made me feel like a squeaky clean zombie. My brain still felt like it was slightly scrambled. I went to the kitchen. There was no way I was going anywhere without coffee, even if I didn't have time for breakfast. I dumped it in a commuter mug, tossed in a few extra sugars for energy, walked to school, and hopped on the elevator.

"Hello, Dorothy. You're looking lovely this morning."

"Oh, stop." She fluttered her eyelashes—green—at me and blushed. At least I think she did. It was hard to tell, because today her skin was a brilliant shade of magenta. She was wearing what appeared to be a 1980's prom gown. To each their own. I gave her a wave and got in a hovercraft.

I went directly to SD and saw I was working with Tom and Sierra. Thank goodness, no Audrey. I didn't think I could tolerate her this morning. Tom and Sierra both worked quietly and kept to themselves, which was perfect for the mood I was in. Dodd hovered around for a while, but he left abruptly mid-morning.

Lunch rolled around. I had pretty much given up the thought of ever seeing Lily in the break room, so when Tom said he was going to the cafeteria, I said, "I'll go with you." This turned out to be another decision I regretted because, although I liked Tom and thought he was a nice guy, I didn't know him that well. We both sat there looking at our sandwiches and saying things like, "Boy, that Audrey" and "I think they shorted me an hour and a half this last paycheck." I was wolfing down my lunch so I could get up and leave when I saw a Hornissen getting a tray. It made me think of something.

"Hey, do you know if they ever found that demon?"

Tom frowned as he popped a French fry in his mouth. "I don't think so. Wherever it went, I don't think it's still in Hell."

"What do demons do, if they escape?"

Tom finished chewing and swallowed. "I think they survive by sucking the souls out of living people. People who are victims of demons start to feel run down, depressed, and they have no energy. Eventually they are so depleted they can't get out of bed, and then they just die. The demon is happy for a while, but then they have to move on to someone else."

"Oh." Great. No mention of feeling sick or blinding headaches.

Tom frowned. "I've also heard sometimes they make their targets physically sick. Like, throwing up, headaches, the whole bit."

I had stopped chewing because my face was frozen. I felt a cold finger of fear tracing up the back of my neck as he spoke. My mouth went dry. "So, what can people do if they suspect a demon is around?"

Tom shrugged. "From what I understand, most people don't suspect until they're almost dead. By then it's too late. I've never heard of anyone recovering from an attempted demon sucking." He gathered up the wrapper from his chips and crumpled them up into a ball. "Ready?"

I had stopped eating and now had a soccer-ball-size lump in my stomach. I nodded, gathered up my lunch, and threw the rest away. We walked back to SD.

At the end of the day, I gave a dejected wave to Dorothy and trudged into the elevator. It lurched up towards the surface, and I grabbed the handrail to steady myself and keep myself from throwing up. At some point I looked up, and on the wall facing me was a sign I had seen about a hundred times but never paid attention to. "In case of fire, do not use the elevator. Use the stairs." I didn't even know there were stairs leading out of Hell. Maybe the sign was just a holdover from the high school.

But that's not the part that caught my attention. "In case of fire. In case of fire." I remembered that I was in the elevator with Lily when I asked what her last name was. I remembered that second of hesitation before she said, "Case." My stomach dropped. I kept thinking how crappy I had been feeling, pretty much ever since Lily had become a presence in my life. But…nah. She was perfectly normal! Just because she seemed to appear just as Hell lost a demon didn't mean anything. And her supposed last name was on the sign in the elevator. Pure coincidence. Right?

CHAPTER TWENTY-NINE

I T WAS A few days later. After my shift in Hell, I waved to Dorothy and got in the elevator. With a lurch the elevator started moving towards the surface. When it stopped, I cautiously poked my head out and looked around the cafeteria. I sighed with relief, got out, and walked quickly to the door.

My emotions were tangled up. On the one hand, the idea that Lily was an escaped demon had been planted in my brain and was taking root. On the other hand, I was tormented by visions of her soft, full lips and amazing body. Yeah, okay, I know I'm shallow. So sue me. I knew I mostly felt like crap after seeing her and thought hard. Was it every time? Certainly when I saw her in Hell I didn't feel like crap afterward. I felt fine. Eager, excited, horny—all those things. It wasn't until she got to Franklin that I started to feel ill every time I saw her. Maybe Courtney was right. If I never kissed her again I should be fine. I liked kissing her, though. It was quite a dilemma. Kiss and be violently ill, or don't kiss and feel fine? I was torn.

I decided I should do an experiment and not see Lily for a day or two. After all, I had been sick every time I saw her for the last week or so, but maybe I really was having some weird illness that was so far undiscovered. I thought, in order to avoid her, I had to go somewhere that we had never gone and she would never think to look for me. So I went to the library. Trust me, no one would ever think to look for me there.

Technically, the library in Franklin is called the Athenaeum because someone decided, in a fit of pretension and possibly unbounded optimism, that this particular library was an "institution for scientific or literary study." Yeah, okay. The rest of us just call it the library. I figured while I was here I should do some research. I turned off my cell phone as I entered. Then I went into settings and hid my location.

"Excuse me," I said, probably too loudly. I saw a few heads jerk up from a few of the scarred wooden tables that occupied the main room.

"Yes?" A woman with steel-rim glasses said. She was kind of frumpy, wearing middle-aged, I've-given-up-on-looking-attractive clothes, but she smiled at me in a nice way.

"I was wondering, where would I find information on demons?"

She frowned. "What sort of demons? Like, Satanism?"

"No, no. Just garden-variety demons. Like mythology kind of stuff."

She looked relieved. "Oh, okay. Follow me. I'll show you where our mythology section is."

I followed her. She wore sensible rubber-soled shoes that made no sound at all. I thought about mentioning she'd make a great thief, but I decided not to. She led me up a short staircase to the second floor. By the landing were a sofa and a small round table perched on a fluffy pink rug. A sign said, "Start your summer reading here!" We walked by that, past a bunch of shelves, and then she gestured down between two of the stacks.

"We don't have a lot on demons specifically, but you'll find mentions of them in many mythology books. Those are…" She ran her finger down the shelves, reading the titles as she went and stopped a shelf up from the bottom. "Here."

"Thanks."

"Certainly," she said as she strode away, looking purposeful.

I sat on the floor, slid out a book called *Demons and Demonology*, and pulled it into my lap. I flipped through it. It was set up like an encyclopedia, with the name of a demon, a painting, and a description of what sort of evil that particular demon spread. Most of the paintings depicting demons seemed to be some combination of human with animal features, or half-human, half-animal. The book did mention demons were a way for unsophisticated cultures to explain evil.

I continued to read, not expecting to find anything useful until an entry for "Lilith" caught my eye. "According to some sources, Lilith was Adam's first wife, but she refused to be subservient to Adam." *Well, good for her,* I thought. "Lilith left Adam. Adam complained to God, who sent his angels after her. She was found by the sea giving birth to hundreds of demon children. God told her to return to Adam, and when she refused God punished her by killing a hundred of her children every day. Lilith was furious, so she killed human newborn babies in the night." I looked at the picture. It was a beautiful demon woman with a snake wrapped around her torso. I studied the picture. It didn't look anything like Lily, but still…Lilith, Lily, Lilith, Lily—it was too close for comfort.

The book said that demons usually served Satan and carried out his evil wishes against humans. "A demon needs to feed on something in order to live outside of Hell." I read on. "The Succubus is a female demon who steals men's souls through sexual intercourse." Wait, what? I read it again. "Repeated exposure to the succubus would lead to sickness, madness, and death." Well, that didn't sound good at all. Assuming Lily even was a demon. The book said that demons ruled in Hell. I hadn't seen Lily in Hell in weeks. Although I did

98

meet her there. And they had no record of her actually working there. And there had been an escaped demon…

Shit.

I searched through the book, trying to see if it had any suggestions for how to get rid of a demon. "Certain demons get attached to a particular human and will stay with that human until they kill them." *Great.* So how to get rid of it? "Sometimes just asking a demon to leave will do the trick. If the demon remains, more elaborate demon banishment techniques will need to be employed." Okay, like what? Naturally it didn't mention any. Stupid book.

Putting the book back on the shelf, I made my way to the public computers on the first floor. I opened the internet and Googled, "Getting rid of a demon." Naturally, there were references to Catholic exorcisms and prayer. "If prayer doesn't work, a priest specializing in demonic possession should be contacted." Through what, the yellow pages? How was I supposed to figure out which priests had experience in demonic possession? I didn't think prayer would work because I was not a religious person, although I had recently come to believe in Hell. And demons.

Then it occurred to me. If Lily was a demon, all I had to do was avoid her. If she couldn't feed off me she would die eventually. Right? Right? I could just explain to her that I had some terrible illness and had to stay home. Eventually she would pack up and go away.

Right.

§ § §

I left the library when it closed at 9 p.m. The thought of just hiding there somewhere and staying the night crossed my mind, but I left. I didn't want to turn my cell phone on until 10:00 p.m., which so far had been when Lily had to be back. If she actually had somewhere to go back to.

I walked around. It was a pleasant summer evening, the heat of the day melting into a balmy softness. I went down by the town green and sat on a bench, not feeling great about myself. Finally, I get a girlfriend, and she's a succubus? Thousands of guys my age have dated thousands upon thousands of girls. Why was I the only guy who wound up with a demon? Why couldn't I just be normal? I suppose someone might reasonably suggest that if you work in Hell, you might meet demons. Well, sure, but that doesn't mean I wanted one to follow me home and feed off of my energy, or my soul, or whatever.

I watched a couple snuggling on a bench, kissing and staring into each other's eyes. There were a couple of kids, twelve, maybe thirteen—Kevin's age—walked around holding hands. They would look at each other, giggle, and then gaze at the ground, the sky, passing traffic—anywhere but at each other. I sighed heavily and glanced at my phone. 9:46 p.m. Almost. Might as well start walking home. If I walked slowly, I would be there by 10:00 p.m., and I didn't want to stay up late anyway. I had to go to work tomorrow. So I might as well go to bed early.

I got to my house at 9:57 p.m., looked around for Lily, and didn't see her. *Whew*. Nevertheless, I snuck across the lawn as if I were breaking into my own house. After swinging the front door open and closing it softly, I leaned against it and took a deep breath.

Now that I was home, I didn't especially care if I had missed a few texts from Lily, so I looked at my phone. I hooked it up to a charger and left it there. Then I got in the shower, enjoying the fact that I was home and not throwing up or fending off evil headaches as I stood under the hot spray. I put a gob of shampoo on my head—tea tree oil scented—washed my hair, and lathered up my body. Finally, I shut it off and wrapped a big, fluffy towel around myself. Suddenly I was exhausted. Maybe it was the hot, relaxing shower or the relief of having made it home with no problems, but I could barely keep my eyes open. Rubbing my hair until it was acceptably dry, I fell into bed. I slept a delightful, dreamless sleep until it was time to wake up for work.

I thought about not turning on my phone, throwing it away, and getting a new phone, possibly under an assumed name, but none of those things seemed feasible. Since my whole family was on one plan—except for Maddie—they would probably wonder why on earth I couldn't use the phone number I've had since I was twelve. I thought about inventing a stalker—Courtney could probably hook me up with someone who would pretend to stalk me—but I wasn't sure it would help anyway. If Lily really was a demon, changing my phone number probably wouldn't stop her for long. I sighed and turned on my phone.

Seven missed calls and a series of increasingly agitated texts. "Where are you?" "I tried to call you, call me back." "Are you still sick?" "Just call me." "Fynn, WTF?" "FYNN!!!" Where was the understanding, just let me know if you're sick? Of course, I hadn't let her know, I just disappeared. I was afraid she'd show up with soup or something. It doesn't sound terrible, does it? No, but then after the soup she would try to suck my soul right out of my body. See, it doesn't sound so good now, does it?

Reluctantly, I responded to the last text. *Sorry—I was really, really sick and I shut off my phone so I could sleep*. Then I waited. After about seven seconds this popped up: "You could've just told me."

Sorry.

"Why did you just vanish off the face of the earth?"

Sorry. Like I said, I was really sick. I inserted a sick guy emoji.

"Just a minute." The phone rang—*Eye of the Tiger*. I love Rocky movies. I wasn't looking forward to being bitched out, though.

"Yeah?"

"I don't understand why you didn't just let me know." I could almost see her tapping her foot impatiently, her nostrils flaring out to the sides like sails.

"I told you, I was sick. I don't know what this virus is, but I was in bed all night."

"No, you weren't." A pause.

"What?"

"You weren't home. I went to your house and asked for you. Your brother said he hadn't seen you."

Fuck me. I sat for a few seconds while my mind scurried around in circles, looking for excuses. "That's because I told Kevin to tell people that if anyone came by." It sounded lame, even to me.

"Why didn't he just say you were sick then?" she said, not unreasonably. It wasn't unreasonable, but I was beginning to feel cornered, which was making me extremely irritated and not reasonable at all.

"I don't know! I didn't want you to worry! Or try to visit! I'm probably contagious." I coughed a few times for emphasis.

"You weren't with that girl?"

"No! What girl?"

"The one who was texting you. Caroline?"

"Cassidy? No, I was not." I briefly pictured my life with Cassidy—a normal, non-demon. It sounded lovely. Even with her son, it sounded lovely. Maybe Maddie and Blake could be play date buddies. Anyway, I was tired of this conversation. "Look, I have to go to work. Are you working today?" I asked. If there was one thing I was sure of, it was that I would never see Lily in Hell again.

"No, I'm off today."

"When do you actually work? I haven't seen you there in weeks."

"What difference does it make? I'm taking some time off—you know, to care for my father? Or did you forget about that?"

I had actually, mostly because I was pretty sure it was bullshit, but whatever. "All right. Go care for your sick father. He must miss you."

"Will I see you after work?" she asked. I thought I detected a hard edge in her voice. Frustrated. Furious.

"I guess I'll have to see how I feel." I would not be killed by a demon, no sirree Bob.

101

"Really."

"Yup. Okay, I have to go. Bye now." I clicked off and took a deep breath. I dressed quickly, went into the kitchen, and grabbed a coffee. I poured it into a to-go cup, took an energy bar, and was on my way.

Was it ironic that the safest place for me was Hell?

CHAPTER THIRTY

I GOT OFF the elevator. Never have I been so happy to get to Hell. I gave Dorothy a big smile. She smiled back, which is when I noticed she had colored her teeth fluorescent green. She was wearing a matching feather boa and a pair of overalls.

"Hi, Dorothy. How are you?" I paused at her desk. I genuinely liked Dorothy. She was always pleasant and friendly.

"Fynn. I'm well, how are you?" She batted her eyelashes, and I think her hair blinked.

"Happy to be here, Dorothy, happy to be here." It was true.

"Fynn, you're so funny."

"Yeah, that's me. Funny." My spirits dipped a little at that. After all, it wasn't going to be so funny when I was dead as a result of a demon attack. I continued on my way, got in the hovercraft, and sped off to SD.

I was pleased to see that I was working with Adrian and Sierra, which meant no Audrey, which meant peace and quiet. Making my way over to my workstation, I started sorting, kept my head down, and just focused on meeting my targets. I had lunch right after Adrian—on busy days we had to go one at a time. Grabbing my sandwich and an orange juice, I sat at a table in the break room, chewing slowly and savoring my alone time. My not-being-pursued-by-any-demons time. I wondered if they had residency programs in Hell. I could be like a landlord or something. Maybe I should ask Mr. Dodd about that.

The afternoon passed much as the morning had. I sorted the souls, packed them carefully in their boxes, and set the boxes to be picked up by Transport. I hit my target with a solid ninety-seven percent. Then I caught a passing hovercraft and zipped off to the elevator.

After my usual motion-sickness-inspiring elevator ride, I got off cautiously, looking for Lily. I sighed with relief when I didn't see her. Maybe she would give up and move onto someone else. After all, I was hardly all that. Wouldn't pretty much any soul do? Now that I had caught on, I would be that much harder to suck the soul from. Right? I had pretty much convinced myself of this entire fairy tale on my walk home. Putting on my headphones and listening to my tunes, I grew more and more confident with every step I took. Lily wasn't stupid. Of course she could find someone else. She could just pretend I was breaking up with her, so she could save demon-face.

I pushed the side door open, taking my headphones out as I did. Maddie's shriek of delight could be heard even from the kitchen. "Hi, Mom," I called out as I smiled to myself.

"Hi, Honey. We're in here."

"Okay." I grabbed a Coke from the fridge and checked my email on my phone. I went to the living room, and what I saw made my blood run cold. Lily was sitting on the floor of the living room, in my house, with my mom and my baby sister.

CHAPTER THIRTY-ONE

ICE WATER RAN through my veins and I froze. Lily was sitting cross-legged on my living room rug, in my house, pointing out something in a book to my baby sister. She looked up at me and smiled—a sort of knowing, cat-that-ate-the-canary smile. Maddie squealed and ran over to me, opening and closing her fists and saying, "Up, up."

I lifted her up and said, "Hey, Maddie. What's up?" She giggled with delight and started to pull at my hair. "Ow, no, Maddie, that hurts. No," I said, gently putting her down on the floor. I looked from Lily to Mom and back again, speechless.

"I hope you don't mind, Fynn. Lily said she was supposed to meet you after work."

"Sure. Lily, can I speak to you for a moment?" Digging my fingers into her upper arm, I yanked her to her feet. I started walking quickly towards the backyard with Lily in tow. Mom raised her eyebrows at me as I went past her.

"Fynn, is there a problem?"

"Nope! No problem at all!" I said as I steered Lily to the patio and closed the sliding glass door behind us. "What do you think you're doing?" I hissed.

"I don't know what you're talking about. I just came here to see you, Fynn." She reached out her arms and tried to pull me into a hug. I held my hands out and took a few steps back.

"I told you I was sick!"

"Well, obviously you're not sick!" She glared at me.

"There is no reason you need to come to my house and invade my family!"

Lily glared. "I knew you weren't sick." I noticed she didn't apologize or anything for the invasion of my privacy. I felt like territory had been invaded by the opposing army.

I glared at her, so furious I couldn't see straight. "You don't even work in Hell, do you?" I said.

"Of course I work in Hell! That's where I met you!" she yelled.

I stood staring at her. Lily was wearing a blue tank top and short shorts. She looked hot, and I wished to God I had never met her. "Are you sure you're not a demon?" I spit out.

She froze. The moment hung in the air like a lead weight. Then she laughed, a high, house-of-horrors laugh. "Of course I'm not a demon."

"Prove it. Prove you're not a demon," I said.

"You can't prove a negative! Prove *you're* not a demon!" She folded her arms across her chest.

She had me there. I couldn't prove I wasn't a demon.

"Come with me to Hell." It was the only thing I could think of that would prove she wasn't a demon. I hadn't seen her there in weeks, and I was pretty sure it was because she had escaped and wasn't going back.

"No," she said with finality.

"Why not?" I shot back.

"I…just don't want to."

"Really? Why not? Is it because you're an escaped demon?" I was almost shouting now. I thought I saw a window open in the neighbor's house next to us and lowered my voice. "I haven't seen you there in weeks, and I get sick every time I kiss you."

"Oh, so that makes me a demon? Are you crazy?" she said.

Maybe. I had often wondered, lately, if maybe I had actually lost my mind. They say you can't tell if it happens to you. You think you make perfect sense until other people around you start talking about your upcoming commitment.

"All right, look. I don't care what or who you are. This relationship is just not working out for me. We need to break up." I probably should've started with that. It was so much easier.

"I'm not…what do you mean, break up?" Her eyes flashed.

"I mean, it's over, done. I don't want to see you, talk to you, kiss you, or text you. Go back to Nebraska, if that's actually where you're from."

She stared at me malevolently. Her eyes smoldered and turned black, inky pools of hate that hinted at catastrophe. I recoiled. Even the very presence of her was making me physically sick.

"Do not fuck with me, Fynn Hardin."

"Who's fucking with you? I just want you out of my life!" I shrieked. I'm sure the neighbor was very entertained.

She looked at me for a long time. Then she said, "Fine. I don't have to have you. One soul is as good as the next. Actually, the younger the soul, the easier it is. Your sister will do nicely."

Wait, what? Did she just admit to being a demon? Then the rest of what she said sunk into the battlefield that was my brain. Maddie? She was going to kill Maddie? She was threatening my sister?

"What did you just say?" I looked at her dark, dead eyes and saw only emptiness and greed.

"You heard me. I can just as easily use your sister."

"What, you're going to date my baby sister now?"

She shook her head and smiled. Then she said, as if explaining something to an overtired kindergartner, "No, you self-absorbed half-wit. I don't need to date the people I steal souls from. That was just the easiest way to get to you. I can drain her energy in any number of ways."

"So, you think I'm just going to let you in to visit? That I'm not going to do whatever it takes to protect my family?" I said. As soon as I said it, I realized it was true. I would. I would do whatever it took to protect and defend my family. I thought about how desperate I was to get a job so I didn't have to spend the summer taking care of Maddie and what a selfish ass I was. Right now I would love to go back in time and be spending the summer with no demons whatsoever.

"Oh, I believe you'll try. But I'll get in. In the middle of the night, when it's dark and you're asleep, I will steal in through a window. I will find your sister, your brother, your mother, your father, and you. There's a nice cache of souls here that will keep me going for quite a while. I have no intention of moving on until the well is dry."

People don't talk about evil these days. People suffer from psychiatric disorders; they have failings, addictions, and Achilles' heels. Calling someone evil seems Puritan in much the same way calling someone insane is a legal defense.

Looking at Lily now, the girl I would have told you I was falling in love with just a week ago, I saw true evil. There was nothing underneath her pretty face but a black husk, an endless void spinning towards bitterness and loss. Eyes as hard and dark as olive pits gazed at me with an air of superiority.

"I will destroy you," I said, as if it were a foregone conclusion. Of course, inside my heart was quivering like a newborn baby bunny, but she couldn't know that.

She laughed again—a laugh without humor, a dry, mean laugh. Her eyes darkened to black holes and her lips curled back to expose pointed teeth. A black cloud seemed to envelop her, and then she was gone.

CHAPTER THIRTY-TWO

OKAY, SO MY ex-girlfriend was a demon. Now what?

There must be some way someone could protect himself and his family from demons. In the days that followed, I feverishly Googled demons and demonology almost non-stop. Afraid to sleep, I sat up at night, drinking coffee and energy drinks, wondering why I didn't know any drug dealers that delivered. I had never used drugs before, but this seemed like a fine time to start.

I set myself and my laptop up on the kitchen table. It provided easy access to the coffee maker and the refrigerator. Also, after hours of research, when my ass started to fall asleep, I could be revived by the sunlight flooding in through the windows. I know it sounds corny, but the sun coming up every morning made me feel there was hope.

Some websites seemed to take the position that demons were something that lay within, and all someone had to do was pray. Nice idea, but I was pretty sure that wasn't going to work at all. I supposed holy water and crucifixes might help some, but I wanted more. I wanted not to feel like my family was dangling on the edge of a precipice that I had created for them. I wanted to be able to sleep and not feel like they were going to be attacked by a demonic force.

Many websites mentioned demons can't tolerate crosses. I thought it was vampires who couldn't tolerate crosses, but who was I to argue? My grandmother gave me a cross once. After some frantic searching, I found it shoved in the back of my underwear drawer. I put it on and tucked it underneath my T-shirt. Would I explode or something if I wore a crucifix to Hell? I decided to chance it. If I was stopped getting out of the elevator by some anti-religious force field, I would just go back to FRHS and hide the cross near the elevator. It was the best idea I could come up with.

I also learned demons can be very tricky beasts. They apparently make you feel depressed, paranoid, or hear voices in your head. Obviously, anyone trying to explain these feelings is suspect and usually placed in locked seclusion. I wondered, briefly, how many of the worlds' mental patients were actually in the same boat I was.

One website recommended salt as a way of keeping demons at bay. I grabbed the salt from the cabinet, ran outside, and poured the salt in a thin line, thinking

I would form a barrier with it. There was only one container, though, and the line I made only went about thirty inches. So I ran to the store and bought all the containers of salt they had. I went back outside, pouring a line of salt around the entire house and hoping it worked, because I really needed to sleep. I was getting extremely tired and on the verge of a mental breakdown.

Mom came downstairs, clutching her robe around her even though it was summer. For a minute, I thought maybe Lily had gotten to her. She looked at me, concerned and a little frightened.

"Fynn?"

"What?" I snapped.

She drew back a bit. "Sweetie, what are you doing?"

Too late, I realized I was clutching six empty containers of salt to my chest. "Uh...summer school project?"

She leaned forward to take a closer look at me. She brushed the hair out of my eyes with her fingers. "When was the last time you slept?"

"Uhm..." I tried to think, but my thoughts kept evaporating before I could catch them.

"You're taking this breakup hard. There will be other girls, hon."

"Yeah, I know. I know." I knew there would be other girls. The question was would I still have a soul left so I could date them? Were there any girls who would consider dating a guy with no soul? I think I saw an episode like that on Dr. Phil.

"I...I'm going to sleep right now. See?" I said as I headed up to my room. I got to the landing, looked down, and saw her looking up at me, perplexed and very worried.

I had no idea if Lily could appear at any time or what. Up to this point, I had only seen her between the hours of six and ten at night. But now that we could dispense with her fabricated life story, for all I knew she could show up at any time. I felt a little better for having made a barrier with the salt, but I wasn't completely confident it would work.

I got in bed and lay there, exhausted but hyper-vigilant. Ears straining and nerves jumping at any unexpected sound, I listened. I heard Mom and Dad talking to each other in low voices. I thought I heard "...since he slept." And then, "Maybe we should take him to a doctor." Then Mom said, "Or a psychiatrist." I heard the clink of breakfast bowls and spoons and heard Maddie's shriek of protest as she was put into her highchair. I lay rigid and uncompromising...until sheer exhaustion overtook me and I fell asleep.

I dreamed of blackness and horror, phantoms, and the smell of rot. I heard whispers. I saw vampires, red mouths dripping blood and vomit, black capes whipping out behind them. I don't know how long I slept, but I awoke with a start. I looked at my cell phone and was shocked that it was four in the afternoon. *Shit*. For all I knew I was the only one still alive, Lily leaving me for last in some sort of perverted order. I ran down the stairs.

The kitchen was empty. I ran into the living room. Empty. Terror gripped me. Where was everyone? I ran upstairs and checked everyone's bedroom. Empty. I ran back downstairs, frantic. Then I saw Mom. She pushed open the kitchen door with her hips because she was holding three clay pots filled with herbs. She took them inside and put them on the windowsill. When she saw me, her face brightened.

"Fynn. You slept. How do you feel?"

"Fine. Great." I was in a T-shirt and boxer shorts. I rubbed the back of my neck with my palm. "Where is everyone?"

"Your father's still at work, Kevin's in the basement playing a game, and Maddie's with me." Again she looked concerned. "Are you feeling okay? Are you still sick?" I imagine she meant to say psychotic but caught herself in time.

I saw Maddie in her saucer chair just beyond our crumbling brick patio. She smiled, delighted to see me. "Inn!" She squawked.

"I'm fine." I went outside and dropped into a deck chair. Maddie reached her little arms out, and I got up and picked her up out of her saucer and put her on the ground. She toddled over to my chair and smiled. I grinned back at her. Then something caught her interest over by the house and she toddled over towards it.

"Do you feel any better?" Mom asked. She followed me back outside and sat on the edge of the chair next to me.

"Yeah. A little."

"I'm sorry I let Lily in. I didn't realize you broke up. She didn't say anything about that."

"Don't let her in again. Ever. For any reason," I said stonily.

Mom studied me for a second. "Is there anything you're not telling me? Should I be concerned?"

Yes, Mom, you should be concerned, because my ex-girlfriend is a demon and is trying to suck the souls out of everyone in my family. I thought this, but what I actually said was, "I just don't want to see her ever again."

"I'm sorry. Break-ups are always so hard."

"Yeah." The less said the better.

"Is there anything I can do for you?"

"No, not really. I'm okay." I turned and looked at her to reassure her. "I'll be okay."

"Well, all right then." She put her hands on her knees and pushed herself up. She nodded at Maddie. "Are you up for watching her for just a bit while I take a shower?"

"Yeah, no problem."

"Okay, I'll be quick."

It rankled me a little that Mom was treating me like an invalid, but on the other hand I was acting a little weird. I sighed and closed my eyes. I had to work tomorrow. I could put another layer of salt around the perimeter of the house, but how to protect my family while I was at work? Was there any way I could convince them to start wearing crucifixes? Some kind of religious epiphany?

I had to figure this out.

§ § §

In the days that followed, I began to notice that it wasn't just me who was affected by Lily. I was pretty sure some of the general weirdness that had been going on in town was caused by her and her idea of fun. I know it seems obvious that a demon would wreak havoc everywhere she could and not just with me personally, but then again, I was kind of an ass.

I anxiously read the news every morning, and usually there was something I was pretty sure was Lily's doing. Accidents—a lot of accidents, of all kinds. Cars, bicycles, skateboards—even people walking along, minding their own business, reported being pushed off the sidewalk by an unseen force. Thankfully none of them had been hit by oncoming traffic, but I knew it was only a matter of time.

She was also fond of stealing people's cars out of their driveways, taking them on joyrides, and then crashing them. This was whipping the townspeople, who were convinced it was some kind of teenage gang, into a frenzy. One old man was explaining how someone took his Buick right out of his garage and left it in front of a crack house. He was quite affronted.

I needed help to figure out my options. The only person I could think of, the only person who believed I worked in Hell in the first place, was Josh.

I told him everything—well, almost everything. I didn't mention how I thought I was falling in love with Lily before I discovered she was a demon, but the sickness, the threats, and every other thing I could think of.

"I thought she seemed evil," Josh said.

I stared. Was it obvious? I mean, I would hardly be the first high school junior to be blinded by lust, but still…I thought she came across as normal. Then I noticed Josh grinning in a sly sort of way.

"You're kidding, right? I know you're kidding. Right?"

"Of course I'm kidding. She seemed like a great girl to me, too. Even Courtney thought she seemed nice." The fact Court had thought Lily was nice made me feel a lot better. Josh could be taken in by how hot she was. Girls usually see past that.

Anyway, Josh agreed to try and help me. Naturally he started by Googling. I had Googled "how to defeat a demon" about a thousand times, but maybe Josh would find something I hadn't. I could use all the help I could get.

"It says here we can trap her by having her fall into a demon hole."

I lifted my head out of my hands to stare at him. "What?"

"It says we can trap her with a demon hole," Josh said patiently.

"What is a 'demon hole' as opposed to a regular hole?" I asked.

Josh turned back to his computer and typed something. "I'm not sure. Apparently demons can't climb out of holes?"

I pondered this. I had never heard demons couldn't climb out of a hole, but I supposed it could be true. "How big a hole are we talking about?"

"Six feet."

"*Six feet?* That's a grave, not a hole."

Josh frowned. "Well, I admit it's going to take us a while."

My mood, which was further down than the depths of Hell as of late, lifted the slightest bit. I really didn't deserve Josh. Then I thought of something. "Where are we going to dig this six-foot hole? Because I'm pretty sure my parents are going to notice if we start tearing up the backyard."

"Yeah. I don't know." We sat in silence for a minute.

"Would she answer a text?" Josh asked.

"Telling her to meet us—me—somewhere? I don't know. Maybe. I haven't texted her in a few days. Why? Where are you thinking we should dig?"

"It doesn't matter, does it? I mean, if we can lure her somewhere, we could dig it anywhere. The woods, maybe."

I mulled this over. "Well, it's worth a try. Where should we dig? Should we get help, like from really strong guys, or possibly a backhoe?"

"A backhoe would be great. I'm not sure where to get one. I think we can rent one?" He typed. "Good news, you can rent a small one for $100 a day. Oh, wait. You have to be eighteen."

I groaned.

"Wait. Don't panic. I know a guy we can give the money to, and he can rent us a backhoe."

"And then where will we dig the damn hole? And I've never operated a backhoe before. I'm not even sure how to do it."

113

"I bet we can figure it out. Jesus, don't be so pessimistic."

"Sorry. A demon is determined to drain my soul, but you're right. I should definitely look on the bright side."

Eventually, Josh got us a very small backhoe. It was small enough to fit into the bed of his truck. We brought it out to the edge of a wooded area. Josh didn't want to drive his truck too far into the woods. I couldn't say I blamed him. He was doing so much for me already. We took turns using the backhoe, watching the crane dig into the black, loamy earth.

After about four hours, we had a hole. Josh had brought a shovel as well, and after we threw a tarp over the hole we used the shovel to cover it with leaves and sticks and clumps of earth.

"Are you sure she can't get out of that?" I said doubtfully.

"No, I'm not sure at all. The website said demons can't climb out of a hole. That's all I know. I have no personal experience with trapping demons in holes."

"Fine." I sighed. I was tired and irritable. I took out my cell phone and texted Lily. *Where R U? I need to talk to you.*

Nothing.

We waited. I sat down, I stood up, and I paced back and forth, trying not to jump out of my skin. Twenty minutes went by.

"About what?" came a text. It was from Lily!

"Josh, it's her!" I said excitedly, "It's her!"

"Well, answer her," Josh said reasonably.

"Shit, what do I say?"

Josh came over and looked at the text Lily just sent. "Say you have to tell her in person."

I texted rapidly and waited for a response. I asked Josh, "How do I explain why I'm out in the middle of nowhere?"

"Uhh...you don't want your parents to find out?" Josh said.

Some texting back and forth. Josh took the opportunity to hide his truck some distance away, with the backhoe in the bed.

"Hold on a minute," Lily texted.

"I think she's coming! Hide!" I yelled to Josh.

I tried to position myself a good enough distance from the hole so that if I kept walking forwards, she would step back into the hole. That's what I was hoping for, anyway.

A rush of cold air blew in and then, poof! There she was. Her nostrils flared, her arms were crossed, and she looked impatient and pissed off. "What?" She said pointedly.

"Uh, I have to talk to you. What will it take for you to stop this?"

She laughed. "I have no intention of ever stopping. It's fun on earth! I can do anything. I didn't deserve to be in Hell, anyway." As she spoke her ponytail bobbed up and down. I wanted to kill her. If only I knew how.

"There must be something I can do, something you want."

Her eyes narrowed. "Your soul."

"I can't give you my soul. Furthermore, as soon as I give you my soul, you'll just go after someone else's."

She smiled again. I got the sense she was enjoying this. "Well, of course I will. I have to stay alive. I'll tell you this, Fynn. I am never, ever going back to Hell. Hell is awful. I wouldn't wish it on my worst enemy, or even on you."

"Gee, thanks." I took a step forward, hoping to get her to take a step back. No such luck.

She glared. "Is that all you wanted? Because I have things to do," she said sweetly. She reached out and tried to grab my arm, but I snatched it out of the way just in time.

"Don't touch me!"

"Aww, poor Fynn." She leaned closer and hissed, "What would make you think I would date a loser like you?" Her black, soulless eyes bored into me.

I flinched. She just said what I was most afraid of, that I was a loser who deserved to be miserable. I stared, unable to think of any reason why she would date me, unable to form words. Just then, Josh flew out of the woods, brandishing the shovel. He swung it at Lily, who jumped out of the way, and—with a surprising amount of grace—*over* the hole we just spent all day digging.

She glared and screeched, "You'll regret that!" Then she disappeared. I saw her moving through the trees, but then she vanished.

Shit.

115

CHAPTER THIRTY-THREE

I HEARD MY parents talking in low, tense voices before I even entered the kitchen. Naturally, as soon as I did, they both jerked their heads up and smiled like they were having the best time ever.

"Hi," I said as I made my way over to the coffee maker. I had to work this morning, and I had gotten in the habit of gazing out the window when I woke up to make sure Lily hadn't destroyed the world while I slept. It seemed okay.

I turned and saw my dad. He looked terrible. The lines around his eyes were deeper, and his hair—when did his hair get so gray?

"Dad, are you okay?" I ventured.

He sighed deeply and rubbed his forehead. "Not really. I don't know—did you do something? To the internet? For some reason, my emails to clients haven't been going through, and now I've lost several sales. My boss is furious."

A very sick feeling in my stomach threatened to spray my recently drunk coffee all over the kitchen. It was Lily. I knew it was Lily. Somehow she had deliberately deleted my father's emails. I wasn't sure if this was revenge for trying to bury her in a hole or if she would have done it anyway. Gripping my coffee mug tightly, I imagined myself strangling Lily. Instead, I whipped out my phone and sent her a text: *Do not mess with my family*. In response she sent the laughing emoji.

"No, Dad, I didn't mess with the internet. Do they go through if you send them from work? Or is it just when you send them from here?"

Dad rubbed his face with his palms. "I'll have to check. I think…no, wait. I definitely sent at least a few from work. I was trying to get a new customer, and I remember telling Jerry about it." Jerry was his boss.

"You can't like, resend them?" I asked.

"It wouldn't matter. They've already moved on to other companies. I really have to step up my game, or I won't have a job at all."

I imagined a scenario where I didn't go back to high school for my senior year but instead kept working in Hell to support my family. It probably wouldn't be the worst thing. Unless, of course, Lily was still running around trying to destroy me. I had to figure out a way to kill her, or at least send her back to Hell.

I trudged off to Hell, pondering my options. Holy water? Rosary beads?

A common theme seemed to be demons did not like religious artifacts. As soon as I got to Soul Destination, Audrey pounced on me.

"Dodd said we have to keep a tally of all the boxes we stack. Here," she said as she thrust a piece of paper at me. It was a form, with a place for the number of the box, the number of souls, and what time we stacked it.

"Did you come up with this, Audrey?" I asked. I glanced at Adrian, who rolled his eyes and nodded his head. Then he made a circular motion near his temple quickly so Audrey couldn't see him.

"No, actually. It's a Hell policy—we just haven't been doing it. But I was reading the handbook the other day and I spotted it." She was trying to be low-key, but she was practically glowing with pride.

What kind of person actually reads the employee handbook?

"Fine," I said. I grabbed my first box and started to sort my souls. She watched me for a minute and then turned away, looking disappointed. I noticed her watching us to make sure we filled out the form. Damn Audrey and her compulsion to make more work for everyone.

After a long shift, I came out of the elevator and through the high school. I walked along and saw Jimmy and Paul, plus another kid I didn't recognize, walking in the middle of the road like they owned it. A car pulled up behind them, and still they walked slowly, maddeningly. The driver honked the horn and made a gesture. The bigger kid in the middle, the one I didn't know, turned around as if he had just noticed the car. He stared at the driver, and then all three of them casually walked over to the sidewalk.

Huh. I wasn't sure what to make of that. Jimmy and Paul were always nice kids. Why were they hanging around with this new kid instead of my brother? I thought about calling to them, but I got distracted by a couple of texts. One was from Josh, and the other one was from Cassidy. I had sent her a text a few days ago, just checking in. I felt like an ass, after ghosting her in favor of Lily. It was cool she texted me back.

Josh wrote, "I have an idea. Come over." I texted back, *Okay, be there in twenty*. I was going to have to borrow a vehicle to get to Josh's.

I texted Cassidy for a few minutes. I really needed to evaluate my life choices. Cassidy may not have been as glittery as Lily, but she was a smart, funny, attractive girl. She even seemed to like me, which was a miracle all by itself.

I managed to borrow the minivan and headed over to Josh's. Sure, getting rid of a demon is fun, if it's someone *else's* demon. I couldn't complain—Josh was really going out of his way to help me get rid of Lily. I was a teeny bit jealous that, for Josh, this was like a video game come to life and, for me, it was torture.

"Okay, I've been doing some research. I've been researching demons in general, and I've learned a lot. For one thing, there's one theory that demons were cast out of heaven for not being subservient to God, or to males. So you could interpret demons as a feminist entity."

"Great. How does this help me?" I asked.

"It doesn't. I just thought it was interesting. Another thing I learned is that demons are attracted to people with negative energy." Josh lifted his eyebrows just a fraction.

Negative energy? Me? Then I winced. I was on a quest to buy a car when I met Lily, because I didn't think anyone would date me without one. Also, I spent a bunch of my parents' money so I could be more competitive in an online video game because I was convinced I would be ostracized if I didn't. I *guess* you could interpret that as negative. Crap, maybe I did bring this on myself.

"But, surely I can't have been the only person working in Hell who had a negative attitude." Right?

"I don't know. Maybe you were just the most convenient target. Another thing I learned is demons do not have a corporeal body. However pretty Lily's package is, that's not really who or what she is."

"I knew that." At least, in theory, I knew that. I couldn't help but think of her as a person because that's who I saw her as. "So how do I get rid of her? Just by having a positive attitude?"

Josh rolled his eyes. "It couldn't hurt. But there are some other things we could try. If you burn sage, it protects a dwelling from demons."

"Really?" That didn't tell me how to get rid of Lily entirely, but maybe it would protect my family, at least when they were in the house. The salt was sort of okay, except that I had to reapply it every time it rained. Also, it was doing weird things to the flowers. If the sage worked, all I had to do was convince my family to work from home and become hermits. "I'll try that. Anything else?"

"We could try to douse her with holy water."

I don't know if I've mentioned it, but I am not a particularly religious person. "Holy water? Is that, like, water blessed by a priest?"

I don't know if I've mentioned it, but Josh is not a particularly religious person either. "I think so."

"So, we somehow have to find a priest and convince him to bless a gallon of water?"

"Actually, Amazon has some."

"Seriously?"

"Yeah, I looked it up. All you have to do is order it."

I leaned over Josh's shoulder to look at his laptop. "How much is it? How soon can they get it here?"

"It's less than twenty bucks. You can have it shipped in two days."

Well, that was good news. I took out my debit card and ordered holy water. As for the sage, I knew of a pot shop that had all kinds of dried herbs for sale, so I could stop there on my way home.

So, I guess my next plan of attack was to go through my house with sage, and then throw holy water at Lily whenever I see her next. Luckily, she thought it was great fun to stalk me as I walked to the high school when I was trying to get to work in the morning, although I noticed that, since she left Hell, she was careful not to go into the high school.

I felt a little better. Maybe I could finally get rid of Lily. After all, it was a known fact that demons can't tolerate holy water. All I had to do was wait for it to arrive, throw it at her, and then she would dissolve. This was much easier than digging a hole. Why didn't we try this first?

CHAPTER THIRTY-FOUR

ON MY WAY home I bought the sage. I had never burned sage before, but the woman who sold it to me assured me it got rid of all kinds of negative energy. My hope was that she knew what she was talking about. She looked like she had left the 1960's with great reluctance, so she probably burned lots of stuff.

She also gave me some instructions. She said I should light the sage and put it in some kind of ceramic pot, or a plate, or something that would not burn. "After a minute or so, blow it out. Then just walk around your house, waving the smoke. I promise you, you'll feel so much lighter and freer!" She nodded enthusiastically, her earrings jangling.

So, I walked around the house, trying to get the smoke in every room. Unfortunately, I discovered sage smells fairly strong, and it was only about twelve seconds before my mother came out of her room, sniffing the air.

"What is that?" She asked as I waved smoke around the hallway.

"Uh…I'm trying to get rid of negative energy?" This was pretty close to the truth, so maybe that's why after a minute she just gave me an odd look and retreated back to her room to get ready for work. Dad was locked in his office, worrying about emails and lost business. If he had an opinion on the sage, he didn't mention it.

I waited. I don't know what I was waiting for, exactly. Ideally, Lily would crumple to the ground after smelling the sage and surrender or something. Naturally, this didn't happen. Actually, nothing happened. I guess that was good—there were no demon attacks of any kind, at least not on my house. Eventually, I fell into an exhausted sleep. I don't think I even dreamed—if I did, I didn't remember them in the morning.

I woke up when the summer sun poked through my window blinds, making shafts of light that hovered over my bed. It was quiet when I sat up. That could either be a good sign—the sage was working—or it could be a very bad sign, as in the Apocalypse had started. I hurried downstairs.

Mom was at the kitchen table, reading the news on her laptop and drinking orange juice. Maddie was wandering around the kitchen clutching a stuffed monkey head with a rattle on the end and gurgling happily. She ran over to me and grabbed my leg as soon as I sat down.

"Hey, Mad," I said as plopped her on my leg. She smiled—I saw she had a tooth coming in—and explained to me in a combination of actual words and ones she made up that the monkey she was holding was hungry. So I pretended to give him a bite of my toast. Then Maddie wanted a bite, too, so the three of us shared my toast. I kept my coffee for myself, though. The last thing we needed was a more energetic Maddie to run after.

Mom smiled and said, "Morning, hon. How'd you sleep?"

"Okay." Maddie grew tired of our game and slid off my lap onto the floor. "Am I watching her today?" I asked.

"Could you? I just need some sleep. I don't have to go back to work tonight, so if I can just sleep for four hours or so, that'd be great."

"Yeah. I don't have any plans today." Other than figuring out how to get rid of a demon who was trying to destroy me.

"Thanks." She drained her orange juice and headed up to her room. I flipped open my laptop and checked the news. Seven cars had been stolen yesterday, and they were found in a remote parking lot. They were in a circle, headlights on, with the radios all blasting the same tune: *Witchy Woman* by the Eagles. It didn't take a genius to figure out who engineered that.

I checked my social media accounts. I'm not really into posting, but I like to read what other people are up to. This morning, it seemed everyone was telling me off. They said I sent them nasty messages yesterday and wanted to know what was up with me. I hastily typed that I was hacked and to ignore any and all messages or posts from me in the future.

Just for the hell of it, I checked Kevin's social media accounts, too. Paul, Jimmy, and this new kid, Noel, had posted some really insulting and obnoxious things on his profile. My blood simmered. I had to figure out how to get them to stop bullying Kevin. First, I had to get rid of Lily.

I passed the morning by looking after Maddie and watching morning talk shows. UPS was supposed to be delivering my holy water today, and I anxiously awaited the arrival. I had to go to Hell tomorrow and wanted to be armed for the walk to the high school. So far the cross had seemed to work in preventing her from touching me, but it wouldn't hurt to have something else.

I was just about to doze off when I heard the UPS truck pull up outside our house. UPS dropped off a box that looked like it could fit a drum set in it. When I opened the box, I found a ton of plastic bubble stuff. Way at the bottom was a tiny bottle marked "Holy Water." It looked like a perfume bottle, sort of, except that it had a cross on the front and a picture of a river. I opened it and smelled it. It didn't smell like anything. It probably wasn't even real. Who orders holy water from Amazon, anyway? I was distracted by a piercing scream right around then, so I threw it down and ran into the kitchen where I found Maddie balanced on the kitchen counter with no idea how to get down.

"Okay, Maddie. C'mon down. What were you looking for?" I grabbed her and put her down. She indignantly pointed to the cookie jar and said, "Cookie!" For emphasis, she grabbed my arm and tried to lead me to the jar. Pretty smart, actually. I gave her a cookie, figuring she had earned it, although when she tried it again four minutes later I had to tell her no. This prompted a tantrum that lasted until Mom woke up. I glanced at the time. It was 2:30 p.m. Mom had slept for almost five hours. I was off the Maddie hook for now.

CHAPTER THIRTY-FIVE

I THINK I found something!" the text from Josh read. My phone pinged as I exited the elevator and snuck through the basement of my high school like someone infiltrating the enemy camp in Splinter Cell.

Okay, what? I texted back.

"A bottle and a mirror."

I hesitated, wondering if he meant to send this to Courtney or something, then replied, *What?*

"Just come over."

I have no car, or did you forget? Sure, ask the guy with no car to drop by, no awkward problems there.

"Fine. I'll come get you."

I wondered if I should just wait inside the high school. Lily seemed reluctant to go near the elevator, probably for fear I would somehow push her in and drag her back to Hell. Then I thought, *This is ridiculous*. I had to leave the high school; if nothing else, Josh's car would never make it down the stairs. Besides, I was wearing my cross. My fingers felt for it around my neck and I was reassured. So out I went.

I tripped over something long and metallic almost as soon as I got onto the sidewalk. She had ripped the metal railing out of the cement and thrown it at me. I staggered as it skidded past me, but some survival instinct told me to stay on my feet—don't fall over or she'll suck your soul out of your body. So I lurched and grabbed onto the metal street sign on the sidewalk.

Lily hissed at me, grinning maniacally. Then she spat fire. I scrambled away from her, having no desire to be set on fire, thank you very much. She laughed and spat at me again. When did she acquire this skill, because frankly it sucked.

I ducked behind a brick half-wall. She flew at me with what felt like inhuman speed, spitting at me. Luckily, she missed me, but she lit a small patch of grass on fire. I threw a trash can at her. She caught it and crushed it between her hands. Then she grinned at me like she was showing off.

"I'll get you in the end, Fynn Hardin!" she hissed.

Shit.

I had to try and run back into the high school, possibly all the way back to Hell. Not only was she going to steal my soul, but she was also going to cook it, too. I guess she was into well-done souls. She zoomed after me as I sprinted for the door. Apparently wearing a cross didn't preclude being set on fire. I could feel her presence, her hot and musty breath on my neck as I slapped at my shoulders where her spit landed. My legs just wouldn't go any faster, I was out of breath, and I wasn't going to last much longer.

"Get in!" A black pick-up truck skidded to a stop, and Josh threw the passenger door open. Never had I been so happy to see him in all my life. I took a hard left and started running towards the truck.

"Go, go, go! C'mon Fynn, *RUN!*" Josh was screaming.

I didn't dare look behind me and just ran faster than I ever had before, launching myself into the truck. As soon as I did, Josh slammed on the accelerator while I struggled to close the door that was hanging open. I grabbed it with both hands and pulled as hard as I could to close it.

A thump hit the back of Josh's truck. I looked back and saw Lily sinking her claws into the tailgate, her eyes tinged blood red.

Josh glanced in his rearview mirror and turned violently to the right. Lily hung on and was trying to put her leg over the edge of the tailgate. Josh jerked the wheel hard to the left. There was a screech of tires, followed by a feral scream, and Lily tumbled into the road. I looked behind me, and she was pulling herself off the ground, staring malevolently at the truck. Then we turned a corner and I couldn't see her.

"Thanks, man." My heart was banging out of my chest, and I was developing a serious anxiety problem. I leaned my head against the back of the seat. "Jesus, I hope your tailgate's okay." Josh glanced back and didn't say anything.

"How do we get rid of her?"

"I was reading an old book my dad has, and it said that you can trap a demon with a bottle and a mirror. Only you have to pee in it first."

"Excuse me?"

Josh glanced over at me apologetically. "Sorry. It has to have something of whoever the demon is after to act as a decoy."

I sighed. "Of course it does."

"You also have to put a mirror in the bottom. So, when the demon goes into the bottle looking for you, she looks at herself in the mirror and becomes fascinated."

"She's a demon, not a teenage girl."

"It doesn't matter."

"I don't think Lily is that stupid." She certainly didn't seem stupid when I dated her...was that really only last week?

"It's worth a try," Josh said and shrugged.

Yes, it was worth a try. After all, only my life was at stake.

We pulled into Josh's driveway. "So, do we need a special kind of bottle or what?" I asked as we scuttled into Josh's house, looking over our shoulders the whole time. I followed him up to his room.

"I don't think so. I saw pictures, and it just looks like a normal bottle. See, look." He grabbed a book that was face down on his bed opened to a page that featured traps for evil spirits. I studied the page. It did look like a regular bottle, a little bigger than a wine bottle. "So, you have a bottle?"

"I thought we could use this." He held up some kind of sports bottle. "I couldn't figure out how to take the bottom of a regular bottle off to put the mirror in the bottom. This opens on both ends to make it easier to clean. Then I got a mirror from a compact I swiped from my mom. And what do you know, it's almost a perfect fit."

I squinted down into the bottle. I saw an anxious-looking geeky kid staring back at me.

"Now you just have to pee in it."

"Okay, great. Then what happens?"

"Well, the book wasn't that specific. It just said the demon would enter the bottle and become trapped."

"Do I cover it with something after she's in there?"

Josh frowned. "It couldn't hurt, I guess. You can just use the screw top it comes with. But they said the demon would be trapped by the mirror."

I sighed. "Fine. Give me the bottle." I went to the bathroom, peed in the bottle, and pondered what my life had become.

"Okay. Now, do I just leave it out, or wave it around, or what?"

"Well, I think you have to set it like a trap, you know. Because she's supposed to think you're in there," Josh said.

"Urine there?"

"Yeah, that too. So I guess I'll just…why don't we put it somewhere far away from my house? Like, maybe back by the high school?"

"Yeah, but not too close. She won't even consider going anywhere near the elevator."

"Okay, well, a safe-ish distance away. After all, you're coming and going to the high school all the time. She may think you've recently decided to hide in a bottle."

I was seriously doubting this, but what do I know? We drove back to Franklin Regional High School. I couldn't help but think I was going to have a very odd relationship with my high school after all of this was over. If it was ever over.

I was pleased to see Lily hadn't burned anything down or left other signs of wanton destruction. Getting out of the truck, I stealthily ran over the grass, hunched over like I was sneaking up on someone. I dropped the bottle on the corner of the soccer field and ran back to the truck.

"Now what?" I asked.

"We wait."

CHAPTER THIRTY-SIX

WE STARED AT the soccer field for what seemed like a very long time. We didn't talk much. I was mentally and physically exhausted. Josh seemed to respect that—either that or he and Courtney were having a very long, drawn-out conversation via text, because he was mostly quiet, too. I wasn't sure what Lily had on her calendar—as near as I could tell, all she had going on was trying to suck my soul through a straw and wreaking havoc wherever she went. It probably seemed odd that I couldn't wait for her to show up and try to kill me. But I was so antsy, so on edge, that I just wanted to hurry up and see if this mirror in a bottle demon trap worked.

After a few hours, a familiar light brown head walked through the parking lot. Lily sniffed the air as if she were suddenly part werewolf and zeroed in on the bottle. We parked Josh's truck on a side street and hoped she didn't notice us. She trekked across the parking lot, over the sidewalk, and across the field. She picked up the bottle and sniffed. All my nerves were stretched to the point of snapping. Was this really going to work?

Alas, no. She sniffed the bottle and squinted inside. This was where she was supposed to be fascinated by the mirror and somehow become trapped, although the book was not really specific on how that was supposed to happen. Possibly because it was bullshit. All that happened was that Lily threw the bottle as hard as she could and shrieked—an inhuman, cutting yowl. The bottle bounced off the scoreboard. Her eyes raked over the field, searching. After a few minutes, she stalked off, furious.

I slouched against the seat, spent. It had been a long night, and I just wanted to go home. I had no idea what to do to get rid of Lily, and I was beginning to doubt it was even possible. After all, how many guys have successfully eradicated a demon? I didn't know of any.

Josh dropped me off. I slunk up the stairs, trying not to wake anyone. For one thing, it would be rude. Also, I didn't want to answer any questions. I just wanted to sleep, ideally without nightmares. Although, quite frankly, most of my nightmares couldn't hold a candle to my everyday reality, so I would take them if it meant I could get some sleep. I crawled into bed and dragged the covers up over my head.

The next day I walked to the high school so I could get to Hell, jumpy as a toddler needing to pee. Lily was getting more determined every day. On the other hand, so was I. I asked Josh to keep an eye on my house while I was at work. He said he would. I poured salt all around and saged the crap out the inside of the house, although Mom was complaining she didn't particularly like the smell. Luckily, she was visiting Grandma today—her mother—and I could sage the house with impunity.

I furtively looked over my shoulder, trying to see if a bouncing, brunette, fire-spitting head was following me. Sneaking through people's backyards, I tried taking different routes, even going through the woods. Lily always found me if she wanted to. Today she must not have wanted to, because I got to the elevator without incident.

As the elevator and my stomach dropped with its usual precipitousness, it occurred to me that maybe Hell had some resources on how to get rid of a demon. After all, wasn't that what they did? Demon management, among other things? Why didn't I think of that before? I couldn't remember seeing a library, but there could be one, I supposed. I would have to ask Dorothy.

So I got off the elevator and, as usual, there was Dorothy. Today she looked rather subdued—gray hair, toffee-colored skin, and a black blouse.

"Hi, Dorothy. Are you in mourning?" I asked.

"No, I just didn't feel like getting all dressed up this morning." She looked a little sad.

"Is there anything wrong?"

She sighed. "Not really. Well, maybe. You know they still can't find the escaped demon. The Hornissens clomp through here every few hours, clicking their jaws and looking at everyone like they're going to shoot them. It's very nerve-wracking. I can't wait until they find the damned thing."

"What if the demon got out of Hell? Do they go to the surface to look?" That would be great. I could identify the local Hornissens and have them reel Lily in. Problem solved.

"I think they do, but not seriously. I mean, Earth is so vast, an escaped demon could be anywhere."

"What if they had a tip? Like, where the demon was, roughly?"

"Why, do you know something?" Dorothy looked at me sharply.

"No! I was just wondering."

"I don't know. Maybe." She shrugged. "How's Hell treating you?"

"It's fine. Hey, do you know where the library is?"

She brightened, pleased she could provide a solid answer. "Well, that's easy. It's behind the conference room." She pointed to the conference room that was just in front of her desk. It was formed from wood panels and glass and curved outwards in a rough semi-circle. A few potted plants stood in front of it. "If you go around, just on the other side there's an unmarked door. Actually, there are two, but the first one is a bathroom. The second door on the right is the one you want."

"Great! Thanks, Dorothy."

I found the second door on the right and pushed open the heavy wooden panel. The plush, red carpet made the door stick, but it opened wide enough so I could walk in. Inside, there was a plain wooden table, a utilitarian chair, and a desktop computer. The walls were lined with stacks of books. Some of them appeared to be modern books, but some looked like ancient scrolls or hand-bound manuscripts. It wasn't a huge room—about the size of the first floor of my house, probably. Above my head hung chandeliers lit with candles that somehow lit the whole room.

A woman looked at me sharply as I entered. She was tiny, barely seeing over the desk she was sitting at. She had a large hooked nose that dominated her face, above which small brown eyes peered at me suspiciously. She was clutching a shawl made of some silken turquoise material. She looked like a large pigeon.

"Can I help you?" she asked.

"Yeah, I…I'm doing a project for school. I was wondering if you had sources on demons."

"That's a broad subject. What exactly about demons? There's demon mythology, demon history, demon education, demon sewing circles…"

"Getting rid of demons? Is that a thing?"

She looked at me as if she was about to say something, and then she shrugged. She got up from the desk—she came to just past my knees—and crooked a finger at me.

"This way."

As I followed her across the room, it seemed my first impression of the room was incorrect. It was huge! As we walked along, it kept expanding, as if it were the closet in Narnia. It just kept going. We walked for about ten minutes. Finally, she stopped. She pointed to a shelf about halfway up the wall. "There's our information on demon eradication. You need a ladder?"

I surveyed the shelf. It was above my head, but not by much.

"I think I'll be okay."

She jerked her head over to a wall a few stacks away. "It's over there if you change your mind." She walked away.

I scanned the bookshelf. They had a whole shelf packed one end to the

131

other with information on "demon eradication," as the pigeon lady put it. I felt the slightest bit of hope. Surely, somewhere in these books I could find something on how to get rid of Lily. I scanned the shelves. *Magical Self-Defense; Damaging Demons; Demons and You; So You're Possessed*. I picked up one called *Defense Against Demons* by Norman Egg, sat on the floor, and started to read.

The first thing I found was that "asking a demon to leave only works if the demon in question wants to go. Otherwise, you'll have to employ more sophisticated methods." Great. What methods might these be?

"The best way to get rid of a demon is to cast them out magically. There are a number of spells that have been proven effective, such as the screamer curse, the banish and vanish curse, and the Holy Roller spell." Well, that doesn't do me a lot of good. I was not magical, nor did I know anyone magical.

"A Night Amulet, originally found in the former empire of Persia, has been effective in the banishing of demons, although it should be noted that the Night Amulet can be a destructive force all by itself. Some reports have pointed to the Night Amulet causing temporary paralysis of limbs, ringing in the ears, and occasional blindness. The blindness is purported to occur at very inconvenient times, such as when driving or when fighting with the demon you are trying to get rid of in the first place."

I studied the text. It said *a* Night Amulet. Did that mean there was more than one? I wasn't sure it mattered, because I had no idea where I would find such an artifact. I read on.

"The Amulet is used by touching it to the demon's skin. This will make the demon shrivel into a shadow of its former self and renders the demon powerless." As far as I could tell, it didn't mention where I could find such a thing. Maybe someone in Hell would know? I sighed and read on.

"There are reports of demons being killed with swords engraved with religious prayers. Ideally, the sword is made of sterling silver, and either the Our Father or the Hail Mary prayers are visible to the demon. When the demon is stabbed with such a sword, they are rendered helpless and easily subdued."

A sterling silver sword? Wouldn't that be expensive? And did they even have swords with prayers on them? I knew nothing about swords. Still, it was worth noting.

I read through some other pages. "A demon hunter may be hired, although, as with hiring anyone, references are important; there is currently no recognized license for demon hunters. All one has to do to call oneself a demon hunter is hang out a shingle."

A demon hunter. Where would I find one of those? The yellow pages? Maybe Dorothy or the pigeon lady knew.

It was time to go to work, so I closed the book and put it back on the shelf. As I walked towards the desk, I figured I might as well ask. "Excuse me, Miss?"

"Mrs. Mrs. Echo."

"Mrs. Echo?" I said.

"Yes, that's what I just said."

"Do you know…where someone might find a demon hunter?"

She raised her skinny eyebrows at me. "For your school project?"

"Yeah. My project."

"Where did you say you went to school?" she asked.

"Does it matter?"

"I'm just wondering what sort of school has you looking for demon hunters." She peered at me, looking at me like a bird that's spied a worm.

"Okay, never mind." I was tired of this and, besides, I was going to be late for work soon.

"Wait." She reached into her desk and pulled out a flyer. Across the top it said: "Edge Valentine: Demon Hunter Extraordinaire." Underneath it said, "Are you plagued with pesky demons? Haunted by the undead? Let Edge Valentine work for you! Services include demon removal, zombie infestations, and succubus eradication. Call for a free quote now!" Underneath was a phone number and a picture of a man with dark, unkempt hair pulled into a man-bun with a big nose and eyes that seemed to stare at me through the flyer.

"Thanks. Okay if I take this?" She nodded and I stuffed it into my pocket. I could feel her beady little eyes on me until I closed the door.

I felt a little better. There was a demon hunter out there. And maybe a sword might work. I would have to figure out where to find a sword with prayers engraved in it. eBay? But at least I felt I had a chance against Lily. That is until I went home that night.

CHAPTER THIRTY-SEVEN

WHERE HAVE YOU been?" Josh said the second he saw me. I had walked home, thinking to myself that maybe things were not as bad as I thought they were. Until I saw Josh. He looked terrible. He was red in the face, he looked like he had been sweating, and his T-shirt was torn at the shoulder.

"What happened to you?" I asked.

"Dude, you have no idea. Your friend, Lily, she's been around here all day, trying to get in through the walls, the windows, the garage…I've been throwing crosses at her all day, but she just laughs and comes right back. It's exhausting."

My stomach fell to somewhere around my knees. "But…but what about the salt?" Wasn't that supposed to be a line she couldn't cross?

"I figured maybe the salt had dissolved. So, I ran around and re-salted everything. That was a challenge. She kept coming at me. Even when I threw crucifixes at her, she laughed and only went away for a few minutes. But finally, I reapplied all the salt and that seemed to work." He glanced outside. "I think."

"Shit."

"Yeah, shit."

"Come inside. It may be safer. Although maybe not. What do I know? But come in anyway." I pushed open my front door, and we went upstairs to my room. I sat down heavily on my bed. Josh slumped into my desk chair. I stared at my room. The floor was covered with laundry, I had my Kate Upton poster on the wall, and there was a laptop at my desk. Under my bed were more clothes and some random cups and dishes I kept meaning to bring to the kitchen but hadn't gotten around to. Car magazines and the latest Auto Trader were on the floor. I couldn't help but think if I had never started working in Hell this would never have happened. I could have met a nice girl at Walmart, who most likely was not a demon.

I told Josh what I had found out in the library, about the Night Amulet, swords, and the demon hunter.

"Amulet? Where do you get that?" Josh turned towards my computer and started typing. He clicked on a page, frowned, and clicked again.

"Anything?" I asked.

"Hmmm…maybe. Tell me about swords." I told him what I knew about swords. He continued clicking away. "Huh."

"What?"

"I didn't know this, but apparently it was relatively common for swords to have a knight's name or a favorite prayer engraved into it. To protect them in battle. What about this demon hunter guy?"

"I don't know. The book said to get references. That anyone could call themselves a demon hunter."

"Well, that librarian had his flyer, so maybe he's legit." He considered. "Where would you get references? Angie's List? Is there a category for demon hunters?"

There was a *thump, thump, thump* on the side of the house. I looked out my window to see Lily hovering outside, even though my room is on the second floor. As I watched, her eyes turned black, and her mouth turned into a black hole with shark-like teeth. Inky black liquid dribbled out of her mouth. She stuck her blood-red tongue out and licked her lips. She didn't look like the beautiful girl I thought I had fallen in love with. She didn't look human. I shuddered involuntarily. She grinned wickedly, as if this were the greatest game ever. I stood up and closed the blinds. The thumping continued.

"Okay, here's what we'll do. I'll go home…in a few minutes…" He glanced towards the now-blinded window. "And research this Amulet thing. You call this demon hunter and see if he has anything we can use."

"Yeah, okay. Sure." Jesus. What I wouldn't give to not be haunted by a vengeful demon.

Eventually, when there was a break in the thumping, Josh was able to run to his car and drive off. I lay on my bed and was so tired. Not physically, but emotionally I was just drained. It's a lot of work trying to get rid of a demon.

CHAPTER THIRTY-EIGHT

I STARED AT the flyer of Edge Valentine, demon hunter, and thought about it for a long time before calling the number. I wasn't sure I liked the look of him. He looked like he thought he was a total bad-ass and all other people were peons underneath his booted feet. But what choice did I have? So I called and got his voicemail.

"Hey, this is Edge. Leave a message and I'll get back to you."

"Um, hi. Edge. My name is Fynn and I can't…I need…I was interested in your demon hunting services." I left my cell phone number and clicked off.

Well, I could research this Night Amulet more. I also scrolled through various websites, looking for swords with prayers that I could afford. I lost hours to searching for swords and night amulets. Apparently, there was an online game where one of the quests was to obtain a Night Amulet so you could defeat the vampire. It looked pretty cool. I'd have to remember that for when I had spare time, assuming I lived through this. I continued to search, but I came up with nothing. Luckily, I had to go to Hell the next day, so I was pretty sure if I got there early I could use the library.

Lily still had my phone number and would occasionally send threatening texts. *Don't think you can hide forever!* Most of them I ignored; I did respond to a few with a series of sad-faced emojis. This just pissed her off. In retrospect, I shouldn't have tried to be funny with a demon.

I got up at the butt-crack of dawn on Thursday so that I could use the library. I greeted Dorothy with a distracted wave and went right for the door behind the conference room. This begs the question, what do they have conferences about in Hell? This would be something to ponder later. I pushed open the door and there, in all her avian glory, was Mrs. Echo.

"Hi."

She looked at me with a blank expression. "Do I know you?"

"Sort of. I was in the day before yesterday, researching demons."

"Oh, right. The school project. How's that going?"

"Good. I need information on something called a Night Amulet."

"Uh huh." She gave me a look like she had creepy teenagers in here all the time, and she didn't trust any of them. Then she rolled her pigeon eyes and said, "Right this way."

Again, the room seemed to extend. There must be thousands upon thousands of books here. There was no telling where it ended.

"Hey, Ms. Echo—how many books are here?" I asked, curiously.

"I don't know. Millions, probably. They've been here long before I started working here, and they'll be here long after I leave." Abruptly, she stopped walking and hauled the ladder over—she was surprisingly strong for someone who resembled a bird—and then climbed up almost to the ceiling. "There is information on historical artifacts and magical relics here." She nimbly climbed down.

Shit. It was a long way up. Have I mentioned I hate heights? I glanced up to the shelf she had indicated. Tentatively, I put my foot on the first rung of the ladder. I swear Mrs. Echo could tell I was nervous because she said, "Don't fall." As she walked away, I thought I saw a little satisfied smile on her face.

I grasped at the slat directly in front of my head and put my other foot one rung up. Okay, this wasn't so bad. I could do this. I reached up for another slat and put another foot up. Easy-peasy. One more slat, one more foot. Now I was about six feet up, with probably another ten feet to go before I got anywhere near the shelf. I was nervous, but holding it together. *Don't look down. Fynn, don't look down.*

I finally got to the shelf in question and studied the books. How was I to know which ones would be useful? I couldn't very well flip through them up here. I grabbed one called *Magical Talismans* and clutched it to my chest. Great, now I only had one hand. I stepped down carefully, one rung, then another. Then I made the mistake of glancing down at the floor. I swear I was higher than the roof of the high school.

I was instantly seized with a whopping case of vertigo as the world swayed sickeningly. *Oh god, oh god, oh god, please let me get down to the floor.* Squeezing my eyes shut, I waited for the sick feeling to go away. If I tucked the book under my arm I could still sort of use my hand. I went down, down, down—finally my foot hit something soft. I looked down and discovered it was the carpet. All the breath I had been holding came out in a rush. I stumbled over to a table and sat down with the book.

I found out the magician who created the Night Amulet created it to protect his third daughter. She was disfigured—it didn't say how—and he thought she needed magical protection. Sadly, he must not have been a great magician, because when he banished the Night Amulet later on, he also banished the daughter. The Night Amulet hadn't been seen since—or, I presumed, the daughter.

Great. I had to somehow find an amulet that no one had seen possibly for centuries. What were my other options, again? I closed the book and went off to Soul Destination, feeling dispirited. There didn't seem to be a lot of viable options. Why was it so hard to get rid of a demon?

Work was horrible. Audrey was working, and she was increasingly irritable with me, Tom, and even Sierra because she perceived, correctly, that we were not taking her seriously. So she adapted by making herself the foremost authority on rules for working in Soul Destination.

"You're supposed to read the tag and sort each soul, not sort them all into a pile and then package them," she said disapprovingly. I found I sorted faster if I just sorted first, packed later. But she didn't like that because it wasn't her way. She preferred to sort, pack, sort, pack.

"Audrey, you do it your way, and I'll do it my way, K?"

She pursed her lips and looked annoyed. "They told us to do it this way." Meaning her way, of course. She watched me sort all my souls and then pack them up, fuming. Not ten minutes later I saw her talking to Mr. Dodd, gesturing at me and shaking her head. I saw Mr. Dodd shrug and Audrey look agitated, and I hid a smile.

"You're not supposed to stack the boxes higher than seven," Audrey pointed out as I placed a box on top of a stack. I took the last box off the top and placed it on the floor to start a new stack. "Happy?"

She continued to work, watching the rest of us carefully, ready to leap into action and make corrections at a moment's notice. No wonder we couldn't stand her.

Anyway, after my ten-hour shift, which felt like thirty-seven hours, I got off the elevator. I walked out into a threatening sky. Thunderstorms were clearly in the forecast. The air had a heavy, thick quality, like sweat. Keeping an eye on the sky, I walked home as quickly as I could. I heard the first rumble of thunder when I turned onto my street. The clouds grew dark and the wind picked up. I broke into a run as it started to rain. Even though I was only a few houses away from my own, I was still drenched by the time I threw the door open and burst through. I found my family sitting at the dinner table. They looked concerned.

"What?" I asked.

"Fynn. Do you know someone named Cassidy Evans?"

My heart gave a lurch. "Yeah," I said slowly, "Why?"

Mom and Dad exchanged glances.

"Okay, what?" I said.

"She's in the hospital. She had some sort of freak accident and got hit by a car this morning," Mom said.

"Oh, my God. Is she okay?"

"She's in critical condition, over at Mercy."

Shit. Poor Cassidy. I took out my cell phone and texted Lily. "WHAT. DID. YOU. DO?" I seethed and waited to see if she would reply. After a few minutes, she texted back with a laughing emoji.

Jesus. She wasn't playing around. Now she was hurting people—physically hurting them. What was I going to do? I had to figure something out. I had to stop this demon creature before she killed everyone I cared about.

CHAPTER THIRTY-NINE

I BORROWED MOM'S minivan and drove to Mercy Hospital, rabid with worry. I should have warned Cassidy. Lily had always been jealous of her. I should've told Cassidy to be careful. Shit, why didn't I say something?

Of course, it probably wouldn't have done much good. How do you stop a demon from flying into you? Lily had run into me before, and she was surprisingly strong. Then again, she was actually a supernatural being. My mind spun in circles, like a hamster. I had the same thoughts, over and over, that I should've done something to prevent this. I worried about Blake, too. Who was going to take care of the poor kid while his mom was out of commission?

I parked the car and walked through the revolving doors. One of the websites said demons could not enter revolving doors—they get stuck and just go around and around—so I was happy about these. At least I knew Cassidy was safe in the hospital.

I took the elevator up to the third floor. Everything was so white and quiet it was creepy. Much to my surprise, I was the only visitor. I was a little relieved. The last thing I wanted to do was explain to her parents that my demon ex-girlfriend pushed Cassidy and that really it was my fault. They were probably taking care of their grandson, or maybe they were just taking a break.

I gazed at Cassidy. She seemed to be sleeping. Her face had cuts and bruises, and her arm was in a cast. My parents said she had a broken arm, broken ribs, and a broken leg. She hadn't suffered any head trauma, thank goodness, but they wanted to keep an eye on her. There was a monitor over her head, and it beeped every minute or so. An IV was attached to her arm. She looked small and vulnerable.

Her eyes fluttered open. "Fynn?"

"Hi, Cassidy," I said.

She smiled. "How are you?"

"Better than you are, I think. How are *you?*"

She started to shrug but winced. "Well, I've been better. But they've got me on a lot of pain meds, I think, so I feel okay."

My heart squeezed painfully. She was such a great girl. What the hell was wrong with me?

"Jesus, what happened?" I asked. I knew what actually happened, but I wondered what she thought happened.

She looked puzzled. "I don't know. I was crossing the street—I didn't see anyone. The next thing I knew, it felt like someone slammed into me. I fell and then—I must have been hit by a car, because I don't remember anything after that. Thank God Blake was with my mom at the time. I don't know what I would do if he were hurt." She glanced down at her sheets, and then back at me.

"Did they say how long you'll be laid up for?"

"At least another week in the hospital. I'm having surgery as soon as I'm stable, to reset the leg. After that, if all goes well, I can go home, but I'll need physical therapy and stuff." She looked hopeful. "But I'm young, so they think I'll recover pretty fast."

"Well, that's good."

"Yeah, and my parents are taking care of Blake, so there's that."

Guilt shuddered through me. "Do you need anything?"

"I'm fine. Between the meds, dozing off, having my vital signs taken, doctors coming in and out—I stay pretty busy."

I laughed, and she did, too. "Don't make me laugh, Fynn Hardin! It hurts my ribs!"

I dramatically drew my hand to my chest. "I haven't been funny at all. You just made me laugh!"

"Oh, right. I'd better stop being funny then."

Just then a nurse in maroon scrubs came bustling in. "How do you feel?" she asked.

"I'm a little tired, but I think I just need a good night's sleep. Oh, you mean her!" I said.

Cassidy rolled her eyes and said, "What did I just tell you?" But she grinned at me, so I think it was okay.

"Sorry."

The nurse said, "She's got to take her meds and get some sleep anyway. And it's almost the end of visiting hours."

"Yeah, okay. I'll come back tomorrow, okay Cassidy?"

Cassidy nodded. "Thanks."

I nodded at the nurse and left.

CHAPTER FORTY

I RACKED MY brains, trying to come up with some way of getting rid of Lily. The demon hunter hadn't called back yet. What were my chances of getting some obscure Night Amulet? Or a sword?

In the meantime, I had to get everyone in my family to wear a crucifix. The smell of sage was driving my mom nuts. I can't say I loved it either, although it did seem to work. Still, I'd feel more comfortable if they had something to take with them when they left the house. Unless I could convince everyone to never go anywhere again, crucifixes seemed like the way to go. The problem would be convincing my family to wear crosses around their necks. We're not religious. Even though I now wore a cross everywhere I went, I haven't been to church for any religious service in the past ten years, except for weddings and funerals. Nevertheless, I had to try.

"Mom, look."

She looked up from her laptop, distracted. "What, honey?"

"Look, I made this for you. What do you think?" I held up a cross that I had embellished with a rhinestone. Okay, so it wasn't artisan-level work— I was in a hurry.

She gave me a weird look. "It's nice." She kept looking at me, evaluating. "What made you decide to make a crucifix for me?"

"Oh, no reason, really. Here, let's put it on." I went around behind her and she pulled her hair out of the way. I fastened the clasp and patted her neck. "That looks nice."

"Hmm…" She picked up the cross and looked at it. "Thank you. It is nice. Is there any particular reason you think I should wear this?"

"Not really. Just wear it, okay? Promise me you'll wear it?" I could not explain it was to protect her from a demon. She'd think I was nuts.

She looked at me curiously. "Fynn, is anything going on with you?"

"No, why do you ask?" As she said this I was checking the doors and windows in the kitchen and chewing my thumbnail.

"You seem a little…preoccupied."

"I'm fine. Really."

As bad as that had gone, I knew trying to get my dad and Kevin to suddenly start wearing crosses was going to go even worse. Kevin just started to laugh, and my dad looked at me the way you look at someone just released from prison. With some empathy, but carefully because they might be dangerous.

"Why do you think I suddenly need to start wearing a cross?"

"Just…so that we all match?" I said. It sounded lame, even to me. I couldn't come up with any reasonable explanation for why we all needed to start wearing crosses. "Just wear it, Dad, okay? Please? Just trust me," I pleaded.

He looked at me with concern and then said, "Okay."

Later, I heard Mom and Dad talking about me. "…hasn't slept at all. Do you think he's religiously preoccupied?"

Dad said, "Maybe. I don't know."

Then I heard Mom. "You know he's almost at the age where a first schizophrenic break can happen."

I knew I sounded fairly unhinged; now they thought I was psychotic. But it was better than having one of them kidnapped by a demon and having their soul drained, so I didn't try to convince them I wasn't crazy.

Kevin just laughed.

"No, really," I hissed. "You have to wear it."

"For what?" he said. "I'm gonna look like a douche wearing a cross. Like Jimmy and Paul…never mind."

"Trust me!" I said.

"No way, man."

Twelve-year-old brothers suck.

"Okay, look. I may have somehow attracted a demon, and she's going to suck your soul from your body if you don't wear the cross. Got it?"

Kevin looked at me like I was nuts, but I was getting used to that. Then he went, "Bah ha ha ha!"

"Kevin, I'm serious."

"Sure you are."

"I…" I was going to kill him myself in a minute. "Just do it."

"What are you, a Nike commercial?"

"I'm serious. Wear it under your shirt so no one sees it if you like."

Kevin shook his head. "Whatever, dude."

I sighed and buried my head in my hands. This was never going to work. I can't say I blamed him. If someone told me I had to start wearing a cross, I probably would have reacted the same way.

Luckily, it was at this moment that Lily slammed into Kevin's bedroom window. We both jerked our heads up. After a second, Kevin said, "What was that?"

I walked over to the window and saw Lily, baring her teeth at me, her eyes pools of black ink. She laughed—a laugh that cut right through me. I pulled the curtains closed and then said, "That's the demon I was telling you about."

Kevin looked from me to the window, from the window to me. Then he said, "Cool!" and got up to nudge the curtain out of his way. Lily was still out there, hissing. Her hair swirled around her, and her eyes were red and threatening. Kevin gasped. Lily licked her lips and laughed.

"Where's that cross again?" Kevin said, looking pale.

I handed him the cross and he put it on, looking shaken. "Someday I'll tell you all about it. For now, just wear that at all times and she can't hurt you. At least, I don't think so."

Now my only problem was Maddie. I didn't think babies who weren't even two yet were supposed to wear crosses because they could choke. Which made sense, but I still had to protect her from Lily. I did the only thing I could think of. I drew a cross under her arm with a sharpie marker. I sighed. For now, everyone was protected. I wasn't stupid enough to think this would last forever. My parents placated me by wearing one, but pretty soon they were going to want to take them off or forget them. I didn't have a lot of time.

CHAPTER FORTY-ONE

S O, I'VE BEEN researching the Night Amulet, and prayer swords, and I think I might have good news for you."

This was a text from Josh, the day after I convinced my family to start wearing crucifixes and then fell into a dark, dreamless sleep. Which was lovely until I woke up and the nightmare of my everyday life came rushing back to me.

I could sure use some good news. What? I texted back.

"The Night Amulet might be within driving distance."

No way! Where?

"Supposedly a collector in Dover Plains, NY has it."

I'm gonna call you, I texted. I punched in his number and he answered on the first ring.

"Hey, I'm at work. But some collector of magical artifacts has what he calls a Night Amulet."

"How did you find that out?"

"I have my ways." Josh is a computer genius. He probably has access to the dark web, or the magical web, or something.

"I guess it's good news, but it's not like he's just gonna let us borrow it. How does this help us?" I said.

"I'm not sure. But it might." I heard someone in the background and then Josh said, "Yes, sir. Yes, sir." To me he said, "Look, I gotta go. I'll come over after work."

"Alright, later."

Someone has a Night Amulet within driving distance. While it was good news, I didn't want to get ahead of myself. For one thing, I don't have that kind of luck. And who was going to let some dorky teenager borrow a precious amulet so they could go destroy their demon ex-girlfriend?

I called Edge Valentine again and left another message. "Hey, man, I could really use your help. Please call." If he really was a demon hunter, you'd think he'd want the business. Unless there were actually demons everywhere, which I supposed was possible. I'd seen reality television.

I also searched Etsy, eBay, and Craigslist for sterling silver swords with prayers engraved in them. "Sterling silver sword" turned up mostly pendants

147

and jewelry. "Sterling silver medieval weaponry" returned nothing, as did "demon removers" and "sterling silver demon weapons." Not that I thought they would.

Eventually, Josh came over. He slammed his truck door, used the fob to lock it, and ran as fast as he could to the front door. I was waiting for him, so I threw it open as soon as he got to the front steps.

"Thanks," he said. He looked a little freaked out. I can't say I blamed him.

"Are you wearing your cross?" I asked.

"Of course I'm wearing my cross. What am I, dumb?" He rolled his eyes and started up the stairs. He had brought his computer with him. When we got to my room he unpacked his laptop and set it up on my desk.

"You know, I have the internet, too. You could have just used mine," I said as he flipped open his screen and let his biometric recognition software let him in.

"What's your password? For the internet?"

"Newcar19. Can't you just tell me about this guy?"

"I can. I just wanted to show you the amulet."

"Well, I don't actually know what one looks like, so I don't know how that helps."

"Patience, padawan." He kept typing and clicking various pages, and finally he said, "Voila! This is what this guy—he bears the unlikely moniker of Torrance Florence—has. He says it's a Night Amulet."

I leaned over Josh's shoulder so I could study the amulet. It looked like a black rock, about two inches across and three inches long. It wasn't shiny, nor did it glow with some kind of divine power. "Why is that an amulet and not a rock? Where did he get it?"

"It says his Great-Aunt Gwendolyn found it at a tag sale. Maybe he stole it."

"I don't know—it looks like it would fit in at a tag sale. It looks like it would be part of the leftovers you put out by the curb with a sign saying 'Free' next to it. How do we know it's really a Night Amulet?"

"Well, he says he knows it's a Night Amulet because, and I quote, 'I was haunted by evil spirits, every night, for months. I was losing weight, I wasn't sleeping. Then my Aunt gave me this amulet, and all my troubles went away.' It sounds like a commercial for anti-depressants."

I sat down heavily on the side of my bed. "This is terrible. I have no idea how to get rid of this bitch."

"Don't despair. We can email this character and see if he'll let us borrow his amulet."

"Why would he let a dip shit he's never met borrow his amulet?"

"Well, I don't know. But I think it's worth a try."

"Yeah, probably." I sighed. I wasn't optimistic. Though I was technically safe in Hell, I was anxious every minute I was there because my family was on their own. Sure, I told them to wear crosses, but still… people take showers, people forget things. Demons never forget.

After Josh left, I brought up Mr. Florence's web page. Actually, it was an array of 'magical objects' he found interesting. I read his little blurb: "I have always been attracted to the magical, the fantastic. I have traveled the world, seeking out strange and wonderful magical artifacts for my collection. Enjoy!" In addition to the amulet, he had a broken stick he claimed was part of a witch's broomstick, a hat which he claimed allowed the wearer to read minds, and the skeleton of a frog which he insisted gave the user the ability to predict the weather. I couldn't help think he was a crackpot, but what did I have to lose?

"Dear Mr. Florence,

My name is Fynn Hardin. I was wondering if I could borrow the amulet that is in your possession, as I have a demon trying to steal my soul and the souls of my family."

I paused. I kept thinking this was futile, but I had to try everything. Otherwise, I wouldn't be working in Hell—I would be a permanent resident. I wondered if they had employee discounts.

"I have heard the amulet in question is effective in banishing demons. I promise I'll give it back. Then you can sell the story and make millions!"

I considered and then deleted that. "Then you can post an update on your website and people will know you are not crazy."

Nope. I deleted that, too. "Then you can post an update on your website and perhaps more people will seek you as an authority in magical artifacts." I thought that might appeal to him. Just a hunch. I signed and sent it. I hoped it worked.

CHAPTER FORTY-TWO

I VISITED CASSIDY in the hospital again. She looked a little better—the swelling had gone down around her face, and the scratches were less angry looking. She was scheduled to have surgery on her broken leg the next day. I gave her a cross. She looked at me like I was a Jehovah's witness planted on her front steps—uh, no thank you. My insides did flips and twists while I tried to think of a reason she needed to wear a cross.

"You know—for good luck. With the surgery."

She raised her eyebrows at me. "When did you become religious?"

Since I've been haunted by a malicious evil demon. "I'm not. Especially. I just think you should wear it."

"Cut the bullshit. Why really?"

I sighed heavily. I guess I should just confess. Why not, right? "Okay. I work in Hell. I have all summer. I get there through the elevator at the high school. While I was there, I met a demon, who looked like a girl—a really cute girl. Somehow I helped her escape Hell, and now she's trying to drain my soul and kill my family. She especially hates you because she's jealous. I think she caused your accident." Well, at least now I would know if we really were a good match. If she was still willing to go out with me, great. If she referred me for psychiatric services, not so much.

She looked at me for a really long time. She searched my eyes, and finally, after I had given up on ever dating again, she said, "Okay."

Now I stared at her in disbelief. "Okay? You don't think I'm crazy?"

I saw her swallow hard. "No." She took a deep breath. "I was getting ready to cross the street, and I saw a car coming so I was waiting. Then I felt a cold, clammy presence, and all of a sudden I couldn't breathe. I felt something— it felt like something was picking me up and tossing me into the street. And I thought I heard…I *thought* I heard something whisper, 'Good riddance.' Like some evil force was trying to kill me."

"Right! That's her!" I said.

I helped her put on the cross. "What are you going to do?"

I sighed. "I've been trying things—everything I can think of, really. So far, no luck."

She gave me a sympathetic look. "If I think of something, I'll let you know. I wish I wasn't in the hospital. I could help you take her down."

My heart sprouted wings and fluttered. Did she just say she wanted to help get rid of my demon? If I had any brains at all, I would've happily been dating Cassidy this whole time and Lily would still be in Hell, where she belonged. Good God, I was dumb.

"Thanks," I said. Do I kiss her? I wasn't sure. She was injured, after all. Instead, I gave her hand a squeeze. Lame, but I felt more would come later. If I survived.

§ § §

I was increasingly frustrated. I had emailed Mr. Florence about the amulet, and I had left several messages on Mr. Valentine's cell phone. It appeared all I could do was wait for people to get back to me. I was an emotional basket-case. I couldn't sleep, I had shadows under my eyes, and I had lost at least ten pounds so far because I was frequently nauseous. My life had turned into one of constant, unrelenting tension, as if I had been stationed in Iraq and was waiting for the enemy to make a move.

On Sunday, the first week in August, I came down to the breakfast table. Mom, Dad, and Kevin were all sitting at the table, looking grave. I should have known something was up when Mom chirped, "Hi, Sweetie!" in that falsely cheery note she always used to use when she was taking us to the dentist.

I stopped short. My shoulders hunched up around my ears. I turned to face them and saw three faces, looking at me anxiously.

"Okay, what?"

They exchanged looks. Finally, my father said, "Have a seat, son." Reluctantly, I made my way to the table.

My mom folded her hands in front of her and said, "Do you want me to start?" to my dad.

"No, I'll go. Fynn, we're very concerned about you. You're not sleeping, you're not eating, at least not that I can see, and you pace around here, checking the locks and looking out the windows. Even though Kevin mentioned he saw Lily lurking outside, it…well, it seems a little paranoid."

I glanced at Kevin. He shrugged. I guess he didn't feel he could report seeing Lily hovering outside the second-floor window, so he went with telling them she was a stalker.

Mom nodded and started in. "We think…that is, we just want what's best for you. We want you to be happy."

"They think you're crazy," Kevin broke in.

Mom and Dad said, "Hey!" at the same time. "That is not true, Kevin. We are just concerned about your brother." The way they said it sounded like they had rehearsed.

"We think maybe you'd like to see someone. I know breaking up with Lily was hard, but you need to take care of yourself," Mom said.

I laughed. I couldn't help it. If only I were nursing a broken heart, my life would be roses and rainbows compared to what it actually was. Again, they looked at each other.

"Look, I'm fine. I'm just...stressed."

"Maybe you should cut back on your hours at work. The world won't come to an end if Big Boxes doesn't get as many hours from you."

"Yeah, I know. But I can't. Not yet." There were only a few weeks left of summer anyway, and Hell had better resources for demon removal. Furthermore, I was close to my goal of being able to buy a nice-ish used car, a goal that I still hadn't let go of. "I'm fine. I feel great." They looked at me silently. They knew I was lying.

"We just want you to make an appointment. It's not a sign of weakness to go to a therapist. I went, after I had Kevin, when I struggled with depression."

Kevin's ears pricked up. "I didn't know that. Were you hoping for a girl or something?"

"Oh, no! No, not at all, sweetie. I was just overwhelmed by having a new baby, and your father was working a lot and I just...I just needed a sympathetic ear. That's all therapy really is. Someone to talk to."

Oh, yeah, I could see it now. "I'm worried the demon I was dating will suck the soul out of my body and then move on to my family." I'd be committed to someplace called Pleasant Acres or something like that and walk around the grounds in a Thorazine shuffle. No, thank you. How on earth would I find an amulet and get rid of Lily if I were locked up somewhere? I needed to convince them that I was fine.

"I just need a few weeks to...uh, get my life together, and then school will start and I'll quit Hell...I mean Big Boxes. Then everything will be fine." Or we'll all be dead.

They exchanged looks. "We want what's best for you," Mom said.

"Yeah, I know. I appreciate it. But I'm fine."

"What's the deal with the crosses?" Dad said.

"You're still wearing them, right?" I said sharply. There was no way I could let them take those off. I drew a cross on Maddie every morning, which seemed to be working, but Mom washed it off every night.

Dad sighed. "Yes, but quite frankly it's a little worrisome you're so adamant about it. Your mom and I…well, sometimes people who…are in trouble become religiously preoccupied," he said carefully.

"Look, just…just promise you'll wear the crosses for a few more weeks. Okay?" I pleaded.

"But, why? Why is it so important?" Mom said. She looked worried and puzzled. I knew I came across as bat shit crazy, but I couldn't let them take those off. Lily would attack.

"Just trust me on this. I'll explain everything in a few weeks. Please."

Again, they exchanged glances. Frankly, I didn't care if they thought I was crazy as long as they wore the crosses and stayed safe.

Mom sighed. "Okay. But if you're not better in two weeks, I'm taking you to see a psychiatrist."

"Great, sounds great."

Right then I heard a whoosh sound. I looked at Mom and Dad, sprang from my chair, and ran to the window. I peered out and saw Lily standing on the front steps, grinning. I lifted my crucifix up from under my shirt and shook it at her. Her demon eyes flashed red, and she hissed. I withdrew from the window. My heart raced. Then my phone pinged.

"You can't hide forever. I'll get you when your guard is down."

I will get YOU. Do you hear me? I will banish you back to Hell! I peered out the window. I saw her reach into her jeans and glance at her phone. Then she laughed.

I had to find that amulet. Or a sword. Or hire a demon hunter. *Something* had to work. Right?

Chapter Forty-Three

I FELT LIKE I was walking a tightrope, caught between keeping Lily at bay, convincing my family I was not insane, and still trying everything I could think of to get rid of her. Not to mention, I also had to work my four shifts in Hell, check my phone for messages from Mr. Valentine, and check my email to see if Mr. Florence had responded. Did none of these people realize that I was in a hurry? What were they doing that was so important they couldn't take two minutes to get back to me? I had a demon to diffuse, dammit.

In order to get back in my parent's good graces, or at least to lend evidence that I was not, in fact, crazy, I agreed to take Maddie to the park. Mom's shift had been particularly horrendous, and she had to go back in that night, so she asked me to watch Maddie. I said I'd take her to the park. Poor Maddie hadn't gotten out much, and I thought she might like to swing and see some other kids. I made sure to draw a cross on her back, under her diaper where no one could see it before we left. No reason for every toddler at the park to think she was a religious fanatic.

I parked the car, slid open the door, and unbuckled Maddie from her car seat. She settled into my arms, and together we walked over to the play area. Before we got there, Maddie was struggling and squirming, trying to get down and run to the swings. I put her down, and she took off like a little drunken sailor, lurching and off-balance but determined.

I put her in a bucket swing and pushed her. "Higher!" she shrieked, the seventeen-month-old dictator that she was. I pushed her higher and higher, and she laughed and clapped and just generally had an amazing time. Actually, after the mess my life had become, I did, too. It was nice watching someone so blissfully happy over something so simple.

After twenty minutes she grew tired of swinging, so she toddled over to the sandbox. Another tiny human was there, a boy about her age. She plunked herself down next to him and grabbed the truck he had been pushing around in the sand. He screamed so loud they could probably hear him in Hell.

"Hey, no, Maddie. You can't just take stuff." I pried the truck out of her chubby fists and returned it to the other kid. Then I offered Maddie a different truck, but she reached for the other kid's truck again. "No, you can't have that one." She screamed. "Give me a break here, kid. Look, this one is nice." She wasn't having it. The other kid's mother came over.

"She likes his truck," I said lamely.

"Leo, can you share?" Leo answered with an unqualified no. "Sorry," she said apologetically. I shrugged.

"We should get going anyway. C'mon, Maddie." She protested vigorously. "Fine. But you have to play with something else. Look, here's a pail and a shovel." I knew that would get her. She loved shoveling sand. Eventually, Leo crept closer to Maddie, and together they sat and played with sand while plotting how to take over the world.

"Okay, Maddie, we really do have to go now. C'mon, Maddie." She opened her mouth to protest, and I said, "C'mon, we'll stop for ice cream on the way home." Instantly she was done with the park and running for the van. She loves ice cream. So do I.

After loading her back in the van, we started to drive over to Stella's, the local creamery. I fiddled with the radio, trying to find a decent song. "Devil Went Down to Georgia" by the Charlie Daniels Band came on. I'm not a country fan, but I still love that song, although I thought the devil played better in their little fiddle competition. In case you're curious, the devil does not actually play the fiddle, although I've heard he sings.

I sang along with the song, and all of a sudden it hit me. Lucifer. What I should do is make a deal with Lucifer. Maybe not my soul, but surely there was something I could offer if he helped me get rid of Lily. But what if he was mad that I was responsible for letting her escape? I could offer to work a certain number of hours for free or something. Surely there was something, some agreement we could make. It worked for Keith Richards.

We drove to get ice cream, and then we went home, happily licking our ice cream cones. Maddie got a good bit all over the back of the passenger seat, but overall I thought it was a good outing.

The next day I was scheduled to work, and I arrived early to see if I could get in to meet with Lucifer. I got off the elevator and greeted Dorothy.

"Hi, Fynn!" She had multi-colored hair today, sort of Rainbow Brite-ish. Her skin was the loveliest shade of orange.

"Hitting the spray tan hard, Dorothy?"

She looked at me blankly.

"Never mind. Say, Dorothy, if a person wanted to meet with Lucifer, how would he go about it?"

"Make an appointment with his secretary, I guess. But I warn you, he hates it when people ask for raises. He gets quite angry."

I did pause for a second as I envisioned an angry Lucifer storming around, but I wasn't going to ask for a raise, so it should be okay. Right?

"Well, how do I get a hold of his secretary?"

"Do you know where his office is?"

"No, not really. I know it's around here somewhere."

She pointed with her pen to an area behind the conference room, on the side opposite the library. "Go around to the right, and you'll see an office marked 'Ester.' That's her."

I thanked Dorothy and went around the conference room, the auditorium, and the Appeals office until I found the one with "Ester" on it. Apparently even Lucifer's secretary gets her own office. I knocked and pushed the door open at the same time.

A disapproving face belonging to what can only be described as an umbrella with a head glared at me. She had broad linebacker shoulders and a skinny pin of a neck which didn't seem like it could support the wrinkled head sitting on top of it.

"Can I help you?" she asked, looking at me as if she had no intention of helping anyone, least of all me.

"I wanted to make an appointment with uh, Mr. Lucifer?"

She looked at me like I was something her cat had killed and left on her front porch. "May I ask what this is regarding?"

"I'd…rather not say."

She kind of "hmmf"ed and looked at her laptop. "He's very busy."

"So, when can I see him?"

She sighed. She typed a few things and clicked a few other things. "I can fit you in next Tuesday at 9:30 a.m."

Today was Thursday. Five days away. "Isn't there anything sooner?"

She glared. "Really, there isn't even anything next Tuesday."

"Okay, great. Thank you so much." Well, five days wasn't too bad. Maybe by then Edge would call back, or I could get the amulet or find a sword, or Lily would just explode and crawl back into the hole she came from. Or she would kill us all. One of those.

CHAPTER FORTY-FOUR

I GOT THROUGH my shift without any hassles, even though Audrey was working, so that was a miracle. She stood off to the side and made that face where she looks like she's sucking lemons, but she kept to herself. After my shift was over I got into the elevator. It was always nerve-wracking getting out into the cafeteria. You never knew when Lily would be there to taunt me. I gripped my crucifix in my fist as the elevator door slid open. No Lily. Walking home as quickly as possible, I looked over my shoulder every so often. I swore I heard laughter.

As soon as I got home, I checked my email. To my surprise, Mr. Florence had written me back.

"Mr. Hardin,

I appreciate your interest in my amulet. It's an important part of my collection. I'm afraid I can't let you borrow it; however, I would be willing to let you rent it, for a small fee. My rate is $100 a week. Please let me know if this is acceptable to you. Best regards, Mr. Florence."

Naturally. Everyone's got an angle. I thought a hundred dollars a week was ridiculous for what looked like, and probably was, a rock. But on the other hand, what if it was the real deal? I had to get rid of Lily before she sucked the soul from my body. If the Night Amulet would help, then I had to rent it. Under his name, Mr. Florence had left a cell phone number. I took my phone out and entered his number on the keypad.

"Hello?"

"Hello, Mr. Florence, this is Fynn Hardin. I'm the one who emailed you about the Night Amulet."

"Oh, yes."

"I believe you said $100 in your email?"

"A hundred a week. If you need to use it for longer than seven days, then it's another $100. I have other people interested, you know."

Sure you do. "Right. That's fine. How do we do this? Can you mail it to me, or can I send you money through PayPal, or—"

"No, no, no. I can't mail it. If you want to rent my amulet, you'll have to come and get it. And I only take cash."

What a pain in the ass. "Where do you live?"

"Peru, New York."

"Great. I can be there tomorrow." I had no idea how far away Peru, New York was, but Josh said it was within driving distance.

"One o'clock. I have things to do in the morning."

"Fine, fine. One o'clock it is. See you tomorrow." Hanging up, I got the impression Mr. Florence was a fussy little man who still lived with his mother. Possibly in a small motel that they ran together.

I told Josh I was going to meet Mr. Florence the next day. Looking it up, it was about a three-hour drive to get to Peru. I managed to convince Josh to drive me by promising him lunch. It was either that or convince Mom I needed to borrow the mini-van, and I didn't think she'd be happy to let me have it all day. What could I possibly tell her I needed to drive to Peru, New York for?

Since Mr. Florence said to come by at 1:00 p.m., Josh showed up in my driveway at 9:30 a.m. I had been up for hours anyway because I couldn't sleep. When I did sleep, I had nightmares of some faceless madman trying to kill me. I would fly away, as far as I could go, but wherever I went, whenever I thought I was safe, there he was waiting for me. I woke up with the sheets twisted around me, damp with sweat.

"Hey," Josh said as I got in the truck.

"Hey."

"You're buying me breakfast, right?" he asked.

"Yeah."

We went through a McDonald's drive-through, and then we were on our way. We drove along the highway for a good while, finally exiting onto a secondary road. The landscape got more rural, green and yellow fields dotted with farmhouses and barns. There were cows and a few horses placidly grazing. I was wondering if Mr. Florence lived on a farm, but eventually we came to the town of Peru. There was a post office, a grocery store, a motel, and a bar. That was it.

Behind the post office was a small apartment building. Mr. Florence had given us his address, but I thought it was a house. I didn't see anything about an apartment number or anything. Josh pulled the truck over in the parking lot. He cut the engine and looked at me.

"Now what?"

A door slammed, and a man came running out of an upstairs apartment. He had a belly so huge he looked like he might topple forward at any moment. He walked to the driver's side.

"Are you Fynn?"

"This is Fynn," Josh said as he pointed to me.

"I'm Mr. Florence." He nodded at me and said, "You can come with me. Only you."

I looked at Josh and shrugged before I followed Mr. Florence to his apartment. As soon as he opened the door it became clear why only one of us could come. The gray shag rug was covered with stacks and stacks of boxes, books, folders, and newspapers. There were clothes and towels hanging over the lamps. On the floor were discarded wrappers, papers, and unidentifiable lumps. There was a single path through the living room to the rooms beyond. It smelled exactly like a rag you had left in the kitchen sink.

"Wait here."

He followed the one path through the apartment and into what I assumed was his bedroom. I stood staring in fascination at all the crap he had accumulated. How did he even know where he put anything?

After a few minutes of what I can only guess was frantic searching, Mr. Florence came out of the bedroom with the amulet in his hand. In person, it was even more underwhelming than on the internet. It was a black rock. It was polished to a high sheen, bits of mica reflecting the light from the 1970's overhead lamp.

"This is it?" I said.

"Of course this is it. It's a beauty, isn't it?"

I stared at it, half expecting it to glow or vibrate or dance or something. But it just laid there in Mr. Florence's hand. "Sure. So, I'll rent it for a week. I give you a hundred bucks now?"

Mr. Florence placed his hands on his hips and pursed his lips. "How do I know you'll bring it back?"

"I'm trustworthy?" I tried to look honest. I don't think it worked.

"What if you sign something? Like a contract?"

"Sure. If that's what…you want." I almost said 'makes you happy' but I thought he might find it offensive. He looked like he found happiness offensive in general.

"Okay—I have some paper…" He started moving boxes in an unfocused way, placing one in a blank space on the floor, looking through the box underneath, and then putting the first one back and moving on to a different stack. I groaned inwardly. This could take all day. Possibly the rest of my life.

"Ah! Here we are. Now, where did I put my pen…"

Finally, he found a pen. He sat at the table and clicked the ballpoint pen a few times. Then he started to write, mumbling to himself as he went. Sometimes he'd cross something out and then write again.

"Okay, sign." He pushed the paper at me with a flourish. I glanced at it quickly—it said I was going to bring back his amulet or face consequences, or something. Frankly, I just wanted to get out of there. For all I knew, I promised him my first born. I took five twenty-dollar bills out of my pocket and handed them to him. He gripped them in one hand, and with the other he reluctantly pushed the amulet into my hand. "Good luck, old girl," he said to the rock. To me, he said nothing. He just watched as I carried his amulet out of his apartment and gave him a half-hearted wave as I closed the door behind me. Then I walked to Josh's truck as fast as I could, afraid Florence would change his mind.

"Jesus, what took you so long?" Josh said.

"Just drive. Trust me."

He peeled out of the parking lot. I half expected Mr. Florence to come running after us, but he didn't.

"You got the amulet?" Josh asked when we were a safe distance away.

"Yeah. It looks like a rock. How is it supposed to get rid of a demon, anyway?"

"I don't really know," he said, swerving to avoid a squirrel. "Maybe we just throw it at her."

I studied the rock in my hand. It really didn't seem all that much different than an ordinary rock. I read that it had destructive powers that included insomnia and temporary paralysis, but I already had insomnia. I would just have to risk the rest.

CHAPTER FORTY-FIVE

THE NEXT DAY was Saturday, a workday. My heart sank when I arrived and saw that I was working with Adrian and Audrey. I went to my table and, after an obligatory "Good morning," I barely looked up. I figured if I didn't make eye contact, maybe Audrey would leave me alone. And it seemed to work. Other than snorting and making "hmmf" noises from time to time, she didn't say anything.

With Audrey staying refreshingly quiet, I decided to use my lunch break to see if the library had anything more about the Night Amulet. Maybe they had pictures or photographs, or something. I couldn't help but think I had just driven to Peru, New York to rent a rock, but maybe not. Mrs. Echo was sitting at her desk when I entered the library. She was eating a donut and hastily put it down and wiped her mouth with a napkin when I entered.

"Can I help you?" she asked as she swallowed the last bite.

"I hope so. Do you know anything about the Night Amulet?"

She looked at me blankly.

"How about, is there anything on nineteenth-century magicians who banished their daughters along with their demons?"

At this, she brightened a little. "Actually, we do have a small section on magicians and magic. Perhaps you'd like to look there?" I nodded and followed her across the expansive, cavernous room. Mrs. Echo's high heels clicked across the floor.

She walked about halfway across and crouched down, balancing on her heels. I wondered if it were harder or easier to balance wearing four-inch heels. She ran her finger along the spines of the books, stopped and slid one out, frowned, and put it back. Then she took out another, glanced at the title, and handed it to me. *Amazing Magicians of the Nineteenth Century.* "Start with that. Let me know if you need more help." She clicked-clicked-clicked across the floor back to her desk.

I sat down at one of the tables and flipped open the book. A puff of dust flew up my nose, and I tried not to cough. The library wasn't busy, but today there were two other patrons. One was a hulking creature, with boulder-like shoulders hunched around his ears and a face that looked like stone. He reminded me of a giant gravestone. The other looked like a very cute girl, which probably meant she was a demon bent on stealing my soul. She smiled at me and I didn't smile back. *Leave me alone, demon girl!*

I flipped the book open to the index, trying to find anything on the Night Amulet. I read about Mervin the Magnificent, the magician credited with discovering nuclear fission, and Blade Haverstock, a necromancer who brought a grave robber back from the dead, and then almost instantly regretted it when they came after him with a scythe. Way in the back of the book, I found a short note about Hamad Zorosht, a Persian magician who created the amulet. Alas, there were no pictures of the Night Amulet.

All I could do was hope for the best: that a fussy little man in New York had somehow come across the Night Amulet. I sighed. I wasn't that hungry, but I wolfed down a protein bar before I had to go back to work.

CHAPTER FORTY-SIX

YOU'RE PROBABLY WONDERING what it's like to be haunted by a demon. It's no fun, I can tell you that. Since Lily's goal was to suck my soul and use it for her own energy, she apparently felt the way to go about this was to get me distracted or injured. The more vulnerable I was, the better. In addition to insomnia and general paranoia, she would also throw things at me when I walked from home to the high school on my way to Hell, or from the high school to home. She threw whatever was lying around—garden tools, packages, potted plants. Since I always wore my cross she couldn't actually touch me.

She could, however, spit fire. It didn't usually land on me—normally I just spent a lot of time stamping out small fires on other peoples' lawns, but once in a while a little tiny fireball would land on me and burn my skin. Sometimes I would see her hiding behind someone's shrubs or under a car. I don't know why she didn't just move on to some other poor, unsuspecting chump. I think because of Maddie. Apparently, if you're a demon, the best souls are the youngest, and Maddie had already met Lily and liked her. I couldn't put a cross necklace on Maddie to protect her, so I just kept drawing crosses with a sharpie, but those were frequently washed off or faded. So Lily watched and waited.

I didn't sleep much. I lay awake at night, staring at the ceiling and wondering how I was going to get rid of her for good.

On Sunday morning I stumbled into the kitchen. Sleep hadn't been going well for me, and I was only half awake. I found my dad staring at his computer in disbelief. "Dad?"

He looked up at me with a tortured expression. "They fired me. I can't believe it. I've worked there for eleven years."

Shit. "Why…why would they do that?" When I was a little kid, I vaguely remember Dad working for some public relations firm, but basically he worked for Digital Trends for most of my life.

"They said my sales have been plummeting since July and they can't—and I quote—afford to carry me anymore." He looked stricken. There was no doubt about it; losing Dad's salary would be a huge blow to our finances, not to mention to Dad's self-esteem.

Wait a minute.

"Your sales have been plummeting since July?" I had a sneaking suspicion I knew who was responsible for Dad's sinking sales.

"Yeah. July. Not even two months." His head was propped up with his hand as if it was too heavy for his neck to hold up. "I can't believe it."

Rage started deep in the pit of my stomach then worked its way up to my chest. I whipped out my cell phone and rapidly texted Lily: *Do NOT mess with my Dad or my family, bitch!*

A series of laughing emojis followed, and then: "Try and stop me."

"Dad, I can still work in He…Big Boxes when school starts. Between me and Mom we'll have enough money, I think," I said.

Dad looked up at me, a ghost of a smile flickered, but only for a second. "No, no. No, you need to focus on school. Don't worry about it. I'll… find something else."

Easy for him to say. There was no limit to what Lily would do next.

I started scouring pawn shops and antique stores, looking for silver swords with prayers carved into them. I had the Night Amulet, but I was not overly optimistic. I also only had it for another four days. There was no way I was paying another $100 to rent a rock.

Seven days after I left a message, Edge Valentine called me back. Naturally, he called while I was at work, so I just found a red dot above the call icon when I got up to the high school.

"Hey, this is Edge. I hear you're looking for a demon hunter, so call me and I'll see if I can help you out. Bye."

I called back as fast as I could type the numbers in.

"Mr. Valentine?"

"Yeah?" A masculine voice grunted at me.

"Yeah, this is Fynn Hardin. I called you about getting rid of a demon?"

"Oh, yeah. Right." I thought I heard another voice in the background, but then nothing.

"I'd like to meet with you, you know, to explain what's been going on."

"Uh, Okay. Where do you live?"

I told him Franklin, Massachusetts. After some back and forth discussion, we agreed that he would come to the coffee shop on Elm Street the following day at 6:30 p.m. I couldn't wait. Finally, someone who knew what they were doing, who could get rid of Lily!

I spent the day checking the time compulsively and swigging Pepto-Bismol, trying to get rid of the nausea I had since Lily came into my life.

Brew Ha Ha Coffee was a fairly new shop. It had good coffee and a variety of muffins, cookies, and little cakes. There were a few round tables in front of the store looking out onto the street. It was usually really busy in the mornings and through to the afternoon, but at 6:30 in the evening it was quiet. I was the only customer, so I got a small coffee, a peanut butter cookie, and settled down to wait for Edge.

I checked my email, drank my coffee, played a game of Hungry Shark Evolution, ate my cookie, and threw the napkin and the coffee cup away. Finally, someone who I assumed was Edge walked in. He had black jeans, a black T-shirt, and motorcycle boots. He looked like one of Hell's Angels. He also looked like he hadn't slept in days—at least we had that in common—and his dirty hair was tied back into a ponytail. He had a scar through his left eyebrow. I wondered if he got that from a demon. On the plus side, his arms were muscular, like he definitely worked out. He said, "Hey," to me and then went over to the counter, where he ordered a large black coffee and a pumpkin muffin.

He sat at the table, legs spread wide, unwrapping his muffin. Sticking a hand out, he said, "Hi. I'm Edge."

"Fynn. Fynn Hardin."

"So, Fynn Hardin, I hear you're having trouble with a demon." While he was talking, he took a small bottle of tequila from his pants pocket and dumped it into his coffee.

"Yes." I told him how I worked in Hell and Mrs. Echo had given me his flyer so I called. Last week.

"Yeah, I'm sorry I didn't get back to you sooner. I was in Thailand at a conference." He took a swig of his coffee, a bite of muffin, and then another swig of coffee.

"A demon conference?" I asked.

"You'd be surprised. There's new technology, new methods of hunting and trapping demons—plus it's good to meet other hunters to swap stories and stuff."

I considered this. "How many of you are there?"

He shrugged. "Couple hundred, give or take. Sometimes more, sometimes less. There was a demon invasion a few years ago in Prague—that kind of set us back some. But enough about me. What's going on that you need a demon hunter?"

I explained how I met Lily and how I thought she was a really cool, beautiful girl. One day she followed me out of Hell, and then I started getting sick every time she kissed me, and then I ended with how she threatened my family, especially my baby sister. "I guess somehow I let her out of Hell. Now all I want to do is put her back there."

Edge nodded. "Was she touching you when you got into the elevator?"

I tried to think back; it seemed like so long ago. I remember saying goodbye to Dorothy and…

"Yeah, I guess she was hanging onto my elbow. I liked it, at the time." Looking back on it, it seemed like such an innocent time in my life. I was optimistic about getting to know Lily, saving up for a car, and I even enjoyed my job. Although I guess I did get to know Lily—it just didn't turn out the way I thought it was going to.

"That's how they escape—they have to be touching someone, preferably a virgin." He said this casually, like it didn't even matter. I felt like I had just fallen from the high dive and did a full-on belly flop. He looked at me and said, as if he could read my mind, "It doesn't have to be a virgin, but that's what they prefer."

My ears burned. Okay, I hadn't gotten a lot of action yet. It wasn't for lack of trying. But I felt my ego shrivel up into a little ball. I didn't realize Lily sought me out for my, uh…lack of experience. "Oh," I said lamely.

"Don't sweat it, kid. We all have to start somewhere. They mostly like virgins because they're more easily manipulated. But obviously you caught on before she ate your soul, so good job. I can't tell you how many people don't catch on until it's too late." Okay, that made me feel a *tiny* bit better.

"So, now we have to discuss expenses. What I do is inherently dangerous, and I have to make a living. To get rid of this demon, I would charge $4,000."

My stomach dropped. $4,000 was almost exactly the amount I had saved up to buy a car, plus a little more. I saw my whole summer's work wiped away by one ghastly expense. I studied his black eyes, trying to see if it was a joke.

"Seriously?"

"You think this shit is easy? It's not easy; it's the opposite of easy. It's rough work trying to eradicate a demon. They tend to fight back. They don't take kindly to it, that's for sure." He studied me with the intensity of a method actor preparing for a role as a stalker.

I tried to think. It might not work, but I had the amulet and maybe I should try it first. Plus, there was always the possibility I could find a silver sword. Also, I had a meeting with Lucifer in three days, assuming I could live that long. I was almost at the end of my rope as it was.

"You want to think about it? I tell ya, demons are hard to get rid of."

"Trust me, I know. Okay, I have to…I need a few days to come up with that much money." I didn't want to tell him I was going to try to do this without him. It took him a week to get back to me when he didn't know he had a job. I was pretty sure if I contacted him again I wouldn't be able to wait that long.

"Yeah, no problem. You have my cell?"

"Yeah. You gonna call back?"

"Yeah, Fred, I told ya—I was at a conference. I'm free for the next little while, so I'll call ya back."

"Fynn."

"What?"

"It's Fynn, not Fred."

"Right. Fynn." He stood up and stretched. For some reason, I found it reassuring that he could touch the ceiling with his arms over his head. I guess I figured a good reach is important when fighting a demon.

He shook my hand and said, "Okay. I'll hear from you in, what? Couple of days?"

"Yeah, a couple. I'll call you. For sure." I winced as his fingers crushed mine, and when he let go I shook my hand out.

I followed him out of the shop, intent on going home. He took a black helmet off the handlebars of his motorcycle and put it on his oversized head. Then he got on the bike, revved the engine a few times, and roared away. Well, he looked impressive, I'll give him that. Still, I really didn't want to pay him $4,000 if I could possibly avoid it.

I had to try this amulet thing before I lost my mind entirely. It was the only thing I had in my possession, so I should try that first. I hoped to God it worked.

CHAPTER FORTY-SEVEN

THINKING ABOUT IT logically, it seemed the first thing I had to try was the Amulet. Not only did I have it in my possession, but it was mine for the low, low price of $100. Not $4,000, not my soul. The question was how did it work? Did I throw it at Lily, force it down her throat, or what? I thought it said something about how to use it, but I couldn't remember since I didn't think I'd ever find it. I ran back to Hell's library and looked it up. I confirmed you were supposed to touch the demon with the Amulet, and then she would shrivel up into a demon shadow. Or something.

I poked my head out of the elevator. It seemed quiet. I walked quickly across the cafeteria and then up to the surface. I was gripping the amulet in my hand, although I wasn't sure how I was supposed to touch Lily with it. "Look here, Lily, I brought you an amulet!" and then press it into her palm? But it was mildly reassuring.

Until it wasn't. Lily came flying at me from behind an old brick munitions factory. She would have barreled into me, but I was wearing my cross. She struck out at me like a cobra, coiled and angry. I held up the Night Amulet. She stopped for a second and shrieked.

It was working! I shook it at her, and she glowered, furious. She whipped around in a circle, a mini-tornado, and screamed.

I should have kept quiet. "Now go away! Go back to Hell!"

Her eyes glowed red and her mouth yawned open to reveal a black abyss of nothingness. "Never." She hissed.

I shook the amulet at her again, and her eyes narrowed as she studied it. Suddenly, a look of relief crossed her face. Then she laughed, made like the Tasmanian devil, and disappeared.

Was that it? I waited, wondering when she was coming back. Did this thing really work? I walked slowly down the street, looking right and then left, expecting her to assault me again at any moment. Then, I walked a little quicker and with more confidence the closer I got to my house. I couldn't believe it. The amulet had worked! I mean, she did say she was never going back to Hell, but for the moment I felt a little better.

171

Now the question was how to bring her back to Hell? I thought the Night Amulet was supposed to banish the demon. Had she been banished? Was she in Hell now? Somehow I didn't think so. That look of relief when she got a good look at the amulet didn't seem to lend itself to happy endings. Not for me, anyway.

My phone pinged. I glanced at the screen and saw I had a text from Josh. It said, "I have something important to tell you. Call me immediately."

Now what? I hit Josh's name and his phone rang. He picked up almost immediately.

"Yeah, I don't think that's really the amulet."

"I wouldn't have thought so either, but I just ran into Lily, showed her the amulet, and she *left!* No spitting fire, no nothing. So maybe it did work."

There was a pause. "I found a picture of the Night Amulet—apparently there really is one somewhere—and it looks nothing like that. For one thing, it's blue. Also, it's the size of a grape."

"Shit." I looked around. "But then, where did she go? Why did she leave?" This didn't bode well at all. I started walking as fast as I could towards home.

"I don't know. I'm pretty sure you have a rock. Although Torrance seems convinced it's real."

I started to run. What was she up to? What destructive plan did she have now? After a minute my sides were splitting and I couldn't breathe. Still, I pressed on, convinced that a smoking ruin would be the only thing left to greet me. I turned the corner and my house came into view. It was still standing. That was a good sign. Right? I wasn't sure. What if she killed everyone?

I pushed open the front door and yelled, "Mom! Dad!"

Mom came out of the kitchen, wiping her hands on a dishtowel and looking at me with a mix of concern and fear. "Fynn? What's the matter?"

"Is...is everyone okay?" My eyes bounced back and forth like the ball at a tennis match. Where was everyone?

Mom looked puzzled. "Dad's on the computer upstairs, Kevin's in the basement, and Maddie's taking a nap. Why do you ask?"

"You're all okay?" I asked.

"Fine. Fynn, what's the matter? Why are you so upset?"

"I just...I don't...Lily made some threats," I said. I had to tell them something. Maybe this way they'd be more careful.

"Oh, my God. Against us?" She put her hand over her heart and looked towards Maddie's room. I nodded. "We should call the police!" Mom said.

I shrugged. I supposed it couldn't hurt, although I was pretty sure it wasn't going to do any good.

"What exactly did she say?" Mom asked.

"I…she wasn't real specific. Just that she was going to hurt my family if she couldn't get to me." Was there some way I could tie this to wearing the cross? Like Lily was some kind of religious zealot?

"Physically harm us?"

I nodded weakly.

"Oh, my God. To think I let her into the house!" she said.

"You didn't know. But don't let her in again. Not for any reason."

"I'm going to call the police. There must be *something* they can do."

A very nice officer took down some information, although it was more difficult than you would think.

"What's her address?" He was pretty young, probably just out of the police academy or something. He had a military-type buzz cut and ears that stuck out from under his hat.

"She's homeless," I said.

He jerked his head up. "Does she go to a shelter or something?"

"I have no idea."

He frowned. "It's not safe for a young girl to sleep outside, you know."

Great, now the police were concerned about Lily's well-being.

"Well, where do her parents live?" he asked.

"I'm not sure."

He studied me, a skeptical look on his face. "I guess you weren't that close?"

"I guess not."

He gave me a hard look. "Did she give you drugs?"

"What? No!" I can't say I blamed him. I would've thought she was my drug connection, too.

He sighed and wrote something down. "Do you have a recent picture? Like on your phone or something?"

"No, I do not."

"Kid, it's gonna be really hard for me to find this girl if I don't know what she looks like or where she lives."

"I know. I'm sorry." I studied the carpet and hoped this would be over soon so I could go back to figuring out how to get Lily back to Hell. He talked with my mother for a minute or two, nodded at me, and left.

"He seemed a little…confused," Mom said.

"Yeah, I know. Look, I met Lily at work, and I never met her parents and I have no idea where she lives. But she's dangerous."

Mom gave me a long look. "Well, we'll deal with it. We can protect ourselves from a teenage girl."

Yes, they could protect themselves from a teenage girl, but probably not from a demon masquerading as a teenage girl.

CHAPTER FORTY-EIGHT

IN RETROSPECT, I probably shouldn't have been excited about meeting with Lucifer.

I was just so mentally and physically exhausted. My joints ached, I had a constant headache, and I got dizzy just standing up, probably because I was eating very little. Lily was hovering outside the house constantly, but she carefully made sure that no one but me saw her. I jumped every time I saw her red eyes staring at me, a smirk on her face, looking at me like a starving dog looks at a rib-eye. I startled every time I heard her singing to herself.

All this jumping, startling, and staring were just adding ammunition to my parents' theory that I was losing my mind. I overheard them seriously thinking of taking me somewhere to be evaluated, possibly committed. Sometimes I thought they were right. I mean, they knew my ex-girlfriend was stalking me and threatening to hurt me and my family, but they were under the impression she was an ordinary teenage girl. How scary could a teenage girl be? They thought if they just locked the doors and windows they would be fine. Ha.

Now that I knew that the "Amulet" was really a rock that left me with few options. When I returned the rock to Mr. Florence, he sniffed and said, "Obviously you didn't develop a rapport with her." Oh, I'm sorry. I didn't realize I had to *get to know* the rock for it to work right. Was everyone I came into contact with a flake? I called Edge again. No answer. *Naturally*. I left a message.

Desperation had brought me to this point. If I didn't hurry up and get rid of Lily she would attack Maddie, or I would be looking at my senior year of high school in some locked psychiatric hospital, probably raving about demons and fitting right in with all the other crazy people.

Maybe I'd make new friends.

I got to Ester's office bright and early Tuesday morning, wearing my cleanest, most presentable clothes—chinos and a button-down shirt. There really isn't a dress code in Hell—most people wear as little as possible because it's so hot—but I wanted to make a good impression. I had never formally met Lucifer, or even seen him up close. I admit I was curious.

"Hi, I'm here for my meeting. With Lucifer," I said, just in case she thought I might want to meet with her.

Ester gave me a look like I was interrupting her day with my trivialities. I really have no idea how many people wanted to meet with Lucifer every day, but if Ester's attitude was any indication, she was juggling his schedule like he was a high-level politician running for office. Or maybe I was interrupting her crossword puzzles.

"Sit over there. I'll let him know you're here."

I sat on a plush, comfortable love seat. There were a few gossip magazines displayed in a fan on a coffee table. I couldn't help but notice that Ester's office was air-conditioned. On the overhead speaker, "Devil in Disguise" by Elvis Presley was playing softly. I tried to calm my breathing down and dug my fingernails into my hand to distract myself from the panic that was threatening to choke me.

Ester picked up her phone and said, "You're 9:30 a.m. is here." Pause. "He wouldn't say. Okay." She hung up and looked at me. "Okay, follow me, Mr. Hardin." I stood up. Only then did I realize that my knees had turned to water. I followed Ester into the office of one Lucifer "fallen angel" Beelzebub.

I had seen Lucifer at Orientation, so I knew he didn't have horns or anything. He looked pretty normal, actually. He had black hair and was wearing a black suit with a black button-down shirt underneath his suit jacket. There was a slight five o'clock shadow on his strong, angular chin. He was handsome. Attractive.

I glanced around his office, trying to take it in quickly. Obviously, he didn't get a window, but it was a nice, luxuriously appointed room. His desk was made of some heavy, dark wood with carvings of flowers and– girls? Angels? Fairies?— and ivy. There was a Pakistani rug on the floor, woven in rich colors of red, orange, and blue. Bookcases lined the back walls. Above his desk was a huge painting of Lucifer himself, looking pensive and posing seated in front of his fireplace. Against the opposite wall was a huge, roaring fire, but oddly it didn't seem to be throwing any heat. In front of his desk was a pair of comfortable chairs upholstered in red velvet.

Lucifer rose to his feet and extended a hand. "Fynn Hardin, Soul Destination. How are you?"

I shook his hand. My mouth was dry. I swallowed quickly and said, "I'm... I'm well, sir. How are you?"

"Fine, fine. Call me Luke." He gestured for me to sit, and he went over to his side of the desk and sat down himself. "I hear you're doing a good job in Soul Destination. Do you enjoy it?"

"Yes, sir, I do."

"Good, good." He looked at me expectantly. "So, what brings you in today?"

I had rehearsed this in my mind about a thousand times, but I still stammered when I started to speak. "I…" I cleared my throat and tried again. "I…I'm having problems with a demon."

"Oh, I see. What sort of problem?" He looked vaguely interested, at least, so I pressed on.

"I met her here. I mean, I thought she was a nice girl, and somehow she followed me into the elevator and back to Massachusetts, and then we started dating, but I got sick, then I figured out she's a demon, and now she wants to steal my soul and my families' souls." I finished in a rush. I thought Lucifer leaned forward a little when I said 'she followed me into the elevator.'

"I see." He leaned back in his chair and crossed his legs. "You met what I imagine looked like a very attractive girl, a very beautiful girl, and she followed you to the surface."

"Right."

"Then when you started spending time with her you grew weak, you stopped sleeping, and you got nauseous. You stayed away from her, and you felt better. You went out again and you immediately felt terrible."

"Exactly!" I beamed. He did understand.

He examined his manicure for a second and then he sighed. "It happens more often than you would think. We've talked about having a unit at Orientation, a "beware of demons disguised as friends" sort of thing, although we catch most of them before they actually escape. Most unfortunate."

"Right."

He made eye contact with me. "So, why are you here? You must have some idea about how I can help you."

I had thought long and hard about this, and I had come to the conclusion that I would do whatever it took to save my family. Still, I had to be careful. I wanted my opening salvo to be appropriate, not showing all my cards at once.

"I thought maybe there was a way you could help. You know, I could work off the debt, or…work extra hours, or…whatever you needed."

He nodded. "And in return, I'll get rid of this demon for you?"

"Yes, sir." I should've done this weeks ago.

There was a pause. I thought he was thinking it over. He rubbed his chin, picked up a pencil, wrote something down, and then he erased it and wrote something else.

He sighed. "I'm afraid I can't help you."

My face fell. *What?* I thought he seemed like he understood, like he even sympathized.

"I often get requests such as yours—you'd be surprised how many people are willing to make deals with me in order to get what they want. But I don't really need any extra help at all. So, I'm sorry." He looked regretful, as if he was sad he couldn't help. Okay, then, I had one more bargain.

"What if I sold my soul to you, in exchange for getting rid of Lily?" This rushed out of my mouth before I lost my courage.

Lucifer looked at me appraisingly. He glanced at the clock that was on the side wall. He leaned forward and folded his hands on the desk. "How long have you been working here in Hell, Fynn?"

"Uh, about…almost two months."

He nodded. "Been at Soul Destination the whole time?"

"Yes, sir."

"And tell me, Fynn, roughly how many souls would you say you sort, on average, in the course of a day?"

I tried to think. Suddenly I got a look into Lucifer's eyes. They were a chasm with no bridge. I glanced at my knees to try to recover my thoughts. "Well, on a good day, I'd say between two and three hundred."

"Of course. So, tell me, Fynn. If you're sorting at least two hundred souls a day, every day—plus I imagine you have co-workers, yes?"

I nodded.

"Two, three coworkers?"

I nodded again. "Usually three of us."

"So between you and your co-workers, you process about 600 souls a day, every day. That's about 4,200 souls a week. With so many souls here, tell me." He stared at me like a cat that had spied a mouse in the grass. "Why on earth would I need your soul?"

I hadn't thought of it. I mean, weren't desperate people in literature always making deals to sell their souls to the devil?

"Uhh…" I was utterly transfixed by his eyes. They were pools of black ink, soulless and empty. I saw the fates of a thousand damned people reflected back at me, endless suffering and crushing pain. I shook my head. This was a bad idea.

"I don't know. I guess you wouldn't." I studied my pants. A thread was coming undone.

"Of course, there is the matter of this demon you helped escape."

I jerked my head up. "I didn't really help her—"

He waved his hands dismissively. "Oh, I know. Nevertheless, I need to get her back. I'm sure you've seen the Hornissens marching around."

"Right. Maybe the Hornissens could, you know, come to the surface and catch the demon?" I asked.

Lucifer shook his head. "I employ them to keep demons from escaping. They're needed here. It's unfortunate, but you do owe me a demon. What are we going to do about that?" He said it softly, but I caught the underlying threat.

I froze. In all my imaginings of how this meeting would go, I hadn't considered that Lucifer might blame me for her disappearance. "I…I'm not sure, sir. If I knew how to get her back, I wouldn't have just offered you my soul."

"Right. Of course. But you're a bright young man. You'll figure it out. Let's say, a week? Yes, I think I can let you have a week." He stood up as if he was done with me. He started towards his office door and gestured for me to follow him. He opened the door, and then closed it halfway as he turned to me. "You know, it would be a tragedy if one moment of carelessness on your part caused you to spend eternity down here. Let's not have that happen, okay?" He smiled and shook my hand, and then said, "Have a nice day. Ester, what does my appointment calendar look like for the rest of the day?" And just like that, he dismissed me from his mind.

It appeared I was worse off than I was before. Now Lucifer knew that I was the reason a demon escaped, and he intended to hold me accountable.

Shit.

You really don't want Lucifer breathing down your neck.

179

CHAPTER FORTY-NINE

I TRUDGED OUT of Lucifer's office, waved at Dorothy, and got on a hovercraft without talking to anyone. I was worse off than before. I still had Lily tormenting my life, threatening my family, and just being a demon from Hell. In addition, I was now in debt to the world's worst mafia don.

Although I worked in Hell, I was under no delusions that it would be a pleasant or even tolerable place to spend any time if you were an inmate. Lucifer had a way of searching your soul for what you feared most of all and then tailoring your sentence accordingly. I wasn't sure what my fate would be, but I thought being tormented by dozens of demons was probably pretty close.

I nodded to Tom and Audrey, although internally I winced. The last thing I needed was Audrey's never-ending pointers to ostensibly make my job easier, but that she really kept giving to establish herself as superior. I just didn't want to deal with it. I just wanted to sort the souls, punch out at six, and be on my way to wrestle with my demon when I got home.

Naturally, Audrey started in immediately.

"I checked with management, and they said that we should only take the lights off the souls once they're safely packed in the box."

"Great," I said. Whatever. Maybe if I just nodded my head she'd go away.

She looked at me, a little puzzled, but she said nothing and turned her attention to her job. I sighed with relief. I had way too much on my mind to deal with Audrey-isms all day.

After an hour she said, "Fynn, when you file your report sheets, be sure to put them with the most recent one on top."

I felt a rush of irritation, but I said, "Sounds good."

Like someone who can't leave a toothache alone, she kept trying, looking for weaknesses.

"I thought we agreed we were going to stack the boxes up only seven high."

I turned and snapped, "You're right, we did. Thank you so much for making my job easier. Is there anything else you'd like to advise me on?"

She looked a little taken aback, but only a little. Then she appeared to take what I said at face value, which made Tom snicker. She turned to him furiously and said, "Is there something funny?"

"Yep," Tom said. Audrey waited for him to say what was funny, but he didn't. Her cheeks got red, but she went back to sorting.

When first lunch rolled around, Audrey looked at the clock and said, "Who wants first lunch?" I know she expected us to say something like 'I don't know, do you want it?' because that's what she would've said, and it's difficult for Audrey to see anything from anyone else's perspective.

What actually happened was Tom said, "I will."

And then, because I didn't want to work with Audrey by myself, having had enough of her already, I said, "I will, too." We both walked out of the room.

"Jesus," Tom said when we were far enough away so she couldn't hear us.

"Yeah, what bug crawled up her ass?"

Tom shrugged. "She's got a permanent bug colony living up there."

I said, "Well, I feel sorry for them. She's so uptight I'm surprised they're not diamonds or something." I'm not sure this made sense, but it sounded good and made Tom laugh.

Lunch was uneventful. I didn't talk much, but neither did Tom. I was thinking about the mess my life was and Tom—well, everyone's got their shit. We just made a few off-hand comments, such as, "Are they cutting back on the salad bar again?" and "What is this?" as we poked at some gelatinous substance with a fork. Tom told me it was going well with Brooklyn, the girl he had started dating. He just told her he worked on an assembly line and couldn't talk or text while he was at work. She seemed to buy it.

After our nine minutes were up, we cleared our trays, gathered up all our wrappers, and threw them away. We walked back to SD slowly, as Audrey was going to be pissy.

She glared at us when we walked in, but she grabbed her purse and off she went. Phew. Nine minutes of peace and quiet. Those nine minutes were the best part of my whole day. No Audrey. I was not being hounded by demons. I was not sick to my stomach. I actually felt fine when I was at work. I guess Lily's demonic influence didn't reach all the way back to Hell.

It was over all too quickly, as fuming Audrey descended upon us at 12:35 p.m. She folded her arms across her chest and said, "I thought only one person went to lunch at a time."

I shrugged. "Normally that's true, but when the other person is you, well, no one wants to work with just you, so Tom and I went to lunch together." I know it was a terrible thing to say, but I was under a lot of stress, and she had been pushing my buttons all day. She looked like I had just slapped her—she got very red in the face, and her eyes looked like they might well up. Without a word, she went to her table and sorted souls, doing nothing but shooting us dirty looks for the rest of the afternoon. I can't say I felt bad. Okay, I felt a little bad, but I appreciated the lack of "advice" more.

Only then did I realize that all that peace and quiet gave me a lot of free time to worry about paying my debt to Lucifer and getting Lily back to Hell. I was loath to call Edge again—how many messages did I have to leave? There must be some way. I just hadn't found it yet. So, the afternoon slowed to a crawl, and I wrestled with my dilemma over and over, never getting anywhere. I still couldn't relax, as I worried obsessively about my family succumbing to Lily while I was safe and sound in Hell.

Eventually, six o'clock rolled around. I punched out, said goodbye to Tom, and I even managed to give Audrey a nod, although she was pointedly looking in some other direction. I took the elevator up and walked quickly out of the high school. No Lily so far.

I had a sudden thought. What if we all just moved away? Could she find us? Would she keep stalking an empty house, until eventually she gave up and went to bother some other poor family? Reality set in pretty quickly, though. How would I convince my whole family we needed to move in a hurry? Like, take your clothes and a few personal items and get in the car? They already thought I was crazy. I turned it over and over in my mind, like looking through a kaleidoscope, trying to get the fractured bits of my life to line up.

CHAPTER FIFTY

SINCE THE AMULET was a rock, Edge hadn't called me back, *and* Lucifer was demanding I return Lily in a mere four days, I decided to try and find a silver sword. I discovered there were lots of silver swords, but very few of them had prayers carved into them—not ones I could actually afford, anyway. Could I maybe just write a prayer on a regular sword? Possibly with a sharpie or something?

I tried eBay—there were lots of reproduction silver swords. Did it matter? I wasn't sure. Nothing else had worked so far. I didn't think I could handle another failure.

I looked in the classifieds, both in the newspapers and on Facebook. While I was on Facebook, I "happened" to scroll through Kevin's feed and noticed that his three goons were still harassing him. Maybe I would just get a sword and practice using it on them. I had to do something about them, too, but first I had to get rid of Lily.

It occurred to me that I could try a pawn shop. Franklin itself didn't have any pawn shops, but there were a few in Chesterfield, which was the nearest city. As I may have mentioned, I don't have a car. However, on Friday Mom said she and Dad were going to do some shopping and asked if I wanted to come. I think she thought I was depressed. Which was true, but not for the reason she thought. Anyway, I asked to borrow the minivan and she said okay.

I've never actually been to a pawn shop. I've seen a few of those reality shows that feature pawn shops, but they look like department stores. This pawn shop did not look like a department store. On the glass windows it said, "We pay top dollar!" Under that was a list of everything they sold: computers, diamonds, gold—gold was in way bigger letters for some reason—iPads, watches…the list went on and on. I searched for anything which might be reasonably construed to mean "sword." In little tiny letters towards the bottom, it said "Collectibles." I guess people collected swords. What else would you want one for? Because you thought you were a pirate?

A bell rang when I walked in, which made me cringe a little because I was hoping to go unnoticed. A bearded man with gray hair tied back in a ponytail looked up from the jewelry counter and said, "Hello. Can I help you?"

He seemed nice, so I said, "I was looking for a sword?"

"Well, I'll show you what we have. This way." He gestured me over to another counter, right underneath where the tools were kept on a pegboard. "We have these three here." He took out each one in turn.

I picked up the longest one. I wasn't sure how big a sword I needed, but it seemed probably the bigger the better, right? "Do any of them have, like, prayers or religious symbols carved on them?" I asked.

He didn't even skip a beat. I guess pawn shops get all kinds. "This one here has a cross engraved in the hilt. See?" He pointed to the shoulder of the hilt of one of the smaller swords. Sure enough, there was a cross engraved into it, and the letters "R.C."

"R.C. Who was R.C?" I asked.

"Probably the knight whose sword this was. They often had religious symbols and their initials carved into them, for protection. So God could watch over them as they went into battle."

I could use someone to watch over me, that was for sure. "How much is this one?" I asked. I gripped it by the leather-covered handle and pretended to swing it around. It had a good weight to it.

"Oh, I could let it go for, let's say, $1,000."

I nearly dropped it. "A thousand dollars?" I had seen reality TV. Never take the first price they offer.

"I can take a little less."

"How much less?" I asked.

"How about…$800?"

I sighed. "What about $500?"

"No, no can do. $700 is my rock bottom price. Sorry."

Reluctantly I took out my debit card. Lily was costing me a fortune. Still, if this sword did the trick, it would be worth it.

CHAPTER FIFTY-ONE

I HAD NO idea where Lily might be hiding, but I had to think of something. She could be anywhere—except Hell, which she was trying to avoid. I was trying to avoid it too at the moment—Lucifer was breathing down my neck about his missing demon, and I was seriously starting to freak out about it. Lucifer's okay as a boss, but utterly miserable to be in debt to.

I thought she might be around Franklin, though—demons usually attach themselves to a place or a person, and Lily had been attached to me. I was the idiot who brought her out of Hell in the first place. Of course, I wasn't sure if there was some kind of limit to that attachment. Would she just cut and run if she thought she was being pursued? I had no idea. I just pinned my hopes on silver swords and flaky demon hunters.

I went to Hell, preoccupied with how to get rid of Lily.

"Hi, Fynn!"

"Hi, Dorothy." I was so anxious I didn't even notice what she was wearing. I just jumped on the first available hovercraft and went to Soul Destination. I caught a glance of her as the hovercraft pulled out of the station and thought she looked a little hurt. *Great, now I pissed off one of my only friends in Hell.*

I'd deal with that later.

I was working with Audrey and Sierra today. I was hoping for peace and quiet. Obviously, before I left the house, I drew a cross on Maddie with as permanent a marker as I could find. I seriously thought of bringing her to a tattoo parlor, but I didn't think you could tattoo a seventeen-month-old girl. I stood at my table and kept my head down, doing my work, and hoping no one would talk to me. That was the sort of situation Audrey lives for.

"Fynn, you're not allowed to wear headphones." I had clamped wireless earbuds in my ears, hoping to drown out the underworld. I removed them and glared at her.

Work went on for another ten minutes before she had more "advice." "Fynn, if you put the souls in the boxes first, you won't keep dropping the lights."

I sighed. "Whatever."

She got a very cross look on her face. "Well, if you don't want to do it the right way, I don't care."

So, to shut her up, I put the souls in the boxes before I took the lights off, not that it matters either way. I was just focusing on my soul sorting, minding my own business, when Audrey said, "Fynn."

I slammed the box I was packing down on the table. "What now?" I could've spit bullets at her.

Her jaw was hanging open, and she was looking somewhere behind me. I turned around and, holy crap, Lucifer himself was standing there.

I gulped.

"Fynn. Nice to see you. May I have a word with you?" He smiled pleasantly, while my insides liquefied and threatened to be expelled out of my mouth.

"Yes, sir," I squeaked. I couldn't remember Lucifer ever coming this far. He mostly stayed in his office or went directly to the Sixth level. He turned and I followed him out into the hallway.

"Are you making any progress with your situation?" He put a friendly hand on my shoulder. My throat was as dry as ash.

"Yes, yes, sir. I'll have her back for you in three days, just as we discussed." *Please don't ask for details, please don't ask for details.*

"Great. I'll look forward to it." He was digging his fingertips into my shoulder. Only they felt more like knives. Pain radiated down my arm, into my chest, like a vise was squeezing my ribs shut. Emotions like razors cut into my skull. I thought I was going to pass out, but then he let go. I watched him walk away. He moved with supernatural grace, almost as if he were made of liquid. I took a deep breath and wondered how on earth I was going to get Lily back here in less than three days. I walked back inside SD.

Audrey was looking at me as if I had just won the lottery. "What did he want?" Awe was in her voice.

"He complimented me on my work here. Said I was the best soul sorter he had ever seen."

Her eyes narrowed a little suspiciously. "Really?"

"Yup. He said I'm doing a great job and he'll miss me at the end of the summer."

She didn't look like she quite believed me, but she was clearly off-balance the rest of the day. She stayed very quiet and didn't speak to me or Sierra at all. It was glorious.

CHAPTER FIFTY-TWO

I WALKED HOME, listening to a podcast on supernatural beings to see if they had any advice. Right now I was really not impressed with myself. I had managed to put my family at risk, gotten a nice girl thrown in front of a car, and indirectly gotten my father fired, and for what? To save up money to get a car so I could date some girl? I realized, finally, that a girl who I was really meant to be with wouldn't care if I had a car or not. Furthermore, I had been a selfish ass. I knew Mom and Dad thought I was working my ass off to save for college. I resolved that when— if—this was over, I would dedicate myself to not being a tool. I would save for college, help around the house, take care of Maddie, spread sunshine and light—I was a changed man.

Of course, none of that would make any difference if my soul was gone. I hoped the sword worked. Lily was getting increasingly brazen and dangerous. Maybe I could strike a deal with her? If I gave her my soul, she could go away and leave my family alone? There was still that debt to pay to Lucifer. But hey, I could adapt. Was there a special place in Hell for people who used to work there?

I was wrestling with these things, almost to my house, when I saw a police cruiser go flying by me, lights flashing. I didn't think anything of it until I saw two more. Then I got a very sick feeling in my stomach.

Lily.

What had she done now? It must be terrible if the police were being called in. Had she killed Mom or Dad? Set our house on fire? I ran home as fast as I could, and I heard tires screeching when I turned the corner onto our street. There were three police cruisers in my driveway. I burst through the front door, and what I saw made my blood turn to antifreeze.

My mom was sitting on the sofa next to my dad. He had his arm around her. Her eyes were red, and she had been crying. She was holding a tissue over her nose. They both looked stricken. Sitting across from them was a police officer, and there was another officer standing next to him. Everyone turned and looked at me as I entered the room.

"Fynn," my mother said, her voice sounding like she was being strangled. She cleared her throat. "Maddie's gone."

189

I stood still for a second, nothing computing. "What?"

"Maddie's gone. Kevin was keeping an eye on her while I slept, and then…I don't know what happened." She started to cry. "We got a note."

"Let me see that." I snatched it out of my mom's hand.

We have your daughter. Wait for instructions. We will call.

For a second, I thought maybe Maddie really had been kidnapped. I mean, stranger things have happened. Stranger things have happened to me, lately. Then it all clicked. I glanced at my cell phone. Sure enough, there was a text from Lily.

"Missing someone?" It was signed with a laughing emoji. I was gripped by a blind fury. *Evil bitch.* I glanced up at my parents, who were looking at me with a combination of concern and fear. The cops were also looking at me with interest.

"I have to go," I said suddenly and bolted up to my room. I heard one of the officers say, "Hey!" Then my dad said, "Leave him alone. He's been under a lot of stress." I vaguely wondered if the police officer thought I kidnapped my own sister, but I didn't worry too much about it. I called Josh and said, "Maddie. Lily took Maddie. She took Maddie, Josh! Her cross must have worn off. Shit. What am I gonna do? She's going to kill her, and she's going to eat her soul. She told me young souls are the best ones! What am I gonna do?"

"Fuck." There was a pause. "All right, calm down. First of all, I think you need to call that demon hunter guy. He'll know what to do."

My heart was racing. I could not let that bitch kill my sister. No way. I had to find her. I had to find her so I could rescue Maddie. Shit!

My fingers were shaking as I tapped in Edge's number.

"Hello?"

"Mr. Valentine, you've got to help me—I'll pay you whatever you want. Lily took my sister! Lily took my sister! You've got to help me."

"Who is this?"

"Fynn Hardin. I met with you last week? At Brew Ha Ha—you have to help me. Lily kidnapped my sister!"

"Oh, right. Okay. Your sister? How old is your sister?"

"She's about a year and a half."

There was a pause, and then I heard a toilet flush. Was he just talking to me from his bathroom? I didn't want to visualize that.

"Okay, Fred. The first thing is we don't have a lot of time. Usually, it takes a demon about a day or so to suck the soul from someone completely. I need payment up front."

"Yeah, yeah, payment up front. Fine! You have to find her."

"All right. Meet me downtown at Brew Ha Ha in…thirty minutes. I take cash, money orders, and cashier's checks. No personal checks." He hung up.

I grabbed my wallet off my dresser and ran downstairs. I didn't even pause as I flew by my parents and the cops, just yelled, "Gotta go, be home soon!" and ran outside.

I had to get to the nearest bank as soon as possible. I called Josh. "Can you pick me up?"

"Where are we going?"

"I need to get a cashiers' check, or a money order, and then I have to meet Edge at Brew Ha Ha in half an hour." I started walking. It was a hike to the bank, but I figured any progress was better than nothing, and I couldn't have just stayed still anyway.

"The banks are closed by now; it's 6:30. But Walmart can cut you a money order. Where are you?"

"I'm walking down Elizabeth Street. I'll be on Franklin by the time you get here."

"Okay, I'm on my way."

Where would she have taken Maddie? Was there some sort of demon club in downtown Franklin? I whipped out my phone and texted her. *Where the fuck are you?*

I waited and walked at the same time. I had a blinding headache. I wasn't sure if it was from Lily or from panic, but I couldn't let it stop me, so I ignored it as best I could. After a few minutes, Josh roared to the curb in front of me, and I opened the door and threw myself inside.

"Jesus, you look terrible."

"Thanks."

He lurched back into traffic and started speeding towards Walmart.

"Be careful not to get caught—I can't imagine how we'd explain that to the cop. 'Officer, we have to get a check to pay the demon hunter, because my demon ex-girlfriend kidnapped my sister.' We'll be at somewhere called Sunnyvale Farm before we know it."

Glancing in the rear-view mirror, Josh said, "It's okay—all the cops in Franklin are at your house anyway."

I chewed on my fingernails and cracked my knuckles. My nerves were screaming, and I was jumping out of my skin. I could barely sit still. Sweat was trickling down the back of my neck and under my armpits. Poor Maddie. She was such a sweet little kid. I thought of her stretching out her little arms and opening and closing her fists when she wanted to be picked up. Edge said we had a day, but was her soul draining away even now?

I ran into Walmart and handed them my debit card. She wrote out a money order for all $4,000 that was in my bank account. I signed it, and then I ran out of the store to go meet Edge at Brew Ha Ha.

CHAPTER FIFTY-THREE

I SAW EDGE before I even entered Brew Ha Ha. He was sitting at a table, seemingly flirting with a waitress. I wanted to kill him.

"Here you go," I said as I thrust the check into Edge's hand. The waitress gave me an irritated look, as I had just interrupted her ego-stroking session. I was not into women at all right at that moment.

Edge glanced at the check, nodded to the waitress, and said, "Okay, Fred, let's go." He threw a ten-dollar bill on the table and winked. "See you later, doll."

Doll. Seriously?

We walked out and Edge said, "Tell me everything that happened."

I talked rapidly, almost without taking a breath. I told him about the Night Amulet, Maddie, and everything else that had happened in the last two hours. He nodded and seemed to listen carefully.

"Can you think of anywhere Lily would have taken Maddie? Someplace Lily considered safe, or at least relatively so, and remote?"

"I was hoping you could tell me, Edge. Isn't that what you do?"

He gave me a hostile look and said, "Yeah, but I've never met this particular demon. You know her better than I do."

I tried to think. Somewhere remote. My mind was spinning in circles— I couldn't grab a hold of any thoughts. Suddenly something smacked me so hard across the face I almost fell down. I grabbed my cheek and blinked, looking around for whatever had just hit me.

"Focus!"

Gradually it dawned on me that Edge had just slapped me across the face. I was about to hit him back when I blurted out, "Small Cove Pond! It was pretty deserted when we went there. Lily might go there."

"Where's that?" He had a knife stashed in his belt, like he was a 19th-century pirate. He rubbed the tip of it with his thumb.

"About twelve miles from here. If you go into woods a ways, there's a cave. It's sort of famous—apparently, some Indian Chief hid in it during the Revolutionary War. It's pretty small, and sometimes it's filled with water." I rubbed my cheek and glared at him.

"It's a thought. You have her cell phone number?"

"I do, but she hasn't been answering texts."

He snorted, or maybe it was a laugh, and said, "Figures. Okay, Fred, what we're going to do is we're going to go down to Small Cove Pond and look for Lily. If she's there, do not approach her. I will use a high-tech, special demon-hunter spell that I know to trap her in a demon-carrying case. Then you can take her back to Hell with you. Okay?"

"What the hell is a special, high-tech demon-hunter spell?"

"You'll find out when we get there. Okay, here." He handed me an enormous red motorcycle helmet. I looked at it, looked at him, and then looked at his bike. "You want me to ride on the back of that with you?"

"Well, how else will I know where to go?"

I hated this idea. I've seen people riding motorcycles, and the person on the back always has his—usually her—arms wrapped around the person in the front. I really didn't relish clamping my arms around Edge's waist. Also, I had never ridden a motorcycle.

He saw my squeamish look and said, "Look, unless you have a car, you got a better idea?"

No. No, I did not have a car. I was never going to have a car, because I had to pay some alleged demon-hunting dick weed all the money I had saved for a car. I didn't say this out loud, but I was screaming it in my head.

Out loud I said, "I guess not."

"Well, then hop on, Fred."

"It's Fynn, dammit!"

"Okay, sorry. Fynn."

I waited for Edge to sit on his bike and put his helmet on. Then I gingerly sat behind him and put my helmet on, bumping it into Edge's back. I stared at his back for a minute. His lats were huge.

"You ready?" He half-turned his head and called out.

I sighed and grabbed him around the waist. My arms got about halfway around. I smelled leather and musky cologne and winced.

Edge flicked the switch, turned the key, and with a roar, we were off. He took off smoothly but so fast that my helmeted face almost fell into him. The wind whipped by, and all I could think of was falling off and smacking the pavement with my head. Turns were especially harrowing. I had to fight the feeling that I was going to slide off. I wasn't sure if Edge would notice if I did. On the plus side, the helmet covered my whole head, so no one I knew would realize I was riding on the back of a bike with some vigilante, demon-hunting cowboy.

Small Pond Cove was about twenty scary minutes away. We stopped in a parking lot above the cove. Edge took off his helmet, so I followed suit.

"Where is this cave?" He turned to me.

"It's over here, probably not even a half mile." There was a trail, blurred at the edges from lack of use but still detectable. I dashed down the trail, with Edge running behind me. The branches whipped my face, and my feet slipped in the thick, gooey, black mud. I splashed across the stream and stopped at the entrance of the cave. Cave probably wasn't even the right word—alcove was more accurate. The point here is that you could see the whole thing from the entrance and Lily wasn't there.

"Shit!" I was frantic. Where had she taken Maddie if not here?

Edge peered over my shoulder. "Any other ideas?"

"No. None at all! We didn't go anywhere else that was remote." I ran my hand through my hair, trying to think. We went here once. We hung out with Josh, but I didn't think she'd bring Maddie to Josh's backyard. We went to a couple of restaurants, but she wasn't going to take Maddie out to a restaurant. "She said she's from Nebraska, but that's not really true, so I don't think she would go there."

Edge shook his head. "She can't bring your sister through Hell. Actually, she can't go through Hell, either. She can only travel on earth."

"Well, that narrows it down," I said.

He glared. "She probably didn't go too far. I mean, from her perspective, she needs a steady supply of souls and somewhere to absorb their energy. Massachusetts is as good a place as any." He paused. "Are there any local places where someone could hide with a baby for a few days?"

I couldn't think of any. "Can I Google?" I asked.

He looked at me like I was an idiot, but he said, "Go ahead."

I pulled out my phone and opened the internet search engine. My fingers hovered over the keys. What to Google? Demon hiding spots? Demon respite? After a few seconds, I typed in 'things to do in Mass.'

Edge said, "What about an abandoned barn, or some abandoned building? A house? I'm getting the sense of a house. Is there anything like that around here? I think I got a ping. You know, from my demon-hunting equipment."

Instantly, the old Randall house came to mind. The Randalls settled in Massachusetts in about 1700 or something, but the farm had been subdivided and sold off over the years. The last remaining Randall, Jenny, died about ten years ago, and the house had been vacant ever since. It was a big, white farmhouse on the outskirts of town. I'm sure as soon as developers thought of something to do with it the house would be toast, but for now it just sat there, abandoned and lonely. I told Edge about it, and he said it was worth a try. So, back we went on his motorcycle, my head encased in a shiny plastic tomb. As we sprinted to the farmhouse, the mantra "Please be okay, Maddie, please be okay," kept playing in my head. I would absolutely never forgive myself if anything bad happened to her.

CHAPTER FIFTY-FOUR

WE PULLED INTO the dirt and gravel driveway, tiny stones kicked up by the heavy wheels of Edge's bike. Leaves dotted the front yard. He killed the engine, and I scrambled off the bike and ran towards the house.

A wide front porch sat like an apron on the front of the house. A few weather-beaten and decaying old chairs still stood in the corner, wallflowers at the party, waiting for someone to notice them. The paint was peeling off the door frame, leaving chips of paint on the wooden floor. I tried the doorknob and the front door creaked open.

I stepped inside to what was once the living room. An old sofa was now a home for nesting field mice, mouse droppings scattered across the floor. To the right was the old farmhouse kitchen, cabinets standing open on ancient hinges. A tattered, woven rug was thrown on the floor. Edge came in behind me.

"You take the downstairs, I'll take the upstairs." He unsheathed his knife and headed up the stairs. I had a sudden thought.

"Hey, Edge. I don't have a knife." Why hadn't I grabbed the sword?

He said, "Yeah. If you get into trouble, scream real loud." He continued up the stairs.

Thanks.

"Maddie?" I called out. I listened for her baby footsteps, for her crying, but I didn't hear anything. Still, I knew she was here. I don't know how I knew. I just did.

I walked cautiously, stirring up little clouds of dust with every step I took. In the kitchen, I opened cabinets and even opened the door of the oven, which made a noise like someone opening a crypt. I peered in the pantry. On one shelf were a few cans of Campbell's Tomato Soup. Curious, I picked it up and blew the dust off. I hoped Maddie wasn't hungry.

I wasn't sure what I would do when I found Lily. Maybe I would have to do what Edge said and scream really loud. I thought I might wave my crucifix around at her, snatch Maddie, and hope for the best.

Standing in the corner of the kitchen was an old wooden door. It had straight lines cut into the frame, marking children's growth through the years. They were labeled with their names and heights, and what years they had achieved them. I peered down the stairs. A musty smell, like rotting cabbage, rose up from the depths of the basement. A single light socket was above the door. The light bulb was missing, naturally.

I took a deep breath. *For Maddie*, I told myself. I wasn't a big fan of creepy basements. When I was a kid, one of my cousins thought it would be a riot to lock me in the root cellar. It was an old farmhouse as well, although this one was inhabited by my mother's family. You would think that would make it less creepy but, if you met my cousin, you wouldn't say that. This cousin was big for his age, and not terribly bright. He had an oversized head which always reminded me of a pumpkin about to fall off its stalk. His ears stuck straight out, too. His name was Jeff, and he had a little brother named Carl.

I was probably about three and naive enough to believe them when they said there was candy behind the old vegetable crate. The door shut followed by hysterical laughter. I caught on pretty quickly and screamed and cried, cried and screamed, until I was hoarse. It felt like I was there for hours, although Mom said it was only about forty-five minutes. I've been anxious in basements ever since.

I stepped on the first step, then the second. I ran one hand on the wall and leaned forward to peer around the wall. It was an old basement, the kind with a dirt floor. The walls were stone. I crept down the stairs, trying to listen for Maddie. My throat was dry as a summer afternoon in August.

"Maddie?" I croaked. I swallowed and tried again. "Maddie?"

I heard laughter. Mean, sharp laughter, jagged as rocks. I turned my head in the direction of the sound, but it was already fading. "Maddie!" I shouted.

Nothing.

I was growing more frantic by the minute. What had that bitch done with my sister? My shin hollered in protest when I tripped over an old crate. I fumbled for my phone and found the flashlight app. I powered it on and swept it in an arc around the basement. Copper pipes ran the length of the space. There were stacks of crates, old clothes, and scrap lumber piled high in the corner. Here and there were scratches on the stone—long, deep scratches. In the corner was another door. Gripping my cell phone so hard my fingers turned white, I tiptoed over to it.

I listened at the door but heard nothing. Jerking it open, I prepared to have Lily fly at me. It appeared to be a wine cellar. There were empty shelves on the walls and a few wooden crates on the floor. Behind one of the crates…was that fabric? I crept closer.

"Maddie!" I rushed over to her. My heart was in my throat. Was she already dead? She was lying so still, so quiet. Maybe Lily had already taken her soul. Relief flooded through me when I saw her little chest going up and down. I picked her up, her body warm and soft against my shoulder. Glancing around, I wondered where Lily had gone. I was sure she was just here. There was a faint odor of carbon and sulfur. I hoisted Maddie onto my shoulder and rushed up the stairs. I'd had enough of the basement.

"Edge!" I shouted as I re-entered the kitchen. I heard his heavy booted footsteps upstairs. He came down, glancing at Maddie and then at me.

"Is that your sister?" he asked me.

No, Edge, this is just some random baby I found in the basement. "Yes," is what I actually said.

"Oh, thank God. Well, at least that's one thing out of the way," he said, as if my sister were just one more task on his list of things to do. "No sign of the demon?"

"No, nothing. But she was here not too long ago. I'd swear to it."

"Okay. Why don't we bring your sister home, and then we can figure out where else to look for Lily."

I stared at him in bewilderment. "I am not toting my seventeen-month-old sister on the back of your motorcycle."

He looked vaguely surprised, but then he nodded. "No, that wouldn't be a good idea. I don't have an extra helmet."

I thought about mentioning the other myriad reasons one should not bring a baby on a motorcycle, but it seemed like too much effort. Furthermore, I just wanted to bring Maddie back to my parents. I hit the call button and then hit the entry for my mom. She answered on the first ring. "Fynn?"

"Mom! I found Maddie! I found Maddie! Someone needs to pick us up. I'm by the old Randall place. I'll explain later." I bounced Maddie up and down, trying to wake her up. I wasn't sure how long the process of stealing someone's soul was. Did it occur all at once or little by little? I wanted to see if Maddie was still Maddie.

"What? What did you say?"

I repeated everything I just said. I heard my mom turn to my dad and say, "He's found Maddie." Then my Dad came on the line.

"Fynn, where are you? How did you find Maddie?"

"I'll explain later. Right now just pick us up."

"You're not…you're not in danger, are you?"

No more than normal, I thought. "No, I'm fine."

I tickled Maddie's stomach, and then her feet. She sighed softly and tried to pull her feet away. I tickled them again. She grunted and opened her eyes.

"Maddie?" I tickled her again. She pushed my hand away from her feet and said, "No!"

She seemed okay. She struggled to get down, to go explore this new environment. I didn't want to put her down, didn't want to let her out of my sight. Naturally, she screamed.

"Down! Down, Inn!"

Edge, who I had completely forgotten about, came up behind me. I jumped. "Sorry. I was just going to tell you that you were right. There was definitely demon activity in the basement just recently."

"Right."

"So, you still want me to find the demon?"

Did I not just pay you $4,000 to find a demon and send her back to Hell? "Yeah. Lucifer told me I have to bring her back to Hell."

Edge shook his big head back and forth so that his hair flapped back and forth. "Yeah, that's a bad scene. You don't want Lucifer pissed at you. Trust me. So, I'll keep looking. She's still close by, I can feel it."

Great.

CHAPTER FIFTY-FIVE

IT HAD TAKEN Edge and me twenty minutes to get from downtown Franklin to the old Randall place. It took my father twelve minutes to arrive in a ten-year-old minivan. I don't even know how that's possible. My parents leaped out of the car, barely waiting for it to stop. My mom cried, "Maddie," took her out of my arms, and crushed Maddie to her chest. Dad wrapped his arms around both of them.

"Thank God. Thank God," he kept saying over and over again. I could tell they were both crying. They kept running their hands over her hair, up and down her back, as if to reassure themselves she was real.

After a minute, Maddie got impatient and started to squirm. "Down!" Neither of them wanted to let her go. Maddie was outraged. "Down! Down!" She arched her back and tried to push away from them.

"Okay, let's just get her home. We can let her down then," Mom said. Dad slid the car door open and Mom wrestled her into her car seat. This made her scream more since she was still facing the back seat and she couldn't see.

"Bottle, Maddie?" I asked her. It's actually a sippy cup, but Maddie reached for it and started sucking on it happily.

Once Maddie was situated, my parents exchanged glances and then looked at me. "Do you want to explain how you managed to find her when the police couldn't?" Dad asked.

"Uh…not really."

Mom looked like she was about to say something, but she sighed and said, "Let's just go home for now."

I climbed in next to Maddie, who stopped chugging juice long enough to smile at me. I grinned at her and poked her in the stomach. She chortled. She went back to sucking on her sippy cup until it was gone. Then her head lolled to the side and she dozed off.

I leaned my head on the window. The glass was cold, which felt good against my throbbing head. I was exhausted, utterly depleted, and I closed my eyes. Thank God I found Maddie. I didn't want to think about the fact I still had to find and capture Lily and return her to Hell before Lucifer killed me.

All I wanted was to go to bed, sleep for a long time, and ideally wake up to discover this had all been an elaborate, extremely screwed-up dream.

What actually happened was that we arrived home. In spite of her insistence of getting down to explore and wreak toddler havoc at the Randall place, Maddie was off in dreamland. Mom lifted her out of her car seat and put her to bed for a nap. I imagine it's stressful being kidnapped by a demon. I could relate.

While Mom was doing that, Dad was calling the police to report that we had found Maddie. Naturally, they were very curious about this and said they would send an officer over ASAP to take a report. With both of my parents busy, I went to my room and grabbed the silver sword. I wasn't sure it would work, but I hadn't liked being unarmed and having to "yell real loud" for Edge. If we were going to go demon hunting, I was bringing my sword.

I walked downstairs as quietly as possible, only to see my parents sitting at the dining room table, waiting for me.

"What's up?"

"We just have a few questions."

"I'm kind of in a hurry," I said.

They looked at me like I had lost my mind. "Where are you going with that sword?" Dad asked.

I looked at the sword as if I were surprised to find it in my hands. "Fencing?" I said.

"I'd appreciate it if you would take this seriously, Fynn," my dad said.

I sighed. "I have to return it. It was for a school project."

They both looked at me like they knew this was bullshit, but decided to drop it in favor of their other concerns. "How did you know where to find Maddie?"

This was a long conversation that I didn't have time for. I sighed. "Okay, look. You know how I told you Lily said she was going to hurt my family? She made threats?" They both nodded. "I knew it was her. I knew she kidnapped Maddie. I also thought I knew where she took her, and I was right."

"*Lily* kidnapped Maddie?" Mom said, incredulous. "Why would she...we have to call the police!"

"Great idea. I got to go." Edge was waiting for me, and he was so flaky I was pretty sure if I waited too long he would either forget he was trying to hunt Lily or go off and take some other job. Time was of the essence.

"Wait!" Dad said. My shoulders crunched up. "Don't you think you should wait until the police get here so you can tell them what you know?"

"Dad, I really need you to trust me right now. I'll be back, and then I'll talk to you, and the police, as long as you want."

They both looked at me like you might look at a rabid squirrel—cute, but dangerous and unpredictable. I was stunned, because I know I had done absolutely nothing to deserve their trust, when Dad said, "Okay."

I hesitated a minute, expecting more. When none was forthcoming, I said, "Great. See ya!" I grabbed my cell phone out of the pocket of my shorts. My fingers fumbled and I dropped it. I stepped forward to get it but ended up kicking it halfway under the couch. When I got down on my knees and peered under it, dust bunnies the size of tigers greeted me. There was also my phone—no cracks, thank goodness—and the holy water I ordered from Amazon and forgot about completely. I stuffed it into the pocket of my shorts. It couldn't hurt. I stood up. My parents were still staring at me, but they didn't say anything. I texted Edge.

Let's go.

CHAPTER FIFTY-SIX

WHERE TO HUNT for Lily? While I knew she went other places in town, I had only ever seen her either at my house or near the high school. Where did she hang out during the day while I was at work? If I were a demon, where would I be?

Then it occurred to me: isn't this what Edge *does?* Like, he has some kind of experience in demon behavior? I texted him: *Where do you think we should look?* Edge: "For who?"

I sighed. *For Lily, you overpriced jackass.* Then I deleted that. *For Lily!* is what I sent.

"Right. Okay. Meet me back at the farm. I'll get a ping on her and we'll go from there."

Finally, some concrete information. I whipped out my phone and texted Josh: *Can you pick me up? Meeting Edge to hunt for Lily.*

After a few seconds, a text back: "What are we doing with Lily?"

I stared at my phone in confusion. I was just talking to Josh not ten minutes ago. Then it dawned on me: I accidentally texted Cassidy, whose number was right under Josh's in my phone. Cassidy, who was trying to recover from being pushed in front of a car. *Nothing. Get some rest. I'll talk to you later.*

I then texted Josh. *Need a ride to Randall's farm.* Josh texted back: "Okay."

I grabbed my sword. On the way out of the house, I caught a glimpse of Kevin. I stopped short. His eye was black and swollen.

"What is that?" I asked him.

"Nothing! Mind your own business," he said, jerking his head away.

"Did that kid Noel do that? They have anti-bullying laws…"

"I said I'm fine." He glared. "I can take care of myself." He looked less angry and said, "Really. I got this."

"Well, okay," I said. I swear, if I ever got rid of Lily, I had a few things to tell this Noel kid.

I paced back and forth across my driveway while I waited. The sharp edge drew blood as I ran my fingers across the blade of the sword. *Good.* I was hoping to cut Lily in half.

After what seemed like about a month but was probably actually half an hour, Josh pulled up. I climbed in and he pulled away. We didn't talk. I guess we were both preoccupied—me with thoughts of my own death, Josh with the difficulties of eradicating a demon.

Josh pulled up in front of the decaying farmhouse. Edge was sitting on his motorcycle like it was a park bench, with his feet crossed at the ankles. When we got out of the car, he stood up.

"I can feel the demon activity here." He held out his palms facing the ground and waved them back and forth. I looked at Josh and rolled my eyes. "I detect that she has moved on...this way!" he announced.

"What way? East?" I said.

Edge pointed vaguely towards the woods bordering the property. "She went that way." Then he tucked his dagger into the waistband of his pants and started trotting towards the trees. I looked at Josh again and shrugged helplessly.

"It's as good a place to look as any," I said. Josh shrugged.

I followed Edge into the woods. The trees hung over the trail as if they were reaching out with hungry branches, waiting to eat me. I shivered even though it wasn't cold.

We followed Edge as best we could, which was more difficult than it sounds. Edge was surprisingly athletic. He slipped through the woods with an easy grace, never tripping, never running into anything. I, on the other hand, kept tripping over various tree branches buried in the dirt and cursing loudly. And Josh was somewhere behind me.

After a few minutes, I came upon Edge just standing still with his arms thrust out to the sides. "Can you detect anything?" I whispered.

"Shhh!" He snapped. "I'm concentrating."

I waited. After a full minute, I said, "So...anything?"

"Ah...I think I lost her. Let's go this way." With a toss of his unkempt hair, he took off in a different direction. I groaned and followed. After a few more minutes, broken up with the occasional loud "Oof!" and other expletives, we came upon Josh.

"Have we been going in circles?" I asked.

"No! Of course not. But I believe Lily has left the woods."

"Great. Do you happen to know where she went?"

"Well, Fre...Fynn. I was hoping you could tell me."

"Why am I...I have no idea! I've seen her at my house, a few pizza places, Josh's house, the high school, and the pond. That's it. How the hell do I know where she goes when she's not tormenting someone?"

"Let's try the high school."

"She's not going to go near the high school—she doesn't want to risk being shoved in the elevator and being dragged back to Hell," I told him.

Edge nodded knowingly. "Yeah but, in her head, there is no danger because she doesn't think anyone's gonna catch her."

I supposed that could be true. Still, why would she go there? I didn't have any better ideas, so off we went.

"Your friend Edge is quite the character," Josh said as he put the truck in gear.

"He is *not* my friend."

Again, there was silence while we rode along. I watched dark houses slide by, holding peacefully sleeping people who were not being taunted by demons. I wondered what their lives were like and if they were happy. I don't know what Josh was thinking, but if I were him I'd be scrolling through my contact list and thinking of how many friends I had who were much less trouble than me.

"Here," I said, handing Josh the holy water. "You should be armed with something."

Josh pulled into the smaller, upper lot of the high school. Edge had leaned his motorcycle against the side of the building. I climbed out of the pick-up, and what I saw made the blood curdle in my veins.

Lily was spitting her demon fire at the base of the building, causing the whole side of the gym to be a raging sea of flames. I could feel the heat from the parking lot.

She was trying to destroy the portal. I suppose she thought that, by burning down the high school, the elevator to Hell would be destroyed and I would never be able to bring her back. I tried to think back—did she not know there were elevators to Hell in high schools around the world? I thought we had talked about this when we talked about her hypothetically being from Nebraska, but maybe not. Or maybe she just chose not to believe me when I talked about it. Either way, FRHS was on its way to being a pile of charred brick. Demon fire, in case you didn't know, burns through anything.

I wondered if I would still have to return Lily if the elevator to Hell burned. After all, if I couldn't get back to Hell, I would never be able to work in Hell. Lucifer would wonder where I went. Then I realized that was ferociously stupid. Lucifer would just come up and get Lily and banish me to some special part of Hell where former employees cleaned Hell's toilets or something. Lucifer didn't venture to the surface very often, but he was capable of it, and when he did there was usually some catastrophic result. The last time he came to the surface, we had World War II.

"Hey!" I had my silver sword tucked down the leg of my pants. Lily turned to me, her eyes glowing with the feverish delight of a pyromaniac. I started to run towards her.

"Stay back!" she hissed. "I'm warning you, Fynn Hardin. I'm not done with you yet." She spit at me, but luckily I was too far back, and instead it set the grass on fire. It did make me reconsider my approach, though. Where was Edge? Where was Josh?

Oh, no.

Behind the far corner of the building, I saw Cassidy awkwardly limping towards Lily, holding a can of mace in one hand with her other hand wrapped around a crutch. *Shit.* Didn't I tell her to stay home and rest? Not that she had to listen to me all the time, but really, now would have been a good time.

Out of the corner of my eye, I saw Josh, who was coming down the hill as quietly as he could. Where was Edge? With four of us, we could surround Lily and hope at least one of the weapons we hit her with did something. Unless she just set us all on fire. That would suck.

Lily stopped spitting fire and whipped around to face Cassidy. "You!" she screamed.

"Yeah, me, you bitch. Come and get me!" Cassidy yelled.

"Gladly!" Lily advanced towards Cassidy, her arms out like she was going to strangle her. Cassidy held out the can of mace. I wasn't sure mace was an effective demon deterrent. But damn, Cassidy was standing there looking so courageous and so vulnerable that it almost brought a tear to my eye. She was the most beautiful girl I had ever seen.

Lily snarled and came towards Cassidy, hissing and spitting like a cobra. Cassidy held her ground, one hand extended with the can of mace and the other hand gripping the crutch and brandishing it like a weapon.

"Hey! Lily, over here!" I yelled.

Lily wheeled around, temporarily turning her back to Cassidy. "I'll get to you!" she screamed. She turned towards Cassidy again. In the meantime, Josh was coming towards her from the left-hand side. On the right was the high school that was on fire. I took the sword out from my pants and held it like a baseball bat.

Lily lunged at Cassidy, who jumped back. I ran ahead with the sword. By this time Josh was almost to Lily. He took the tiny bottle of holy water and threw it at her. I don't know if it was because it was real holy water, or if it was because she just got water tossed in her face, but it made Lily stop for a second and blink. When she stopped to blink, Cassidy sprayed her with mace. Then I took the sword and thrust it at her. It went all the way through her, and a screeching, inhuman scream split the night. I got a glimpse of a small, shriveled creature made up of blackness and hate before it collapsed into the dirt, a small pile of bones and ash.

I stared. All three of us stared at what used to be Lily. None of us said anything for a minute.

"What did I miss?" I turned around and there was Edge, sauntering up to us as if we were just waiting around for him to show up. I wanted to kill him.

I nodded towards the pile. "Well, we seem to have killed the demon. Where the hell were you?"

Edge seemed surprised. He recovered pretty quickly. "I was setting up a demon detection network. It's basically what made it possible for your weapons to work so well." He nodded.

"You just made that up," I said.

"I did not. Look, you don't want to leave the demon on the ground before it regenerates. Look…" He took what looked like a plastic box, rectangular, and about the size of a shoebox. He scooped up Lily's remains and poured them into the box. Then he handed it to me.

"There ya go, Fred. All's well that ends well, you know what I'm saying? Just return her to Hell, and uh, yeah. It's all good." He looked pleased with himself, as if he was the hero here.

"You are nothing but a con man!" I yelled. "You haven't done one single helpful thing since I hired you! I want my money back!"

At this, he took a step back and held up his hands. "Uh, no can do, Fred. My contract clearly states no refunds. Demon hunting is a risky business. I can't guarantee success every time." He glanced at the three of us and said, "Well, I'm gonna go now. Pleasure doing business with you." Then he walked back to his motorcycle, which was parked up on the upper lot, and he roared off.

I shook my head. Four thousand dollars for nothing. *Asshole.*

The flames were growing higher and hotter. Sweat ran down our faces. In the distance, I heard sirens.

"Who called the fire department?" I asked.

"I did," Cassidy said. "As soon as I got here."

"Oh, my God. I think I love you," I said, and I gently wrapped my arms around her and folded her into a hug. I laughed. I laughed until tears ran down my cheeks. I was so relieved. Lily was gone. Lily was gone! I was free. I've never felt so tired, so happy, and so drained.

Josh cleared his throat and said, "I think we should get out of here. Otherwise, someone's gonna think we set the school on fire."

"Good idea." I grabbed the box with Lily in it. "How did you know Lily would be here?" I asked Cassidy.

She shrugged. "I guessed. I mean, I remembered you went to Hell from the high school and that's where you met Lily, so I came here. It was the best idea I could come up with." She looked over her shoulder. "I really should get back. If Blake wakes up, he'll wonder where I am. I mean, my mom is home with him, but it's not the same." She shrugged and smiled at me. Should I kiss her?

Hell yeah, I should. I pulled her into a sweet, sweet kiss. She smiled shyly and then said, "I'll call you tomorrow," as she limped across the grass, down to the lower parking lot. I watched her until she disappeared below the hill.

"Hey, Romeo, get in the truck," Josh said.

I climbed into the passenger seat, still holding the box Lily was in. At least Edge gave me *that*.

We drove away just as the first fire trucks were pulling in.

CHAPTER FIFTY-SEVEN

I DIDN'T GET home until a little after midnight. Slipping into my house, I tried to be quiet so no one would ask where I had been and why I smelled like smoke. I quickly checked on Maddie, and then Kevin. For good measure, I peered in at my parents. Everyone was safe. Thank God. I technically had Lily trapped in some demon escape-proof box, or so Edge told me, but I wasn't entirely sure I believed it.

I placed the box in my closet, underneath a piece of plywood I meant to turn into a hockey game for Kevin but never got around to. I kept my shirt wrapped around the box because, although it seemed soundproof, it was clear glass or plastic and I had no desire to look at Lily. As Edge had mentioned, the demon that had been Lily did re-form, sort of. She bore no resemblance to the girl I fell in love with. Now she was black with blood-red eyes and a mouth full of razor-sharp teeth. She looked like a mound of wet, sticky tar. I put her under the plywood and went to bed.

I couldn't sleep, afraid she would somehow get out and start terrorizing my family. Not to mention the fact I would be taking up permanent residence in Hell. Hell was a nice place to work, but you wouldn't want to live there. So I tossed and turned. Every hour or so I got up and poked the box in the closet. It responded with an angry thump, so I figured she was still there. It was the longest night of my life. I had lots of time to ponder my shortcomings and curse my stupidity.

Finally, the sun shimmered below the horizon, and the world started to brighten. I yawned and got dressed. I quickly lifted up the box and whipped off the shirt to ascertain she was still in there. Yep. I stuffed her into my backpack so my parents wouldn't have to ask any questions.

I went to the kitchen—thankfully no one else was up. I made myself coffee and a bagel, which I was just frosting with cream cheese when my mom came down. She looked as if she hadn't slept either.

"Hi, Mom."

"Hi, sweetie."

"How'd you sleep?" I asked.

She frowned. "Terrible. It's the weirdest thing—I just couldn't sleep, and the few minutes I did sleep I had terrible nightmares." She shook her head and hit the button on the coffee maker. "How about you?"

"I didn't sleep well either."

She took a sip of coffee and sat at the table. "I think I'm still worried about Maddie. I mean, I know she's safe now, but…I just can't stop thinking about it." She shuddered.

I saw something in my backpack thump, but I had kicked it under the table so Mom didn't notice. I sat across from her.

"On a brighter note, it's almost the end of the summer. I imagine you'll put in your notice soon for Big Box?" she asked.

"Oh, yeah. Today, in fact." *Thank God.*

She nodded. "I'm glad. What happened with Lily?"

"Oh, she was arrested. She won't bother us anymore."

"Good. That's a relief. So sad. She's such a pretty girl. You would never guess she was so disturbed." She shrugged and took a sip of coffee. "I was going to ask you, do you need anything for school? It's your senior year."

I felt a brief flash of regret and anger. I had long fantasized about starting my senior year in my new-to-me car or pickup. I shook it off. The whole summer was a disaster of my own making. I was just happy everyone was still alive and not possessed.

"Uh, maybe a few pairs of jeans. I'm mostly good."

"Okay. You want to go shopping with me, or do you just want to take the car and some money?"

"Uh, no offense, but…"

She laughed. "Oh, please. I was seventeen once. There was no way I was going shopping with my mother. It's fine."

I felt a rush of affection. I really do have a great family. I grinned. Then I looked at the clock.

"Oops, gotta go." I jumped up and kissed her on the cheek.

"What was that for?" she said.

"Oh, nothing. Just…thanks for being awesome."

"Well, thank you for being awesome."

I brushed my bagel crumbs into my hand and threw them away, and then I waved at Mom and walked out of the house. Humming to myself, I strolled down the street. It was a walk I had taken many times over the summer, only now there was no demon taunting me. The August sunshine was in full force, preparing for one last summer heat wave. As I approached my high school, I smelled the after effects of last night's fire. The whole side of the building was scorched, but it was still standing. It didn't even look that bad—just black halfway up the sides. I snuck inside and took the elevator to Hell.

"Hi, Dorothy!" I called.

"Hi, Fynn! Do you like my hair?" It was purple ombré today. Her skin was periwinkle blue.

"Lovely! Hey, I need to get in to see the boss." I jerked my head over my shoulder in the general direction of his office.

"Oh?"

I leaned forward conspiratorially. "I have something for him."

"Well, good luck. You'll have to ask Ester if he's free. But he's been holed up in his office a while this morning, so it might be a good time to catch him."

"Great. Thanks." I went around the circular wood-paneled wall and down the hallway to Ester's office.

She looked up, annoyed. "Do you have an appointment?" Her eyes narrowed under her cat-eye glasses.

"I don't have an appointment, but I'm pretty sure Lucifer will see me. He gave me a project and I finished it."

She made a face like she just bit into a grapefruit and picked up the phone. "I have Fynn Hardin here." Apparently, Lucifer said okay because she said, "Fine." Then she hung up and said, "You can go in."

I nodded and then walked into the big boss's office.

He stood up as soon as I came in. "Fynn. Nice to see you. How are you?" He reached out a hand to shake mine. He crushed my fingers.

"I'm doing well, sir. How about yourself?"

"Oh, I can't complain." He gestured to the chair in front of his desk. "Have a seat. What can I do for you?" he said as he sat down.

I cleared my throat. "I got the demon. She's in my backpack."

He looked surprised. He leaned forward. "Delightful. Can I see her?"

I stood up and shrugged my backpack off my shoulders. It slid to the plush carpet. I unzipped it and took out the demon-proof box with Lily inside and handed her to Lucifer.

He shook the box a little and watched, like a snake studying his prey, as Lily slid back and forth. She cowered as his shark eyes watched her. "Splendid. I'm very happy you were able to get her back. You know, Fynn, I don't enjoy sentencing people to Hell; it's just my job." He looked regretful, as if he applied for a variety of jobs and the only one he could get was being the Antichrist.

I nodded. "Also, I have to tell you I'm going back to school the week after next, so I'm giving you my two weeks' notice."

"Oh, I'm sorry to hear that. You've done such a good job for us this summer."

213

He looked thoughtful. "You know, I do have a small number of part-time positions available. You could just work on weekends. How about it?"

I hesitated. Hell paid pretty well. He saw my hesitation—not for nothing is he in charge of deciding the punishment people will hate the most—and said, "Well, think about it, all right?" I stood up and he clapped me on the shoulder, making me think I might sink through the floor. He slid Lily back and forth in the box. She clapped her hands on the sides and opened her mouth to say something to me. Her face was pleading, desperate. I almost felt sorry for her. Almost.

I had a sudden thought.

"Uh, sir? Do you have a business card I could have?"

"Certainly." He reached into the top drawer of his desk and handed me a black business card. In red letters it said, "Lucifer," and under that, "Prince of Darkness. Manager of Hell." The letters were like veins, the red ink flowing through them like blood. The card pulsed with malevolent power.

"Perfect. Have a nice day, Sir." I nodded at him. He looked at the box like it was the Xbox he wanted for Christmas but never got. Actually, I'm fairly sure he doesn't celebrate Christmas, but you get the idea.

I put in a fairly ordinary day at Soul Destination. I was so happy Lily was back in Hell I wasn't even fazed by Audrey's general obnoxiousness. In fact, I smiled at her and thanked her for her help, which confused her so much it was fun to watch. Then I clocked out.

I walked down Smith Avenue, whistling. No Lily, no demons. I enjoyed the late August sunshine. It was warm, but the humidity of summer melted away as September lurked around the corner. I walked slowly, enjoying myself.

As I turned the corner onto Ellis Road I saw three kids goofing around. Paul, Jimmy, and Noel. I waited.

Noel looked up and caught me staring at him. "What's up?" he said.

"Can I speak to you a minute?" I said.

He looked at Paul and Jimmy, and then he looked at me with an insolent expression. "What?"

I walked over. "I'd like to introduce myself. I'm Fynn Hardin, Kevin's brother?" Paul and Jimmy looked at the ground, embarrassed. They already knew who I was. Noel shrugged and laughed. I smiled and reached into my pocket. I gave him Lucifer's card. Then I grabbed him by the collar and pushed him up against a fence.

"I've spent the entire summer working in Hell. Lucifer, aka the devil, is a personal friend of mine. If you ever, *ever* so much as look at Kevin the wrong way again, I'll have Lucifer himself come after you." I let go of him and smiled. "Understood?"

He looked a little shaken. He looked at the card, then at me, then at the card. "Aww, there's no way this is real. Gimme a break. There's no such thing as Hell." But as he looked at the card again, his eyes opened a fraction wider.

I turned around and walked the rest of the way home. Summer was almost over. My senior year of high school was about to begin.

Epilogue — Two Months Later

MY SENIOR YEAR was flying by. Cassidy and I were still together. She was the most fantastic human being I had ever met. I fell in love with her the night she showed up, basically on one leg, to help me take down a demon. I was the luckiest guy in the world. We usually went to the movies, or out to eat if her mom could watch Blake. If she couldn't, that was okay, too. I just grabbed Maddie, and the two of them had a play date while Cassidy and I had a real date. Blake and Maddie got along, mostly. I figured it was good for Maddie's social skills. After all, she would be going to preschool next year.

Kevin started eighth grade. Noel, Jimmy, and Paul no longer bothered him. He started hanging out with kids he knew from elementary school, Dave and Dave. I know—it's ridiculous, but yes, his two friends both had the same name. Kevin said people just called them Dave S. and Dave T.

My dad got a new job. One of his old customers contacted him and asked him to come work for him. The new job had better benefits, and he was even making a little more money than he was before he got fired.

Mom got a day job! As a result, she was less tired and cranky, and she was around more. It was mostly cool, until she got after me to do my homework or pick up my room. Maddie started going to daycare two days a week.

Josh and Courtney were still together. Josh applied early decision to Harvard, but he hadn't heard back yet. I guess that would mean the end of them, unless by some quirk of fate Courtney went to Harvard, too. But who knows?

I hadn't figured out where I was going to college yet. I didn't want to think about leaving Cassidy, so I might just go to the local branch of the State school. But graduation was still pretty far away. I had time to figure it all out.

I also hadn't decided whether or not to go back to Hell next summer. After all, I had the hang of it. I was not going to be tempted by any demons so it should be fine. Right?

Of course it would.

Guardian's Return
Darren Simon

Theodora lives, and if Charlee's dreams of death and fields of spilled blood are true, her great aunt has avenged herself on that world across the dimensional divide. Charlee knows what she must do. Can Charlee defeat Theodora—for good—or will evil consume her? Can she even survive so far from home? Her only hope may rest in the Dragon Lord, but that beast turned his back on her grandfather long ago...

They're Here You Know
Steve Pricone

Will Annie's Goth friend Caden hold the answer to Annie's quest for the supernatural, or does the a haunted nursing home that has become her grandmother's residence as her Nonna is slowly enveloped by the shadow of Alzheimer's disease hold the key? Can science prove the existence of the unknown and that they're here, or will it take a little faith...

The Entropy of Knowledge
Mark Dellandre and Britton Learnard

We've all had moments when we felt like we were surrounded by idiots…Babylon Briggs feels that pain every day because his town, his planet, even his galaxy, is jam-packed with the most thick-headed simpletons imaginable. When his home world is invaded by a group of equally clueless conquerors, it's up to Babylon to save the day. The only question:

Is he smart enough?

www.ingramcontent.com/pod-product-compliance
Lightning Source LLC
Chambersburg PA
CBHW070821180626
46818CB00001B/355